By ALLISON CASSATTA

NOVELS
Beast

SIN & SEDUCTION SERIES
Sin & Seduction
Lies & Seduction
The Final Seduction

NOVELLAS
Kissing Is Easy
This Is Love

DEAR DIARY SERIES
Dear Diary
Pride
Relationships 101

Published by DREAMSPINNER PRESS
http://www.dreamspinnerpress.com

The FINAL Seduction

ALLISON CASSATTA

Dreamspinner Press

Published by
Dreamspinner Press
5032 Capital Circle SW
Suite 2, PMB# 279
Tallahassee, FL 32305-7886
USA
http://www.dreamspinnerpress.com/

The Final Seduction
© 2014 Allison Cassatta.

Cover Art
© 2014 Allison Cassatta.
www.allisoncassatta.com
Cover content is for illustrative purposes only
and any person depicted on the cover is a model.

ISBN: 978-1-62798-787-5
Digital ISBN: 978-1-62798-788-2

Printed in the United States of America
First Edition
April 2014

This book is dedicated to everyone who walked into the world of Sin & Seduction… and never walked out.

ACKNOWLEDGMENTS

As always, I would like to thank the staff at Dreamspinner Press for being so amazing to work with and giving my naughty boys a home. I would also like to thank my beta readers for always dropping everything to read a manuscript for me. I'm not the most patient person in the world, but they take great care of me.

PROLOGUE

"DORIAN GRANT, you're under arrest for the murder of Leonard Antonio Cabrezzi."

Dorian stood in the doorway, shoulders squared, chin held high, knowing good and well the law didn't have a damn thing on him. Yeah, he knew Leonard Cabrezzi and had probably been seen throwing punches with the lowlife a time or two, but he sure as shit didn't commit the crime the 5-0 were accusing him of.

Leo was the guy who'd shot Jansen and a general piece of shit in Dorian's honest opinion. Leo'd had that bullet coming to him. Dorian's only regret was not being the one to deliver.

"You have the right to remain silent," the cop continued as he wrenched Dorian around by the arm. Damn near jerked it right out of the socket. "Anything you say can and will be—"

"Get the fuck off me," Dorian demanded, yanking his arms back with a force strong enough to knock the cop right on his ass. The officer stumbled back a few steps, landing square against his partner's chest.

With a growl, the obviously younger of the two jerked up and started forward, charging after Dorian so fast that when they connected, the force sent Dorian toppling back inside the house. The small of his back cracked the hard edge of this stupid, fancy foyer table his mom had bought back in the seventies but no one had the heart to get rid of. Damn thing was going to storage as soon as Dorian sorted all this crap out.

Pain erupted along Dorian's backside. A stream of curses worthy of making a sailor flinch hurled from his lips. And while he wanted to tear that pig from limb to limb, Dorian had promised a long time ago to be a good boy, so he kept his hands to himself. Worst thing about all of this, he couldn't keep Jansen from seeing any of it.

"You can't come in here," Dorian declared, jerking his torso and wrenching his arms. The weight of one man kept him pinned to the edge of the table. Dorian bucked and fought. Somehow they both ended up on the floor, tumbling around on the marble as if they were two kids in a schoolyard tussle. Dorian could hardly move. The cop locked around him had him by a good fifty pounds and probably five inches of height, which didn't sound like much until everyone was horizontal. Then, a body had a habit of turning to deadweight fast.

"Get the fuck off me!"

"Son," the gray-haired cop standing over the fray in the floor said, "we can do what we want. We can tear this place apart and say we had a hard time findin' ya. Know why?" Dorian glared, and the other man grinned wider as he held up a very official-looking document. "This here warrant says we can."

The first cop pushed up off him, and Dorian lay with back flat against the floor, staring up at Jansen, who looked like he was about to burst into tears. Well, that just pissed Dorian right off. No one was going to come into his house, interrupt his romantic evening, and bring tears to his husband's eyes. No way in hell.

"Fuck you, cop." He pushed his elbows against the cool floor. "I want my lawyer."

A boot connected with Dorian's chest, putting him right back against the marble.

"Stop it!" Jansen screamed. "You're hurting him!"

By God, the pain in Jansen's voice was enough to crush Dorian's hardened heart. By the look on his face and the glisten in his eyes, Jansen couldn't deal with seeing Dorian being bullied the way he was. Dorian couldn't deal with not soothing the man he loved.

At least the cops backed off. They didn't help him up from the floor, but they stopped beating him down like a felon trying to resist. They left him lying there, sucking wind and holding his chest. By then, every inch of his body had started to throb. Older age was catching up, apparently. Revenge was looking rather tasty.

"Can I see the warrant?" Jansen asked rather calmly, holding out his hand.

Dorian knew damn well Jansen wouldn't know the difference between a genuine, court-issued, judge-signed warrant for his arrest versus a fake made by one of Dorian's many enemies. But he also knew that, if nothing else, his husband could put on a damn good show. That's what he did. That's what he was best at… performing.

The gray-haired officer slapped the paper against Jansen's palm. Dorian climbed back to his feet and eased in next to his husband so he could look the paper over. Both cops kept one hand on their guns, as if Jansen or Dorian would do anything. Sure, Dorian had been a bad guy for a long time, but he'd backed off his criminal ways a while ago, even before they'd gotten married. He didn't act like a freakin' thug anymore. He was just a businessman who wanted to provide for his family.

"Dor," Jansen said, voice quivering. "It's the real thing." He'd said it like a statement, but Dorian knew Jansen needed confirmation, that those trembling words were really a question Jansen needed to have answered. Dorian gave a little jerk of the chin, a subtle nod he knew Jansen would catch but everyone else would probably miss. "They have it signed by the judge and everything," Jansen added for good measure. "You, um… you…."

As Dorian sucked in a breath so deep it made his big, tattooed chest expand, he closed his eyes and lowered his head, scrubbed his hand down his face, then exhaled. He had to resign himself to the idea of being behind bars. He'd come close to being thrown in jail before, and done enough shit to deserve a few years in prison, but the closest he'd ever come was a night here and there just to quench his temper. Nothing like this, though. Nothing close to being charged with murder.

"Fine," Dorian said, raising his chin and squaring his shoulders. Being thrown in a cage like an animal didn't scare him. He could protect himself. He hated the idea of losing his freedom, of not being able to keep Jansen safe, but he could do this with dignity.

"Baby, I need—"

"Can I at least get him a shirt?" Jansen asked in a low, shattered voice as if he hadn't heard Dorian speaking at all.

"We should take him like this," the younger cop said.

"No," the gray-haired guy immediately responded. "There's that stupid civil rights shit you rookies don't know nothin' 'bout." He looked over at Jansen. "Make it quick. We ain't waitin' long."

HEART BEATING wildly, Jansen took off in a run toward the laundry room. He knew Maria had done their clothes earlier that day and knew there would be a T-shirt in there for Dorian to throw on, something ratty and unimportant, something Dorian wouldn't miss if it got destroyed.

God, he couldn't believe this was happening. Dorian didn't deserve this, not now, not after all the changing he'd done. He was a good man now. He took care of his businesses in an honorable and legal way, took care of his family and friends, gave back to the community. The man had a damn heart of gold, and now they chose to shit on him.

"This can't be happening," Jansen whispered to himself.

He pulled a plain white tee out of the dryer, then rushed back to where the cops had been manhandling his husband. He stopped dead in his tracks when he found Dorian's arms wrenched back and a cop at each wrist. Dorian's lip looked like it had been busted wide open. A spot of blood clung to the stubble on his chin.

"Did you fucking hit him?" Jansen yelled as he charged forward.

"Nah, we didn't hit him. He fell down while trying to get away from us."

"Screw you, pig," Dorian spat.

They wrenched him up again, pulling his arms back so hard his pecs flexed and he stood on the tips of his toes to give his arms a hint of relief.

"You resisting us, Grant?" The rookie right-hooked Dorian in the ribs. "You don't want to resist us."

Dorian's legs shook so badly Jansen could see them tremble, as if they just couldn't hold his weight anymore and needed a break from trying to keep Dorian upright. He almost buckled. Jansen could tell he was putting up a hell of a fight to stay on his feet.

"Can you stop beating him up, please?" Jansen cried out.

"Baby, I'm fine. It's okay," Dorian swore. "These two ass… gentlemen are going to take damn good care of me from here on out, right boys?" He looked back at the two cops. "I mean, since your boss's boss is my golf buddy and shit."

Gray-haired's eyes widened.

The rookie arched a brow as if he didn't get it.

Jansen smirked and Dorian smiled wickedly.

"Cuff him, Bloom," the old one said.

The rookie slapped the cuffs on Dorian's wrists, and for the first time since their arrival on the mansion's doorstep, he actually acted like a real cop. He started reciting the Miranda Rights… again. "You have the right to remain silent. Anything you say can and will be used against you in a court of law…."

Dorian let them handle him and this time didn't put up a fight at all. In fact, he kept a smile on his face, kept giving Jansen the same loving, caring stare he'd been giving him right before the cops interrupted the candlelit dinner Maria had prepared for them. The remains of the enchiladas still filled their plates. Wine still filled their glasses. They'd barely started eating when this bullshit had broken loose.

And amazingly, Dorian looked as calm as he had before, as if the something inside of him keeping him sane had either snapped, or snapped back into place.

With all of Dorian's bravado, Jansen thought he could take some of his husband's strength and use it as his own, but he couldn't. He was falling apart on the inside. The man he loved, the man who'd protected him and cared for him the last three years was being carted off in handcuffs and being charged with murder, and there wasn't a damn thing Jansen could do to stop them.

"Baby," Dorian said, ripping Jansen right out of his internal meltdown. "Get my phone. Call my lawyer. Her number's in there. Tell her to get her ass down to the precinct now."

Jansen couldn't do much more than nod. Tears began to flow down his cheeks. While everything once felt surreal, now it felt very, very real. They were taking Dorian to jail and God only knew when Jansen would see the man he loved again.

Dorian's pissed-off expression softened significantly. Jansen saw his arm jerk, as if he was trying to reach out and touch him. "Baby, listen to me," Dorian said. Their gazes locked as soon as Dorian spoke his command. Jansen sniffled back his tears and Dorian continued. "They ain't gonna put me away. Got it? They ain't got shit on me. Go call my lawyer, and get her to the precinct, okay?"

Jansen nodded again.

"I love you," Dorian told him.

"I love you too."

Through his watery eyes, he watched the blue lights atop the cop cars flicker. They made a clicking noise as they strobed—a noise Jansen would no doubt hear as he fought to go to sleep later that night... if he was able to lie down long enough to try.

The older cop clamped his hand over Dorian's head, pressing his once neatly styled hair against his scalp. He guided Dorian into the backseat and slammed the door, then joined his partner in the front of the car. Dorian kept his eyes glued on Jansen, and Jansen could've sworn he'd seen the glistening of tears clinging to Dorian's thick, dark lashes. His husband didn't cry. It just wasn't something he did, but in a situation like this, tears were okay. God knew Jansen would certainly shed his own fair share after they pulled away from the house.

After the cars disappeared down the driveway, Jansen spent one silent moment—a moment longer than any other—trying to collect himself. He stood there in the heat of a June New Orleans night with humid wind beating against his wet cheeks and the blazing-red memory of the squad car's taillights traveling down the driveway. He was left standing there with all the despair and emptiness he felt after those officers had pushed Dorian into the car. In the heat of the bayou night, he felt his world falling apart around him and all the safety Dorian had promised him had just been taken away.

"I love you," he said, bringing his ringed hand up to his heart. He held his fist there while his mind checked out for a bit. He needed a minute, maybe two, to feel nothing and think nothing and be nothing. He needed the numbness before he completely broke down, and once the urge to spontaneously combust passed, everything was... not okay... not right... but better.

He put his head on straight as best as he could. It needed to be clear if he wanted to be the man Dorian needed him to be. And there was nothing he wanted more in the world right now. He had to pull it together and handle business so he could get his man back home—where he belonged.

1

Six months later

CLANK. CLANK. Bang. Those sounds didn't come from the sand and ocean, or the seagulls flying over Davi's head. The sounds confused him, but didn't concern him enough to make him open his eyes. *Clank. Bang. Boom.*

What the…?

He bolted straight up and peeled his eyes open. The room around him was dark as night, a blur of color here and there. Where were the sun and sand and ocean he'd fallen asleep to? Where had his tropical paradise gone?

"Sorry, guy," a scruffy voice called from the corner of the room. Davi blinked once, twice. The third time everything came into focus. The beautiful blue horizon he'd been staring out at had turned into filthy, black-painted cinder-block walls. The blurred color came from neon signs advertising American beers. The voice wasn't the hot cabana boy he'd been ogling in his mind's eye, but an old, balding plumber they'd hired to fix a busted drain behind the VIP bar. That old man just utterly ruined Davi's nap.

Davi hefted himself up from the booth. He'd just wanted an hour, maybe two to sleep before the festivities got started. Honestly, he wasn't even sure why he'd agreed to partake in Thanksgiving dinner with the guys. That was an American holiday. While he appreciated the invite, he didn't exactly understand the meaning of the tradition. People were so thankful for something they turned into face-stuffing gluttons, watched football, then went shopping? It just didn't make sense.

Muttering curses in Portuguese, Davi started down the walkway overlooking the empty club. He balled both hands and rubbed the edges of his fists against his eye sockets to get rid of the remaining sleep. His feet dragged the carpet. His muttered curses turned into soft grumbles.

Voices bled out from the door to his right. That lonesome door led into the offices of what everyone called "General Management," meaning anyone who got called up there would most likely find themselves in hot water. And the voice he'd heard belonged to a man Davi respected more than most: Jason… his boss.

"Deus, perdoe-me," he whispered before taking the few steps closer to the door. Eavesdropping had been considered a sin in his boyhood home, but he

couldn't help doing it now. The voices behind that door didn't sound happy, and if Jason was in trouble....

"The club's closin', Jason," someone said.

Davi jerked his head back. With widened eyes, he stared at the translucent glass and the dark, distorted shadows beyond it. His English might not have been the greatest, but he understood what "the club's closin'" meant, and he assumed with a fair amount of certainty it meant trouble for him—not the violent kind of in-fear-for-your-life trouble, but the kind that meant his world would be turned upside down.

Oh merda!

That blast of bad news had him good and awake now. Worry had him on the verge of panic. He wasn't in the States legally and probably couldn't land another job unless it was in a seedier club than Sin & Seduction. He would have no way to pay his rent and put food on his table. He'd have no means to care for himself and had no family here to run to.

This was bad. So bad.

What the hell would he do?

Where would he go?

He pressed his ear back to the glass. The faint sound of different voices bounced back and forth. The only person he recognized was Jason, the stage manager. The others, he couldn't put a face or a name to. He didn't know any of those people, and yet they hid behind that door deciding his fate.

Jason said, "There has to be something we can do."

Sim, please, do something.

"Afraid not, kid. The latest raid from the cops really put a damper on business."

"Then we'll do something to boost it."

"We're losing money hand over fist here."

"Then we'll pull people off the streets. We'll have dancers at the door. Who wouldn't want to come in then?"

Someone let out a hearty chuckle. A chorus of much smaller laughs promptly followed. Davi's stomach knotted. He couldn't believe they were laughing. People were losing their jobs and these assholes were laughing.

Then the noise abruptly stopped. "I'm serious, Hank." Jason's voice sounded desperate now. "It's a good idea."

"I'm too damn old to be hangin' out in nightclubs, kid. The smoke bothers my sinuses. The booze is killing my liver. The music has me half-deaf."

"Hank...."

"Jason."

"Some of these guys need this place. Some of your dancers have nothing else," Jason said, voice rising in pitch. "What will they do? Where will they go?"

"You act like dancing here is the runway to riches."

"Seriously?"

"Yeah, kid, I think I sound pretty damn serious."

"Hank, do you have any idea what goes on in the VIP area?"

"Drugs. Sex. Booze."

"No." Jason paused. "Well, yes, but no. I'm not saying it's right, but a lot of money changes hands up there and some of your customers leave here a hell of a lot happier than they were when they got here, and your dancers reap the benefits."

"I see."

"Do you?"

Everything went quiet inside that room. Davi wished like hell he could see what was going on behind the office door. He wished he could see their faces so he could judge their expressions. He couldn't, though. Davi was a fly on the wall, someone unimportant to the business of the club. He was just a pretty face and a nice ass for people to stare at and spend money on.

"I'm gettin' too tired for this lifestyle, Jason," Hank said.

"Then get out of it. That doesn't mean the club has to close."

"I'm looking for someone to buy the place, investors or new owners, something. But it ain't lookin' pretty, kid. We're all preparin' for the worst here. So, for right now, we're goin' with the club's closin'."

There was another short pause, a pause that lasted way too long for Davi's comfort. He shifted back and forth on his heels, wishing like hell he could melt into the walls just so he could see and hear everything going on in that office. Then Hank said, "So I was thinkin'… if you can get a closing show together, we'll have a big New Year's Eve celebration and when we lock the doors New Year's Day, we'll lock 'em for good… unless something changes. That gives you over a month to put something together. Think you can do it?"

Davi really didn't process a whole lot after that. The world sort of shut down on him. Through a narrowing tunnel, he stared at the office door, willing himself not to tear up and not to fall apart.

"*Eu não quero ir para casa*," he mumbled in his native tongue as he slowly backed away, fearing he would have no choice but to return to Portugal and give up on living the American dream, worse yet, give up on being true to himself.

While he loved his family with all his heart, he didn't want to go back home. Going back home meant he had to face certain skeletons in his closet, demons his good Catholic *mamãe* and *papai* would never, *ever* understand. To be outcast from his family—the people who were supposed to love him unconditionally—scared the hell out of him. Not to mention the idea of facing a man he once loved so much he would've given the last breath in his body for. To see Paulo with another man would be devastating at best.

There was no way he could go back home.

Not now.

Not ever.

He charged down the walkway, running at full speed, then down the steps without slowing. He galloped to a halt in the backstage area where the dancers always congregated while the shows were going on. Davi doubled over and gripped his knees, sucking in short bursts of air that really didn't feed his lungs with anything useful. His heart thumped so hard he could feel the thudding in his temples. He blinked back the tiny beads of sweat dripping down into his eyes.

The smell of food nailed him hard. In the madness and sadness, he'd forgotten all about the feast he'd been invited to. A tradition he simply didn't understand, but participated in anyway. Since none of the dancers had any family to go home to or their loved ones also had jobs, they celebrated here. Together. Like a real family. Something Davi no longer had outside of the club.

He looked over the spread of food—the giant turkey in the center of the folding table, the dishes filled to their rims with other traditional American dishes. Someone had even brought a pie of some kind. It all smelled so wonderful, like cinnamon and nutmeg, and everything autumny. And everyone looked so happy, as a true family should be.

"*Não. Não. Não.*" He shook his head, ruefully watching the seven other main-stage dancers gleefully laughing and talking as they filled their plates with food. He almost felt guilty for knowing the club's fate. It wasn't fair for him to have to be the one to spoil their fun.

"Não," he said once more, this time a little louder than he had before.

One head rose, looking in his direction, then another and another. Within seconds every eye in the room was on him. The clatter of utensils against dishes completely ceased. Dead quiet replaced the eager chatter. Davi swallowed hard, gaze trickling over every curious face.

"The club... it is... it is closing," he finally said. Then he braced himself for the onslaught of a million questions he couldn't answer.

Bodies stilled; seven sets of eyes widened. Seven faces stared at him as if he'd just prophesied the apocalypse. "I hear the owners talking to Meester Jason. They don't want the club anymore." There was a breathlessness to his voice—not just from running all the way from the offices upstairs to the backstage area downstairs, but because the weight of what that meant to not only himself, but his fellow dancers, had become utterly suffocating.

"Wait. What?" One single voice cut through the thick silence. It was the dancer they called Golden Boy, one whom Davi had a schoolboy-type crush on ever since he'd come to Sin & Seduction. Backstage, among their little family, he was simply Lance.

Lance set his plate on the edge of the table and stepped forward, lean, lithe body moving with the kind of grace true dancers dreamed of. He wasn't so tall his thin figure made him lanky, but he wasn't short, either. Somewhere in the area of the perfect build, if Davi had to guess. His pink lips were framed with deep dimples, high cheeks spilling up toward sky-blue eyes.

"Are you sure?" Lance asked.

Davi nodded.

"Where did you hear that?"

"*Senhor* Jason is with the owners now. I heard it through the door."

"And you're positive that's what you heard?"

Davi nodded again. "I don't wanna go home. I…."

"Shh…," Lance said, pulling Davi into a hug. "No one is going to make you go home."

"I cannot work. If I cannot work, I cannot live."

"Don't worry about it."

Those wonderfully strong arms of Lance's tightened around Davi's body. His embrace felt so warm, so comforting and caring that Davi felt compelled to relax, to close his eyes and simply… relax. He honestly didn't want to worry about it, and with Lance stepping into such a protective role, Davi thought he could let go of the worry.

But that was all fairy-tale fun and happily ever afters. In reality, Lance had as little power as Davi did. He was just a dancer too. Lance couldn't change fate. He couldn't change the inevitable. If the club closed, Davi was screwed. Bottom. Line.

He must've stiffened or something, because Lance's arms flexed and two warm lips found the crown of Davi's head. They lingered there, waiting—he supposed—for him to panic again. He didn't. Maybe he wouldn't. The lips moved, and Lance said a soft, "We'll figure it out."

2

"WE'LL FIGURE it out" came with a whole lot of promises and a whole lot of assumed responsibilities. Responsibilities Lance wasn't in any position to shoulder. First of all, he barely knew this guy. Well, not on an intimate level. He'd admired Davi from afar like every other living, breathing man with a pulse and a hot spot for dick. That admiration didn't mean Lance wanted to know the guy's woes.

But damn it if he didn't keep his arms locked around Davi's body, and he was definitely trying to think of a way to be as helpful as he could without getting too involved. He could make idle suggestions and hope for the best. He could offer Davi a couch to crash on if all else failed.

"I know people," Lance quietly suggested. He knew he could get Davi another job, probably making a lot less money for a lot less prestigious work, but it would be a job....

As his mind got to work on thinking up a solution, he kept his arms around Davi and held the poor kid as tight as he could without crushing him. Davi curled against his chest, head on Lance's shoulder, each breath a hot burst of air across Lance's neck. It had been much more than a minute since he'd been close enough to another man to feel those subtle inhalations and exhalations gusting over his skin. Not to say the little shivers that came with each breath were welcome, but they did make him feel more human and less... mmm, frigid.

Looking over Davi's shoulder, Lance took in the entire backstage view— the rack of old, worn-out costumes, the vanities with blown bulbs, the chairs with cracks racing through their vinyl... every single human being he'd come to consider his family. Some of those dancers looked worried. Some didn't seem to care or hid their fears well by going right back to the feast Davi's blast of news had interrupted. They piled mashed potatoes and slivers of turkey onto their plates, topped it off with gravy and green beans, and let's not forget a healthy dose of carbs to round out the meal. God, it all smelled so good and Lance's stomach had started actively campaigning to be filled over an hour ago, but he couldn't very well stuff his face with something so bad, so final, and so life-changing hanging in the air and leaving a trail of unanswered questions. He knew he needed to get to the bottom of the rumors about the club for his sake and everyone else's.

"The show must go on," Lance whispered against Davi's ear.

He slowly released the dancer he'd been holding on to for far too long, exhaled, and took a step back. Even if the club did close, Lance knew life would carry on. It had to. Sin & Seduction wasn't the be-all and end-all. The world wouldn't cease and neither would life. Sure, things would have to change. Money would be tight. But life wouldn't end. For anyone.

Life. Ha.

Yeah, Lance vaguely remembered having one of those before becoming completely engrossed in the world of Sin & Seduction, before he was either dancing on the stage or dancing in VIP, or… the other many extracurriculars that came with the job. If he wasn't onstage shaking what God gave him, then he was in someone's bedroom or the back of their limo doing things naughty confessions on Sunday morning were made of. His nine-to-five involved tubes of lube and used condoms, happy men, and an even happier bank account.

That sounded so bad. He sounded like a cheap whore, but there was nothing cheap or even whorish about him. He kept clean. Kept safe. He stuck to the same handful of men. Thank God they all had pretty insatiable appetites for cock. It kept him paid well. But it wasn't exactly the life he would've picked for himself. When his fifth-grade teacher had asked the class what they wanted to be when they grew up, Lance was pretty damn sure he didn't raise his hand and say, "Ms. Fleming, I want to be a male prostitute."

Maybe, if the doors closed on this place, he could have a real life, a real career. The closing could actually be a good thing. It could be his chance to change some things—like his love life, or lack thereof. Maybe he wouldn't be so jaded by the shit he saw going on in the club that he could finally trust a man enough to settle down with him. Not that he considered monogamy a life goal.

"You guys," he said, raising his voice and speaking over his shoulder for his colleagues to hear. "Please don't say anything about what you heard until I talk to Jason." The other dancers grumbled their agreement. Lance looked back at Davi. "I'm gonna find out what's going on. So don't freak out."

"Thank you," Davi whispered, big brown puppy-dog eyes looking up at Lance as if he were the freaking Savior or something.

"Go get some food. I'll be back."

Lance let Davi go, then spun on his heel and started toward the mouth of the hallway when the low thumping of tennis shoes against concrete echoing down the hall stopped him in his tracks. With each somber step, the footfalls grew louder and louder, as though whoever was attached to those slowly marching feet was getting closer and closer.

Jason emerged from the darkness, looking as delicious as ever. He had his auburn hair cut a bit shorter than normal, showing off his defined features and his rigid jaw. He had a long, slender neck begging for a night's worth of kisses. That man would always be Lance's one big regret, the one who got away—at least, that was how it felt right now.

"You ladies enjoying your dinner?" Jason asked as he stepped farther into the light.

All eyes turned in his direction. He wore the fakest smile Lance had ever seen—fake because the shifty nervousness in his gaze and the stern set of his chin gave away the truth. The tick in his jaw spoke volumes about his ill-hidden worry.

A few dancers responded with words that melded together and came across as nonsensical noise. One of them suggested Jason grab a plate and have a seat. Their boss man hesitated a moment. The look passing over his face at the mention of food made him appear nauseated, as though his stomach was too knotted to even consider holding down a single bite—much like Lance's. But Jason made a good show of digging in with the crew.

What better way to hide hard truths?

Lance simply couldn't partake. He had too much on his mind, too much bothering him. He hadn't been prepared for the kick in the gut Davi had so harshly delivered not fifteen minutes ago. Maybe a few of the others saw this coming, what with all the bad press the club had been getting lately and the seemingly unending string of drug busts, but he hadn't.

The dancers had the worst of it. For them, Sin & Seduction wasn't about getting high and getting off, or about partying all night long... well, not for the most part, anyway. Most of those men relied on the club and its patrons to pay their bills and put food on the table. Some had sugar daddies or mommas who took care of their needs. Some of them walked away with enough cash in their Speedos to supplement their other jobs. The point was the bulk of their money slipped between hands. Big paydays weren't recorded on paper and were not something they could get unemployment for. They were completely screwed.

Thankfully, Lance had always been pretty smart about his money. He'd been stashing back as much as he could as often as he could. So his nest egg was decent, but that was material bullshit. All those rent-a-lovers may have padded his wallet well, but they didn't do a damn thing for his heart. That was where the guys from the club became an essential part of Lance's day-to-day.

Outside of the club, the dancers and the lovers he'd found there, Lance didn't have jack shit in the way of a support system. He hadn't talked to his mom or dad since they'd kicked him out of the house at sixteen. His one sister had come to find him a few years ago, after she'd turned eighteen and moved away from home, but she didn't agree with his sexuality or his lifestyle. So their relationship never blossomed, either.

Outside the club, he really had abso-fucking-lutely nothing.

Indeed, the show must go on....

"Mario and Scott, you're up first. Followed by Jake, then Davi...," Jason said as he stood from the table.

Apparently, Lance had missed the entire freaking meal and they were back to business.

Jason kept calling off the dancers' names as if nothing had happened. The dancers kept stuffing their faces as if they didn't eat the other 364 days of the year. No one stopped him. They didn't give away the fact they'd heard about the club shutting down, just like Lance had asked.

Good job, guys.

"Got it?" Jason asked, clamping his palm against the back of the clipboard.

Everyone in the room, save for Lance, yelled out a harmonic yes.

Everyone in the room, save for Lance, went right back to what they'd been doing.

Jason turned and headed down the hall toward his office. Lance didn't stop staring. He watched every footfall, even watched the way Jason's shoulders rounded the moment he thought no one was watching him, as if all the wind had been knocked out of his body or all his hard-won composure had been lost. It must've taken a whole lot of effort to look every dancer in the eye and carry on as if nothing was wrong. And Lance didn't know whether to respect that or detest it for being an outright lie.

Lance glanced back over his shoulder one more time. He found everyone still going through the normal motions—a few gossiped and laughed, a few fawned over Davi. Mario and Scott were in the middle of changing into their stage costumes. No one paid Lance any attention. No one would notice him chasing Jason down the hall like a maniac.

Right before Jason managed to close the door, Lance slammed his palm down and stopped it from meeting the jamb. Jason's head shot up. Lance stepped into the dimly lit office and closed the door behind him. He said, "Tell me what's going on."

"What are you talking about?"

"Really?" Lance crossed his arms and arched a brow, lips pursed and pinched at the corners. "Let's try this again."

Jason shrugged.

"Don't play games with me, Jason. Tell me what's happening to the club."

For a long moment, Jason stared as if he didn't have a clue what Lance was talking about. The longer Jason held that stoic expression, the more willpower it took to keep Lance on the opposite side of the desk and not all up in Jason's grill giving him the third degree.

"C'mon. It's me." Lance's voice softened. "You tell me everything."

Sighing, Jason sat down behind his desk, and instead of sitting back in his chair with his arms tucked behind his head and that handsomely smug expression he often sported, he looked tense. His shoulders remained square as a box as he rested his forearms on the desk's metal surface. He locked his hands together—one thumb tucked under the other. His jawline rippled as he clenched his teeth.

"Jason...."

"What have you heard?" he finally asked.

Lance sank down in the seat across from his boss and a man he considered a good friend. He tucked his right foot under his left thigh and crossed his arms over his chest. "I think you know exactly what I heard." He didn't mean to smirk, but he could feel the height of his eyebrow arching up into his forehead, felt one corner of his lips tugging.

Jason remained silent and stoic.

"The club's closing," Lance finally said matter-of-factly, not leaving Jason any room to avoid the subject.

JASON'S MOUTH pinched shut. He kept his stare on Lance—focus not faltering, eyes not shifting. The silence and hesitation spoke volumes, but Jason wasn't sure what to say. He couldn't very well confirm the rumors were true. Not yet. The owners were working their asses off to keep things going. As long as there were dancers and staff and a reason to invest, there was still a very, very small chance the place could be saved. If everyone got scared and jumped ship, there wouldn't be anything left to save.

Jason raked his fingers through his shorter than normal hair—yet another dead giveaway he had something to hide. "Where did you hear that?"

Smooth. Answer a question with a question. Good thing you don't play poker, you ass.

"It's true, isn't it?"

"I'm not at liberty—"

"Jason, c'mon, man. I'm the closest thing you have to a best friend right now."

Shit. That epic truth hurt... epically.

"Tell me what the hell is going on." Lance sat forward and hooked both hands on the edge of Jason's desk, getting all up in his face. "Don't I deserve to know?"

Jason pressed his thumb and forefinger to his eye sockets and rubbed tight circles. He nodded, but the movement was so subtle Lance might've missed it had he not been eyeing Jason so hard. Jason was about to do exactly what Hank had asked him not to, but what else could he do? Lying never suited him and Lance had him over the fire right now.

"Please don't tell the other dancers yet," Jason said, exhaustion dripping from his voice. "It's still very up in the air. The owners don't want the club, but they're looking for investors. Problem is, with the bad press, no one wants to touch the place."

"Why don't you and Brad buy them out?"

Jason snorted. "You're kidding, right?"

"No." Lance shrugged. "Why not?"

"I don't have shit to my name and no credit. Brad doesn't have that kind of money either, man. His daughter and ex-wife get a good portion of what he makes. The rest goes into our house and savings."

"What about your friend? Jansen... and his husband? Aren't they loaded?"

"Dorian's in prison and Jansen is... well, he isn't exactly stable right now."

"Dammit," Lance said with a sigh.

It was Jason's turn to slump down in his chair and fidget with his fingers. He lowered his head and stared a hole straight through Lance's cranium. It felt as though they were both waiting for the other one to come up with something that resembled a good plan.

Silence.

Apparently, neither one of them had enough neurons firing to think up something good enough to consider. And the quiet staring, the fidgeting, and the despair Lance kept trying to hide had gotten old like ten minutes ago.

"Did you need something else?" Jason asked.

Lance frowned. "Am I being dismissed?"

"Lance...."

"No. No." Lance held up both hands defensively. "Would hate to be an imposition."

"C'mon, man."

"No. It's okay. I should go back out there anyway."

3

IN THE dark space of Jason's little closet office, it was hard to read someone's expression if that someone hid within the shadow. Lucky for Lance, the only light sat on the edge of the desk, sprinkling a soft golden glow over Jason's clipboard and the schedule for the night. But while he may have been able to hide his face, he knew he wouldn't be able to hide his anger behind empty words and a stiff body. He needed to get out of there. Fast.

Lance stood from his seat, heart hammering harder than it should've been. For good reason, though. His heart hurt. Hurt more than Lance would've owned up to for anyone. He considered Jason one of his best friends. Hell, there was a time not too long ago when he'd dreamed of something romantic with the hot-bodied ginger. Now they were reduced to… to what—employee and employer?

Ouch.

"See you out there," he said, thumbing over his shoulder.

"Lance, wait…."

Midstep, Lance froze, but he refused to turn back around. That would've been a dire mistake; facing Jason wouldn't have gotten him anywhere he needed to be. Jason had this uncanny way of reducing Lance's willpower to dust, even with Bradley Britt—local legend and ex-breeder—in the picture.

"What?" he asked. As soon as he heard that wobbly, one-syllable word, Lance wished he'd kept on walking.

"Don't do this to me."

This time, Lance *did* spin back around. He slammed one flattened palm down on Jason's shitty desk and leaned in close, nostrils flared, lips peeling back. "Don't do *what* to you?" he asked in a frighteningly low, even voice. It wasn't exactly calm, but wasn't blistering with rage, either. "You're the one who's lying to the people who trust and respect you the most. I'm looking out for you, trying to watch your back. I'm *trying* to be a good friend, like I've always been, and you're dismissing me like I'm nothing to you. That fucking hurt. For you to know how I feel about you, and you *still*"—Lance popped the desk again—"treat me like I'm nothing, that hurts more than you can possibly imagine."

"Lance, I'm—"

"I don't care, Jason. I'm done. I'm here to be a dancer. Nothing more. My station is crystal clear. I won't mistake it again."

"Lance, c'mon."

He only stayed long enough to give Jason one last look, then headed out the door and back to where he belonged, with the other underlings, not chumming it up in the boss's office.

When the door closed behind him, the loud cracking sound echoing in the quiet hallway gave him a start. Lance's already edgy heart skipped a beat. He rolled his eyes, silently cursing himself for letting Jason get to him like that. Seriously. He couldn't remember the last time he'd made such an ass of himself, but he would almost bet two nights with Howard Gordon at a whopping two grand a pop that Jason had been the reason he'd embarrassed himself then as well. He scrubbed his hand over his messy blond hair and continued down the hall.

Why are you obsessing... still?

He reached the mouth of the hallway, where it opened up to the backstage area, and found everyone moving about as if the news of their little world crumbling down around them didn't matter. Some of the club's other workers and not-so-well-known dancers were stuffing their faces, now joined by a couple of bartenders. A few sorted through the costumes. Everything had returned to business as usual and it was one of the most heartbreaking things to watch, even if part of him prayed Davi's blast of news had been a bad dream and the conversation he'd just had with Jason had never happened. All of his coworkers, his only family, acted as though life wasn't about to change for them all, oblivious and happily meandering through their normal Thursday evening.

In a few hours, patrons would leak in and the music would sing out through the club, the dancers would take the stage, and the lights would flicker and bounce and strobe, each piece playing its part in the big show. They would all wear smiles—fake or not—and they would do their best to make every person who walked through the hallowed front doors of Sin & Seduction feel like they could own the world. That was why the clientele loved them. That was what had once made this place so magical, so wonderful, and one of the greatest nightclubs in the Big Easy.

Lance turned his gaze away from his friends and headed over to the costumes. The two dancers who'd been there before him moved on to the second rack. Like, what? Did the look on his face run them off? Sure, he wasn't sunshine and rainbows right now, but was it really *that* bad?

He dug through outfit after outfit, mechanically sliding the coat hangers down the metal rail without even paying attention to the garments hanging from them. The hangers raked against the rack, letting out a high-pitched squeal. The sound normally would've gnarled his fingers and made him cringe, but tonight, it didn't really bother him. He barely even noticed. He was half there and half not.

Lance just couldn't seem to get his head in the game, and honestly considered sitting his first performance out.

"Lance?" a soft voice said from somewhere behind him. "Can we talk?"

He recognized the voice—the silkiness of it, the awkward enunciation, but more importantly, the way it was not too bassy and not high-pitched. Perfect. Just the right amount of everything.

He turned around slowly, subduing the half-smile plastered onto his face.

Apparently, Davi had been practicing his routine while Lance had been lamenting over love never had. Sweat clung to his bare chest. The florescent lights hanging from the rafters twinkled in the moist beads on his beautiful bronze skin. Wet strings of long black hair stuck to his cheeks. Lance had to fight the urge to reach out, push the tiny tendrils back, and tuck them behind Davi's pierced ear.

"What's up?" he asked only after clearing his throat.

"I saw you." Davi leaned in to whisper. "You went to talk to Jason, didn't you?"

"Maybe."

"What'd he say?"

The pleading look in Davi's puppy-dog eyes could've softened the hardest heart. Fortunately, Lance had been doing a good job of keeping his on lockdown, reserving it only for Jason's beck and call... unfortunately. He swore to himself no one else would get past the guard dogs, the barbed-wire fence, and the high-tech security system his brain had in place.

Oh, but Davi was so damn adorable and so scared, and so on his way to climbing right over into no-man's-land. Well, maybe not that close, but Lance would freely take some carnal comforting, or maybe even give it, if that was Davi's thing. Either way.

"Davi, I"—Lance shook his head—"can't."

"Please."

"I promised not to talk about it."

"Lance, please."

That look. That voice. The helplessness and innocence, the pleading and the misery. If Lance had one weak spot, it was for cute damsels in distress. While Davi was way too masculine to be a damsel, he had the distress part down pat. And boy, didn't that make Lance's heart go all pitter-patter?

Shit.

Clenching his jaw, Lance silently cursed himself for not having the willpower to tell Davi he couldn't talk about his impromptu meeting with Jason and stand firm on the fact. The longer Davi stood there looking all desperate, handsome, and completely delicious, the more Lance's wavering will crumbled.

What would it hurt? Everyone would know everything soon enough, right?

Sinking ship, Lance. Sinking. Fucking. Ship.

"It's not looking good," Lance finally said. The very second the words left his lips, he wished he could've taken them back because they betrayed the trust Jason had given him. *Too late. You messed up.* "Promise you won't tell anyone else. None of us are supposed to know. They don't want people getting scared and leaving. Besides, if it gets out that I perpetuated your little rumor, Jason will never trust me again, okay?"

Davi nodded. The pleading look in his eyes grew sadder, as though he was on the verge of crying now. *No crying. Please no crying.* If there was one thing Lance wouldn't be able to deal with right now, it was watching Hot and Helpless let tears rain down his cute dimpled cheeks. Tears would surely make him melt.

"We should get ready for tonight, don't you think?" Lance softly asked.

Again, Davi nodded.

Lance gently laid his hand against Davi's shoulder and guided him to the rack. Maybe Davi would have more luck than him finding a costume for tonight.

Together they dug through all the corny themes that had gone out of style twenty years ago. There was seriously a bullfighter costume with a fading red cloak hanging there, and for the briefest moment he imagined Davi all decked out in gold sequins and black velvet, with a cloak of silk flowing behind him as he sauntered onto the stage. Even he wasn't hot enough to make something so ridiculous look good. Sadly, ratty costumes were the least of their worries right now.

He stopped at a white lab coat, plastic stethoscope hanging from the pocket, and the little lightbulb in Lance's head fired up like the Fourth of July. "I got it!" he declared as he yanked the costume from the hanger. "Do you have a red Speedo?"

"Yeah…," Davi drawled, curiosity and nervousness clear in the one word.

"Doctor Love." Lance grinned. "You can dance to the song. You know, the one by KISS."

"KISS?" Davi frowned.

"It's a band. From the eighties. You know? Corny glam metal?"

Davi shook his head.

"Trust me. It's perfect."

4

Friday

THE THIRTY or more minutes spent in the car twice a week to get from Dorian Grant's mansion to the Orleans Parish Prison had started turning into a blur three months ago—after the first dozen trips.

He'd put his entire life on hold to see Dorian. Not that he would ever complain about any of it. The prison's visiting hours interfered with dance rehearsal, so the dance company Dorian had gotten him in had no choice but to let him go. Jansen hadn't shared that tidbit with his husband. He didn't see any point in adding bad news to an already horrible situation. Besides, Jansen had more important things to do with his time, like seeing to his husband's legal woes. Dorian's well-being became his central focus. Now, twice a week, he went on the most cumbersome ride of his life, and he did it out of pure love.

When Jansen had first begun visiting Dorian through a disgusting plate of marred glass, he'd spent those long, seemingly never-ending minutes chewing his nails down to the quick and quietly cursing every driver on the road, or cursing the state of Louisiana for the perpetual construction that led to detour after freakin' detour. The more anxious he became, the more it felt as if everyone else in the world had ground to a crawl. It was agonizing. Maddening.

During the last few visits, Dorian had remained quiet and distant. He hadn't appeared excited to see Jansen at all. Not like he had been in the beginning, six months ago. Where relieved smiles once greeted him, now all he got was pinched lips and a gaze that seemed to take in everything but Jansen. The very worst of those visits had been about three months ago, right after an incident Dorian had refused to discuss. The slit across his brow and the swelling in his cheek had told a story his lips refused to tell.

As soon as Dorian appeared in the window, Jansen's eyes bulged. He went all fish-mouthed—opening and closing, opening and closing. He sank down in the hard plastic chair and absently reached for the phone on the partition wall. This time, he didn't give a shit about pulling out a Kleenex to lift the receiver from the hook. He didn't care about the germs and the filth. "What happened to you?" he all but gasped when he finally found the fortitude to speak.

"Nothin'. I'm fine." Dorian had one of the greatest poker faces known to man, but even he couldn't hide behind such a blatant lie. "Did you put some money on my account?"

"Yeah, a hundred bucks, just like you asked."

"Good. Have you talked to Rebecca lately?"

"No. I called her, but—"

"Shit."

When Dorian dragged his hand down his face, Jansen noticed his busted, bloodied knuckles. Dorian had been fighting. Jansen distantly wondered what the other guy looked like.

"I miss you," Jansen finally said.

"Shhh..." Dorian quickly looked around the room. "Someone might hear you."

Whatever that meant. Guess he'd have to save the "I love you" for another time.

Dorian wasn't the man he'd married anymore. This man didn't have the strength and confidence Dorian Grant had. He didn't exude power. He seemed scared and alone, and Jansen would've given anything to have him back home.

Dorian wouldn't have even been left in that shitty prison had the damn judge not denied his bail. The reason for keeping Dorian behind bars had to be the dumbest crap Jansen had ever heard in his life. The big decision maker, sitting on his hefty ass behind a bench the good people of New Orleans had given him, had said Dorian had enough money to make him a flight risk. The judge claimed Dorian could leave the country on a whim and never be heard from again, thus not paying for the crime they were all so certain he'd committed. The district attorney had put that little bug in the judge's ear. According to Rebecca Chambers—Dorian's trusted lawyer—that was how it worked. In cases like this, the judge always listened to the DA over anyone else. As if *that* was true justice.

God, if Jansen had a violent streak like Dorian....

Cheek pressed against the cool window, he exhaled a breath he didn't know he'd been holding. A lot of things in his life had become like that since they'd hauled his husband away. Jansen had to remind himself to get out of bed, to eat, to shower, to breathe, to keep living. His body was on autopilot and his brain had shut down. Those menial tasks got lost to things like hiding in the bed and staring at the ceiling. That hopelessness came immediately after the local authorities hauled the love of his life away in the middle of the night.

And people said horrible things to him about his husband, things like "Dorian belongs in jail" and "Dorian is a monster" and "Dorian got what he deserved." These were people Jansen considered friends, people Dorian had invited to their home, people whom Dorian did business with. Yeah, some of the friends Jansen had brought into the relationship had expressed concern when he'd married the slightly less than moral businessman, but they'd warmed up to him. They had claimed to like him. Plus, Dorian had changed so much and he lived to make Jansen happy. Didn't that earn him some compassion? Did becoming a better man not matter?

Well, it mattered to Jansen. Screw what everyone else thought.

The sedan slowed to a stop right outside the front entrance of the Orleans Parish Prison—better known as OPP to the natives. It was the equivalent of a county lockup and the place all the parishes around the greater New Orleans area dumped the people they intended to keep for a while. It was no better than a freakin' zoo, and a man like Dorian Grant didn't deserve to be there, no matter how horrible people thought he was.

As always, the driver parked right outside OPP's ominous front doors. He let Jansen climb out just before pulling across the street to park the car, where he would wait and watch for Jansen to emerge again. After it was all said and done, he would hastily swing around and corral Jansen into the car before any danger could come to him, because that was what Angelo had told him to do. More like, "So help me God, nothing's gonna happen to that kid while he's on my watch. I ain't tellin' Dorian we got his husband killed. Got it?" Couple that with Angelo's nothin'-but-business stare, and even the pope's knees would've been knocking.

Looking around, Jansen hugged himself tightly as people from the rougher side of the tracks looked at him like they wanted to take his life or rob him blind. Right there on the street, in broad daylight, with cops milling about, like they didn't give a shit or weren't afraid of ending up in the very place they were visiting freely for now. The slim-slit windows and barbed wiring, the graffiti and litter made OPP look like urban hell, and it wasn't too far from the illustrious French Quarter.

Wonder what the tourists would think.

God, he hated coming to this place.

Today he could ignore the threatening stares and the stench of piss on the sidewalks. He could ignore the bum who always asked him for money, and ignore the feeling he was on the verge of getting mugged. Today wasn't about going to see the love of his life behind bars, rotting in jail while fat, greedy law-dogs played a game of who had the biggest balls. Today was supposed to be different. Oh, the same nervousness and anticipation was there. He still felt the dread of seeing Dorian in that bright orange jumpsuit and those handcuffs, but today things had a very good chance of changing for the two of them.

The lawyer had called Wednesday afternoon and told Jansen she would meet him at the prison on Friday because she had some damn good news for them. Over the phone, she didn't give any details, but the excitement in her voice had been enough to give Jansen hope. He'd needed hope. The many, many hours he'd spent silent, curled on the bed, hugging Dorian's pillow and refusing anyone who tried to get near him, the waiting for Dorian to get out of prison had seriously taken its toll on him. He was a few more disappointing letters and bad phone calls from completely flipping his lid.

The phone call the day before Thanksgiving had Jansen finally seeing a silver lining in those gloomy clouds, even if it had made for a very anxious holiday. Maybe now they could get an innocent man out of jail and back at home where he belonged.

Granted, Dorian wasn't a saint and wasn't innocent in the most general of terms. He'd done his fair share of bad stuff in the past, but the guy they were accusing him of killing, he never touched. Oh, Dorian had wanted to, and it had been Jansen's fault… sort of. It was the guy who'd shot Jansen through the opened car window at the dark end of Bourbon Street the night Dorian was trying to make things up to him.

The night hadn't been going well to begin with, even with Dorian trying so hard to make things right by Jansen. The dinner had been romantic—the table had been in a cozy corner, the lights low, and the wine divine. Dorian had really gone all out to make Jansen feel special, but the one thing Jansen had needed him to bend on, Dorian wouldn't: the violence. Dorian's reason had been his businesses and his reputation, but in Jansen's mind, his unwillingness to budge on his mean streak meant Dorian didn't love him. So Jansen had stormed out of the restaurant that night and stalked down the dark end of Bourbon Street alone, and that was where he'd gotten shot.

Jansen had lain in the street feeling his life slip away, but miraculously, Dorian had found him in time. He'd been rushed to the hospital where he'd stayed on life support for a while, and that had been the wake-up call Dorian had needed. But that didn't mean Jansen's assailant was going to go free. Not even close.

Angelo had been the one to handle the guy—or that was the general belief, anyway. No one ever told Jansen the specifics of what had gone down while he was in the hospital fighting for his life. He only knew Dorian didn't do the deed, but his husband damn sure wouldn't have let the guy go. He assumed Angelo had handled it since the big guy handled all of Dorian's "business," but Dorian wouldn't let Angelo go down for the crime. No, Dorian would take the rap before rolling over on the best friend he'd ever had. It didn't matter if Jansen was losing his ever-loving mind over this crap.

"Let them try to pin some evidence on me," Dorian had said the first time they'd all met with Rebecca Chambers—less than forty-eight hours after he'd been hauled in to the precinct. "They got nothin'."

Maybe not, but the fact they had no evidence didn't get Dorian out of that cage and back into their bed.

People lined up right outside the prison's doors, waiting to step through the metal detectors and into the main seating area where family and friends would sit and pass time until they could see the convicts they loved. The thought of sitting on a single chair or touching one of the door handles made Jansen's stomach turn. Maybe it was his imagination, but he swore he could see a dingy gray layer of filth clinging to every single surface. The yellowish flickering lights overhead didn't help matters, either.

He couldn't even believe he was doing this, that his life had gotten to such a point. Who the hell fell in love with a murderer? Who in their right mind would love someone like Dorian Grant?

He did.

Without doubt.

Without question.

"Mr. Grant?" a familiar feminine voice called Jansen's name. He spun around to find their lawyer charging across the broken, busted parking lot, waving her arm in the air and clutching a briefcase while her Prada heels clacked against the pavement.

When Rebecca Chambers finally reached him, she held her hand out for Jansen to take. Her dark-brown stare narrowed on him. Her chocolate-colored hair was pulled back in a painfully tight bun. She wore a business suit and heels made for kicking serious ass. The bright makeup he'd always seen her in was now subdued and neutral, unlike Rebecca's true personality.

They shook hands, but there was nothing friendly in either one's demeanor, even though they'd spent weekends by the pool, nights at the bar, and dinners in elegant restaurants—she and her wife, Jansen and his husband. Even though they were close enough to be considered great friends, she was all business and Jansen was all curious concern.

"So what is this 'news' you have for me?" he asked, cutting to the chase.

"We were able to get the staff members who tended to you at the hospital to officially corroborate Dorian's alibi. He didn't leave your side the entire time."

"I knew that. I said that."

"Yes"—she dismissively shook her hand in front of her—"but the judge and DA didn't believe it and wouldn't take your word because you'd been in and out of consciousness. Plus, they probably thought you might lie just to get your husband off."

"So...." He quirked a brow, impatiently waiting for her to tell him what this all meant.

"So, if Dorian didn't leave the hospital, he couldn't have possibly killed that man."

"Seriously? And here I thought he could've been in two places at one time."

She rolled her eyes.

Jansen sighed. "What about the DNA evidence they claim to have?"

"Well, after a second interview, the victim's sister said he'd gone to see Dorian about a week before the murder. She told the police he came back looking like he'd been in a fight. So I'm guessing the blood they found on his shirt was from Dorian's busted knuckles. Didn't you say when you saw him, he had a few gashes on his hand?"

"Yeah, that was normal for him back then."

"It was?" She curled her nose as if the idea of his violence disgusted her. Though Jansen was offended by that now, there was a time when he would've completely agreed with her.

"You've been working for him longer than we've been together," he said. "You've never noticed it before?"

"He didn't let me get that close to him until the two of you got married. Hell, he never let anyone close to him."

"I guess love has a way of changing people," Jansen said in a solemn voice.

"Yes, I suppose it does."

Rebecca's expression softened significantly, as if she actually felt badly about Dorian being in this predicament now that they were all friends. Jansen wondered if she would've felt so badly all those years ago, or if she would've been just as happy to see Dorian go down as the rest of his husband's naysayers.

With a sigh, he crossed his arms and cut his eyes toward the building. Exhaustion and frustration had been getting the better of him for a long time, and the two made him grumpy as shit.

"So...," he hesitantly began, "does this mean Dorian gets to come home today?"

"Not today. I presented the evidence to the DA and he said he would get it in front of the judge—"

"In his sweet time," Jansen said with a huff.

"No." She held up both hands. "No, I told them if they don't get that *wrongly accused* man out from behind those bars soon, expect a media storm and lawsuit, and there was also that little matter of police brutality."

"Beautiful," Jansen said with a relieved sigh. "Does Dorian know yet?"

"No, I was going to tell him in person. Would you like to come with me?"

"Please."

She nodded toward the automatic glass doors—away from the general audience of people waiting where Jansen normally went to visit Dorian—

signaling for him to follow her. He did as she obviously wanted, listening closely to the *clickity-clack* of her designer heels as she made her way down the hall and toward a guard standing by yet another metal detector. When she approached him, he stiffened, giving both her and Jansen the most hardened, curious stare. She set her briefcase down on the little battered table next to the metal detector and opened it wide so he could inspect its contents.

"I'm Rebecca Chambers, Dorian Grant's attorney, and this is my clerk. We're here to see my client."

The guard looked back and forth between them. Jansen dropped his stare down the line of his high-dollar gray tie and deep purple dress shirt, his dark gray slacks and black Italian loafers. The only thing Jansen could think was thank God he always dressed up for Dorian, because he hadn't been prepared to be tossed in the middle of a little white lie.

"Either one of ya got any contraband on ya?" the guard asked, and his thick, bassy voice was twice as intimidating as his tall, wide build.

"Contraband?" Jansen frowned.

The guard nodded toward a list hanging on the wall. It included everything a MacGyver-type criminal could conceivably use to escape—from ballpoint pens and paper clips, to dental floss and sticks of gum.

"No," Rebecca said, answering for them both.

After being patted down, they were waved through the metal detector and down another tunnel. It spilled into a room of people who all looked like professionals—all dressed in business suits with briefcases at their feet. Probably lawyers if Jansen wanted to take a guess. She led him over to a row of seats and they both sat down at the very end, far away from all the others.

"Will there be a piece of glass between us again?" he quietly asked, hoping like hell the round tables in the center of the room were meant for people to sit with the inmates.

On his previous visits, they'd put their hands to the window for a pseudotouch, but it wasn't the same as the real thing. He didn't get that tingly, happy feeling when skin met skin.

"No," Rebecca answered. "Not this time. He's allowed time to confer with his attorney… and his attorney's clerk." She gave Jansen a little wink.

A rush of excitement wound through him. The happy fluttering pushed through him so hard and so fast it forced his lips into a smile. It had been six months since he'd sincerely smiled, six lonely months without the other half of his soul, of sleeping alone when he'd gotten so used to having Dorian lying beneath him and holding him in those incredibly muscled, tattooed arms.

God, he missed Dorian.

This was killing him.

The door on the far edge of the room opened and a train of people came through. Most of them were wearing orange jumpsuits, so unless Jansen paid very close attention, he feared missing the love of his life. He knew from the last visit, Dorian's once-shaved hair had grown out a few inches. The facial hair he never kept had grown as well, leaving a full beard and mustache that actually looked very debonair. It gave his handsomeness a healthy dose of ruggedness. Dorian hated it. Jansen liked it.

Jansen sat on the very painful edge of the plastic seat, so close to falling off his legs were probably holding more of his weight than the actual chair was, and when he saw his partner's face, Jansen bounded to his feet. He started toward Dorian when he felt someone tugging him back. He looked down and found Rebecca with a death grip on his wrist.

"Calm down," she suggested, keeping her voice low so everyone in the room wouldn't catch on to their lie. "Don't act so excited."

"I can't help it," Jansen whispered from the corner of his mouth. "It feels like it's been a lifetime since I last touched him."

"Well you can't touch him. If you do, we'll get kicked out of here."

"I won't. I promise."

"Good," she said, rising to her feet.

Jansen held back and let Rebecca approach Dorian first, even though it was absolutely killing him not to rush over and throw his arms around his husband's body.

When Dorian laid eyes on Jansen, his entire face started to glow, as though Jansen was the only thing in the world that gave him happiness and the longer they spent apart from each other made Dorian's light dim. It was a stark contrast to the way Dorian had greeted him during the last few visits. If Jansen had to guess, he would attribute the change to the lack of security devices between them. Maybe it helped Dorian feel a little closer to freedom.

"Mr. Grant," Rebecca said in an especially loud voice. "This is my associate." She touched Jansen's arm and his back straightened. "He'll be taking notes as we talk. Can you please have a seat with us? We're here to talk about your case."

For a brief moment, Dorian looked confused. His stare ping-ponged between Jansen and Rebecca. Then his eyes widened and he nodded slowly, as if what they were doing had finally sunk in.

Dorian sat down at one side of the table. Rebecca pulled out the chair closest to Dorian and nodded for Jansen to sit down. He didn't so much sit, but absently sank down into the chair as if his body had a mind of its own and his legs kind of just quit holding his weight. Jansen realized then he hadn't stopped staring at Dorian and any chance of coherent conversation flew out the window when Dorian had crossed the threshold.

"Dorian," Rebecca said as she leaned in a little closer. "We're going to get you out of here. The charges haven't been formally dropped, but the DA realizes he screwed up badly. Your alibi checked out, and by 'checked out,' I mean almost the entire hospital staff made official statements saying you never left Jansen's side."

"That's perfect." Dorian smiled wide, so wide it filled his eyes with the glow of genuine hopefulness. "You think you can get the charges dropped?"

"I don't know. I'm pretty sure they're still going to put you in front of a jury, but—"

"But you get to come home, Dorian," Jansen said. He couldn't help himself.

"When?" Dorian asked.

"Not so fast, guys. The DA is meeting with the judge," Rebecca said. "We're trying to get you another bail hearing. A week. Three weeks tops."

"That's better than waiting years for a trial," Dorian said.

"Yes, it is," Rebecca said.

"I might even be home for Christmas...."

5

JASON RESTED his forearms on the thick wooden railing of the VIP balcony—a normal preshow place for him even when circumstances were at their best, which was a far cry from the here and now. The view from high above the club gave a hell of a lot of perspective of what was going on down below—the size of the crowd, the performance of the dancers, the business at the bar, and overall sound. But the club hadn't opened yet. He only stayed up there now because the quiet gave him a means to think about everything happening in and around his life, and what he would do to keep things copacetic for everyone. In reality, though, Jason knew he would have to take a step back and let everything run its course. He didn't have the means to save the club, so why bother worrying about it?

Simple. Because he cared.

If last night was any indication of how the weekend would end up going, he sure the hell wouldn't be any closer to keeping the doors open. *Don't forget, it was Thanksgiving too.* Maybe people had stayed home with their families. *Today's Black Friday.* Maybe they were out shopping or still staying home with their families.

Why didn't that make him feel any better?

With a sigh, he sank down on the edge of the semicircular booth closest to the railing so he could still see everything down below. The dancers all milled about the stage, getting ready for Friday as if it were any other normal night at the club and they weren't all standing on the edge of doom. The music grew louder, inching up to that sweet spot—the volume where the bass rattled the heart, the mids could be felt on the flesh, and the highs were at that perfect place right before ear-piercing.

Everything was running like a well-oiled machine… as always.

He lay back on the bench and closed his eyes, thoughts of for-sale signs and hot-bodied dancers prancing through his head. A sigh slipped through his pinched lips. Exhaustion bore down on him. He wanted to hide, for twenty minutes or two hours, he didn't care. He just needed some time to decompress and relax, then he promised himself everything would go back to normal. It had to.

According to the clock on his phone, at least an hour had passed when Jason finally sat back up and looked down at the club below. A few patrons had trickled in and they were dancing as though they'd been there all night. One of the warm-up dancers was gyrating all over the stage, getting everyone hyped up for the real shows. Everything looked great, business as usual, and yet his mind and heart weren't any more settled than they had been.

Looking out over the crowd and the stage from the balcony, watching those people dancing and his guys performing was magical. The dancers always looked larger than life, and the patrons—with their smiling faces, sensually moving bodies, and sweat-moistened skin—appeared to be in nothing less than a state of true bliss. Drug-and-alcohol-induced bliss or not, they seemed to love Sin & Seduction almost as much as Jason did.

Too bad such a great thing had to come to an end.

Over the years, that club had become his home. Whenever he was sad and lonely, he knew there would be people there to make him laugh and forget about his problems. Whenever he didn't want to sit around the house, staring at the walls, he knew he could find something to occupy him at the club. He'd met the only two men he'd ever really, *truly* loved there. The place *was* home, better than any home he'd ever known.

Friday nights were always their best night, but as Jason looked out over the spattering of heads and the slow trickle at the door, he understood why the owners wanted to close the club. It had to be a major drain on their wallets, especially with the legal fees that came from fighting with the New Orleans PD. At their ages, with so much to lose, who would want to keep fighting to stay afloat? Who would want to waste the energy?

So yeah, he got it. Didn't like it, but understood.

He ran his hand over the leather surface of the seat. In that booth, on that seat, he'd met the man he'd fallen in love with—a man he'd never expected, a man he knew he would love for the rest of his life, who still made him incredibly happy even two years later. They'd had their first rendezvous up there, hidden in the dark of the VIP balcony in a booth with walls so high no one could see them. It had been a tense, and yet somehow magical, moment between the two of them, and Jason knew when his lips met Brad's he would love that man for the rest of his life.

Whenever he needed a break from the club and the dancers, the owners and the patrons, he always went back to that spot, closed his eyes, and remembered that night with Bradley. Just like magic, whatever had been bothering him at the time faded away.

"You okay?"

Jason heard the voice behind him at the exact moment he felt a hand clamp down on his shoulder. He looked back, sort of hoping Brad had decided to make a surprise visit because he could use his partner's company right now, but he found Lance staring down at him instead.

"I'm fine," Jason said flatly.

"Sure you are."

As Jason turned his scrutinizing stare back down to the floor, the unwelcomed hand left his shoulder. He had all of about two seconds to be thankful Lance was going to leave him alone before the opposite end of the booth seat dipped and from the corner of his eye, he caught Lance settling into a spot across the table.

"Don't you have somewhere to be?" Jason asked without looking away from the stage.

"You know what?" Lance said. "Don't give me that abrasive cold-shoulder routine. I ain't buyin' it. You're just as worried as the rest of us." Lance paused, and the absence of sound made Jason turn his head. Lance wore an intense frown now. He said, "I'm sorry for what I said to you. It was uncalled for."

Truth be told, he couldn't be angry at Lance for pointing out the obvious or the thorough ass-chewing he'd given him. Jason knew good and damn well his whole demeanor had changed the moment he'd left the boss's office and knew the people he called family would see straight through his bullshit. Sure, he'd tried to keep a stoic expression on his face. He'd been trying like hell to pretend everything was okay, but he knew a few of the dancers—Lance in particular— were able to see right through him. And unfortunately, Lance got the brunt of it.

"So. You gonna talk to me now? Or am I still just an employee? Want me to get back to work, boss?" Lance asked.

Jason glared.

Lance smirked.

"You know you're not just an employee to me." Jason's shoulders sagged and his head drooped.

"Talk to me," Lance said, tone all genuine now. "And I don't mean about saving the club. You need to get this shit off your chest. It's bothering you. Talk about it."

"My worry *is* about saving the club, about keeping it open so you guys can keep your jobs. I'm worried about my friends, Lance."

Lance gave him a thoughtful look. "So, what did you come up with?"

"I've been sitting here trying to think of some way to save this place. I thought about going to the bank and *trying* to take out a loan. I thought about asking the owners to be silent partners or… something. I even thought about going to Dorian and Jansen like you suggested. Every single idea I came up with led me right back to the fact I don't have any sort of business skills and I can't ask my friends to invest in something so risky."

"You should give yourself a little more credit."

"I don't know how to manage a nightclub."

"I think you do just fine."

"Okay, sure, the stage runs like a well-oiled machine, thanks to you guys. But what about the bars? What about the bouncers? What about maintenance? What about keeping up with lawyers and accountants? It's way too much. I'm not qualified."

He leaned forward—elbows pressed to the tabletop, knotting his fingers in his hair. The slightly curling locks fell down in front of his face, cloaking him from Lance. "I don't know shit about running a nightclub," he muttered with self-disappointment. "Not a damn thing."

"I happen to think you could do it."

"There's no way."

"Jason," Lance said. He moved to stand in front of Jason, and again Lance had his damn hand right back on Jason's shoulder. "Sweetheart, you're smart. You're a leader. And if anyone has the kind of drive it takes to make this place a success, you do." He gave Jason's shoulder a soft pat. "You need to trust yourself. You need to believe in yourself."

"Right," Jason muttered.

Lance shrugged and started to walk away. He stopped long enough to tell Jason, "I have faith in you, even if you don't. And I know you'll figure it out. You always seem to figure everything out." Then he disappeared.

With the end of that overly clichéd pep talk clinging to the air and somehow echoing over and over, drowning out the sound of the music and the cheering, happy people below, Jason sat back in the seat. Even if he thought for one second he could pull off saving the club, it was a huge undertaking—one that would take a hell of a lot of time away from his new family, one that would wear down his patience and boost his stress. God, if he became one of those men who brought their work home and took it out on his family....

No. He would never, *ever* be that guy.

Sad thing was, at one point in time, Jason had had more self-confidence than any one person needed. He would've dived headfirst into taking over the club and not batted a lash. No pep talk would've been needed and no one could've told him he couldn't do it. Hell, he'd once tiptoed on the tightrope of being downright vain. Not anymore. Between Jansen breaking his heart, Brad putting it back together again, helping raise a toddler, and the responsibilities of pretty much being a housemother to a bunch of twentysomething kids, he'd learned to get over himself. Some might've called it "growing up," but Jason considered it facing reality.

The music below changed from the slow and almost sensual electronica song that Mario and Scott liked to dance to together, into something a little more edgy and, dare he say, discoesque. He hated that style of music, but the newest addition to their team moved like fluid to it and the patrons seemed to enjoy it, so Jason suffered through.

Admittedly, the kid had moves. Mario wasn't Jansen, wasn't Lance or Davi, but people liked him and in the matter of six short months, he'd made a few fans. He even brought in some new faces, which was what the club needed more than anything right now.

A shadow passed by the edge of his sight seconds before he felt lips on his cheek and a hand on his thigh. He jumped and whipped his head around, only to find Brad staring at him wickedly.

"Mmm… looks like I was able to surprise you," Brad said. "How did I know you would be sitting up here in our spot?"

Jason gave him a crooked half-grin. "Because you know me so well?"

"You think so?"

Jason nodded, grin growing wider by the second.

Brad eased into the booth, then slid all the way around. The length of his body pressed against Jason's side. He placed his hand on Jason's thigh again, but now he slowly stroked his fingers back and forth, back and forth. The sensual hand play was a welcome relief from the ramblings of Jason's mind, and yet, he only half enjoyed the feel of those strong fingers massaging tight muscles. Poor Brad was giving it his all, and being so damn sweet. All this, and he had no clue about the club closing down and how stressed Jason had been all night. It didn't matter. Brad wanted to make him feel good. Brad *always* wanted to make him feel good.

Jason wrapped his fingers around his partner's hand and held it tight. There was so much strength in Bradley, so much intelligence and love. He looked at Brad one more time and gave him a tight-lipped, hard-staged smile, and said, "The club is closing down after the New Year. I um… I won't have a job anymore."

"I told you a long time ago I make more than enough money to take care of you."

"I know, but I need to pull my weight. Plus, you have your family to support too."

"Jason, you're my family as well now."

"I know. I know." Jason brushed his fingers over Brad's knuckles. "I still need to pull my own weight and I don't have any skills. I mean, I managed a bunch of dancers and I managed a deli for a little while."

"So you have management experience."

Jason rolled his eyes. "Not the kind of experience I need to get a good job, honey."

"You shouldn't worry about it. Either you'll find something or you won't. It's not a big deal. Like I said—"

"I know. You can take care of me." Jason sighed and sat back against the booth. "It's not just about me having a job. It's about saving something I love, something that might not be great to people who don't know it like I do, but it's great to me. I mean, God, Brad, I met you here. Jansen met his husband here. More than a few great romances started here, and there's the potential for a few more. I don't want to lose that."

"So what are you going to do about it?" Brad cocked his brow.

"Come again."

"Are you going to just sit here and whine about not wanting to lose the club and mope around until its last day, or are you going to do something about it?"

"What the hell am I supposed to do about it? I don't have the means. I can't—"

"No." Brad interrupted. "Don't ever say you *can't* do something. That'll guarantee your failure. Say you'll try, but don't say you can't."

Funny, Jason didn't remember signing up for *another* motivational drilling, and when the hell did his lover become the Little Engine That Could?

Jason opened his mouth, but Brad cut him off by saying, "The man I fell in love with would've moved mountains for what he wanted. Last I knew, I hadn't lost him."

Ouch. That wasn't a motivation speech. That was a kick in the ass.

Sighing, Jason dragged his hand down the front of his face. He knew Brad was right. If Jason kept telling himself he couldn't do it, if he set himself up for failure, they would all lose the club for sure, and yeah, when Jason wanted something, he went after it. Case in point—the man sitting beside him.

Maybe he did need to seriously explore his options, consider taking over and bailing the owners out of being there around the clock. They just needed to keep the doors open, and let Jason do the rest.

This could work.

It *had* to work.

6

WHEN LANCE returned to the backstage area, he found Davi sitting in the very center of the sofa tucked against the wall right outside Jason's office. He had his legs drawn up to his chest, hugging them tight, face buried against the tops of his knees. His pitch-black, cheek-length hair fell down around his eyes and covered his face enough that Lance couldn't see his expression. He was supposed to be getting dressed with the other dancers, but Davi still had on the sweatpants and T-shirt he'd come in wearing earlier that afternoon.

Lance spent a long moment quietly watching the kid all the dancers and most of the patrons of Sin & Seduction adored. Davi was oblivious to the fact someone had their eyes on him, studying him as he sulked. Lance wondered if Davi would raise his head, get up, and get over it—the *it* most likely being the club closing down. He hadn't been right since the news surfaced, since Lance had confirmed everything Davi had heard.

"Whatcha doin', Golden Boy?" one of the other dancers said as he passed between Davi and Lance's field of vision.

"None of your business," Lance said in return.

The dancer smirked, but shimmied on back to the dressing room where he belonged. As soon as he cleared Lance's line of sight though, Lance caught a glimpse of Davi's face, and what he saw was the puffy red eyes of someone who'd been crying. It didn't make much sense to Lance. People lost their jobs all the time. They found new ones. No big deal, especially in a place like New Orleans where entertaining was a way of life. Someone as sexy as Davi would get scooped up in a heartbeat. So why the tears?

Cautiously, Lance started toward him. He wished there was something he could do to make Davi at least a little less miserable. Pep talks and motivational speeches weren't a strong suit for Lance, though. He fell short when it came to rallying the troops. That was why Jason made an awesome leader and Lance remained a happy follower. But hey, he'd give it a try.

"Why aren't you in costume?" Lance asked, taking the seat right beside him. Okay, maybe that wasn't motivational speaking at its finest but....

Davi didn't even acknowledge his presence.

Fail.

Lance reached over and pushed a few tendrils of fallen hair back behind Davi's ear, exposing a hint of his beautiful, tanned face. What he found was a silvery, glistening streak running the length of Davi's cheek, trailing down over his jaw. The tear that made the shiny trail found its doom at the tip of Davi's chin. While Lance had seen his red eyes before, he hadn't seen the actual tears and, well, that just broke his heart a little more.

So why not change the subject? Maybe try to make him feel better, you asshole?

Lance stole a peek of the clock hanging right at the entrance backstage. His eyes widened when he saw the time. "You go on in like"—*That's not changing the subject, idiot*—"twenty minutes, don't you?"

"*Sim*," Davi said. "I don't want to dance. I have sad."

"You *are* sad," Lance corrected.

He wrapped his arms around Davi's shoulders and pulled him into a hug. Davi willingly went exactly where Lance guided him, as if he had no control over his body, or maybe he needed a hug *that* badly.

"How long have you been sitting here?"

"I don't know."

"*Why* are you sitting here?"

There wasn't an immediate answer. Davi didn't so much as flex a muscle. He didn't raise his head. He sat frozen, eyes focused on what Lance had to assume was the floor. The longer they sat there in silence with an intrusive question lingering unanswered between them, the more uncomfortable Lance became. When Davi finally decided to speak, his voice sounded more broken than Lance had ever heard from the kid who normally wore a smile on his face and brought cheer to any situation.

"I called home."

"Oh...." *Why is that so bad?* "And?"

"*Mamãe e Papai* do not want me anymore. I have no home in Portugal."

Oh. Wow. Okay, this was way worse than the club closing down.

"Well.... Who said you have to go home? You have family here." Lance shrugged. "We'll be your family."

"But... but they don't want me."

"Sweetheart, my family doesn't want me, either. I haven't seen them since I was a teenager. They kicked me out and told me not to come back. I didn't and I'm perfectly fine."

Davi gave him a sad smile—a false show of hope, a genuine show of appreciation.

Lance held on to that poor kid for a long time, simply comforting him, which was something Lance wasn't used to doing. Quick and dirty trysts in Jacuzzis or VIP booths or manager's offices he had a lock on, but caring about anyone other than himself—and people who were clearly off-limits—he just couldn't do. Although, Davi didn't seem to want to complain about the company.

So, why this kid was easy to comfort, Lance didn't know. Sure, as he sat there, he didn't mind holding Davi in his arms and didn't mind the idea of the kid crying on his shoulder. If Davi needed five minutes or five hours, Lance thought he could give it to him without taking him into Jason's office and having his way with him.

Whoa. That wasn't normal.

"You should get up and get ready," Lance said as he eased Davi out of the hug, voice soft and hoarse and foreign to him. It sounded so careful and tender, and so damn wrong.

"I don't want to dance," Davi said again. "Can you tell Meester Jason I have a sick?"

"You *are* sick," Lance corrected... again.

"I don't want to dance." Davi's big brown eyes were so sad and pleading, and nothing in the world would make Lance say no to him right now.

Lance cleared his throat and squared his shoulders, mentally facepalming the hell out of himself. He was tiptoeing through uncharted territory, and who knew what doom he faced if he kept on going. He needed air and space and distance, and all the tools that kept his heart guarded inside its happy little barrier. The longer he sat there soothing Davi, though, the more Lance realized he wasn't in a big hurry to go anywhere.

"I completely understand."

Davi lifted his head and promptly laid it on Lance's shoulder. Lance turned to a puddle of goo. Everything inside him melted, even that steadfast wall around his very fragile heart. He swallowed hard, closed his eyes, and pressed his lips to the crown of Davi's head. He didn't speak because he didn't need to. When Lance got like this, he put himself and his heart out there, he made offers he always ended up regretting.

"I have no home now," Davi muttered, tragedy filling his voice.

Lance could certainly sympathize with his pain, even if he didn't know a whole lot about Davi's home. Sure, Davi had always spoken of Portugal fondly. He talked about the beauty—the ancient, towering buildings and lush countryside, the immaculate beaches and the sights—but he never spoke of the people who shared his bloodline, the people who made Portugal home. He never spoke of his mother and father. No one knew if he had siblings or someone he loved back home. It was a mystery just like the sexy, adored dancer also known as Amante Quente.

Hugging him tighter, Lance brushed his hand over Davi's flowing black hair, brushed down until he had the nape of Davi's neck cradled in his hand. He pressed his cheek to the dancer's temple and whispered, "This is your home. You're not going to lose it, or lose any of us. You have a family and a home and we'll figure this out. You're not going to be left out in the cold. We'll... we'll fix it, I promise."

He had no freaking clue why he'd made that promise to Davi. It wasn't as though Lance could bathe in bills. He had a nice life, but it was because he lived fairly modestly and he only had to take care of his own needs. If it wasn't for all the rich older men who wanted a hot young guy in their laps, riding their cocks and telling them how great they were, Lance wouldn't have shit to his name, either.

For some reason, though, the fact he couldn't afford to take care of another person didn't matter. What mattered right now was Davi. The kid was scared, and the fear in his eyes nagged Lance in a way nothing had in a very long time. In fact, the last time something had gotten to him so badly was high school, when the only kid Lance had been able to relate to had to be taken away for trying to kill himself. Those were the darkest days of Lance's life. As far as he could tell, he never really got over that. Years. Therapy. Distance.

Nope, that loss was still a problem for him, and the main reason he took such care when it came to letting people get close to him. People couldn't be relied on. They always disappointed. Case in point—Davi's family.

One of the other dancers came racing by, no doubt on his way to smoke before having to fit into another costume and grace the stage again. Sweat clung to his muscled arms. Locks of his normally light brown hair clumped together in thick, dark chunks. Lance called out to him and his body whipped around. He kept jogging backward toward the door.

Lance said, "Can you guys skip over Davi? He's not feeling so well."

"Jason'll have a stroke."

"He'll have to deal. Davi won't be any good to anyone trying to dance right now."

Scott shrugged. "Whatever. I guess so."

"Thanks."

The other dancer took off out the back door and Davi raised his watery stare. There was something undeniably grateful in the way he looked at Lance, and had it been anyone else, Lance might've taken the look as an opportunity to worm his way in for a quick-and-easy lay. He couldn't do that to Davi. Attraction wasn't the problem. The kid was hot, beyond drop-dead gorgeous, but for whatever reason, Lance couldn't make himself look at him like that. Maybe it was the innocence in Davi's eyes. Maybe it was the seven years age difference between the two of them. Maybe it was simply the fact Lance actually cared.

"Hey," Lance said, giving him a gentle nudge. "You wanna go for a walk or something? Maybe get some air? I think I could stand to get outta this place for a bit. How about you?"

"That sounds nice, but what about Meester Jason? Won't he get mad if you no here?"

"*Not* here, and he can get over it. I'm not scheduled to dance for another forty-five minutes anyway. Come on. Go with me."

Lance slid off the couch and popped up to his feet. He held out one single hand all knight-in-shining-armor-like and gave Davi the most sincere grin, which Davi returned with a bright, stellar smile that pushed dimples into his cheeks and filled his eyes with a glow Lance hadn't seen in too many days. It was that very charming, joyful, in-love-with-the-world attitude that made Davi so special to everyone he came in contact with. And it was great to have it back.

Davi took Lance's hand and rose to his feet.

Crazy as it was, Lance didn't let go as he probably should have. In fact, he became very aware of their fingers threading together. He looked down in time to catch the weave forming in slow motion—dark, bronze skin against lightly tanned flesh. They were holding hands, more connected to each other than Lance wanted to be with another human being, doing something sweet and tender, not hot and hungry. Did he actually care that much about this kid?

Nah. Not possible.

The sight of their hands locked together tightened Lance's throat momentarily. It hitched his breath and widened his eyes. A little wave of panic rushed through him, and every instinct inside him told him to pull his hand away before he found himself in the kind of trouble that led to heartbreak.

Lance didn't hold hands, he held cocks. He didn't do caring and cuddly. He did rough and rude. But as startling as the need to be kind to Davi was, even more startling, he didn't want to stop.

They stepped out into the cool, November New Orleans night. The spicy ambrosia of Cajun food and the mighty Mississippi River gave the Big Easy a scent all its own. It was unlike anything Lance had ever experienced, and though he'd been living there since the ripe old age of sixteen—after he'd left his home up north—every time a gust of eastern wind wound through the French Quarter, the experience became new again.

He cut his eyes toward Davi, who still walked close beside him, not close enough to be confused as intimate lovers, but close enough to be considered good friends. Close enough they were still holding hands and close enough for Lance to be very, very aware of Davi's breathing and his stare and the twinkle in his dark eyes and his subtle half-smile and his annoyingly adorable dimples.

Fuck.

"So, um… you feel any better?" Lance asked, caution and nervousness spilling into his voice.

"Sim," Davi said with a faint smile. He had a thankful look about him. It did wonders for that big brown puppy-dog stare of his, and honestly, nearly melted Lance's heart all over again. "Thank you for walking with me."

"Eh, it's no problem." Lance released Davi's hand and rubbed the back of his own suddenly warm neck. He feared the pink evidence of a stupid blush creeping into his cheeks. "Just wanted you to feel better."

There was a second or two, maybe more, of silent staring. No matter how much Lance wanted to look away, he couldn't do it. Something about Davi drew him and held him there.

He opened his mouth, frowned, and closed it again. Without a sound, he spun on his heel, starting back in the direction of the club, back to normalcy, back to a place where Lance felt like himself.

"We should go inside," he said without turning around and without missing a step. "I'm sure everyone is wondering where we are."

"I'm not ready to go back."

"We have to."

"Why?" Davi stopped him by laying his hand over Lance's wrist.

Lance knew that move all too well, had used it a few times in the past to steal a kiss he'd been craving. He silently prayed that wasn't what Davi wanted, though why he was so adamant not to kiss Davi, he wasn't sure.

Their eyes locked, and the weight of Davi's warm, innocent expression hit Lance so hard it made him swallow. He licked his parched lips, noticing the way Davi's gaze followed the brush of his tongue.

Davi took a step closer.

Lance froze.

Their lips collided.

7

WITH THURSDAY came almost an entire week since Rebecca had told him about Dorian's chances of getting out of OPP, an entire week of anxiously waiting for news of his release, of sleepless nights and staying close to the phone. None of which did anything for Jansen's increasingly gloomy demeanor. The longer he went without hearing from Rebecca Chambers, the closer to five-alarm-fire level his frustration became. He found himself snapping at the help for no reason, and even barking at Angelo.

Angelo—a man who could've ripped Jansen in half without a second thought.

Through all the forcing himself to eat and forcing himself to sleep, pacing the expanse of the too-empty-for-comfort mansion, and working out in the weight room just to blow off steam, he managed to completely exhaust himself. Now, all these days later, he could barely do much more than move from the couch and blankly stare at the television screen, but he still couldn't catch the first damn Z. It was as if his brain wanted to keep doing the hula, rather than chill out for a quick siesta. Enough of the round and round and round would drive anyone insane, and Jansen was only a few miles north of Looneytown to begin with.

The phone ringing on the end table beside him cut through the silence of Dorian's mansion and nearly scared Jansen right out of his skin. Those hours— no, days—of waiting for a good-news call, waiting to hear that abrasive ringtone, culminated in a single heart-stopping moment.

When he picked up the cell and saw the name on the caller ID, the world became a much happier, much brighter place. Like birds singing and sun shining and flowers blossoming under a clear blue sky. All that corny shit. It was Rebecca Chambers, and God, did he hope she had good news for him.

"Hello?" he said, voice gravelly from not speaking for too many days.

"Get the bail bondsman on the horn," she said. "Dorian's getting a new bail hearing. The DA is asking for a million dollar bond, and I'm pretty sure he'll get it."

"Okay…."

"You'll need ten percent of that up front. Do you have access to Dorian's money?"

"Yes. I… I do."

"Then, I suggest you get everything in order. I have a pretty strong feeling Dorian's going to want to break free as soon as he's allowed."

"When will he be released?"

"The hearing will be on Friday next week. If it's early enough, maybe that night. Maybe Saturday morning. The judge will have to rule on the bond and your bondsman will have to file paperwork. They'll start processing him through the system as soon as the paperwork goes through. Then he's all yours until we go to trial."

All mine. The thought pulled Jansen's lips into a high smile.

"I'll get on it right away."

Immediately hanging up, he then slid the phone into the loose pocket of a pair of flannel sleep pants he'd been wearing for far too many days and nights. Had Dorian been there, they would've slept completely naked and curled against each other's bodies. They would've climbed out of bed together, then into the shower where they would've scrubbed each other from head to toe and back again—maybe making a pit stop for a little playtime. They would've headed down to breakfast hand in hand, then spent the day doing whatever their hearts desired.

He bounded up the staircase, taking the steps two at a time without even having to think about it. Thankfully, being a dancer gave him the kind of grace that wouldn't land him on his ass in a crumpled heap at the foot of the stairs. He didn't stop running until he burst through the door of Dorian's office, but once he got there, he skidded to a halt. He looked around the darkened room and had no clue where to begin.

Between Dorian's keen sense of keeping business nice and tidy, and Maria's unwavering OCD, when it came to the cleanliness of the mansion, everything looked absolutely immaculate. That might've been in part due to the fact the man of the house hadn't been there to rummage through papers in six months, but didn't change the fact the place was pristine. All the pens were in their holder. Papers and files were in a neat stack. Dorian's laptop sat in the middle of the desk with the lid closed, and right on top of it was his cell phone. Jansen had left it there after making the call to Rebecca, *after* he'd forwarded all calls to Angelo for him to handle. Dorian would've wanted it that way anyway. Angelo was his right-hand man when it came to business, and Jansen just didn't have the wherewithal or the knowledge to deal with any of it.

He sat down on Dorian's plush leather high-back office chair and laid his hands on top of the antique mahogany desk. They'd made love on that surface more than a few times in their years together, had even left a little knick on the edge when things had gotten especially kinky one night. The metal of Jansen's wedding band had carved the wood away when Dorian had pinned his arms back. God, that was some of the hottest sex they'd ever had. Dorian had made him come three times that night, and when it was over, they'd cuddled on the office floor until their legs became solid and they could walk again.

Jansen rubbed his thumb over the indention in the dark wood. That night had been pretty damn magical and Dorian had made him feel so loved. He'd been hot and rowdy, then tender and sweet, and everything Jansen had ever wanted in a lover.

God, I miss him.

As if he didn't have enough reasons to burst into tears already....

It had been six long, cold months since he'd laid his hand over his husband's heart, since he'd laughed at one of Dorian's ridiculously corny jokes, since he'd watched Dorian feed him bites of cheesecake with the most incredible smile. Sure, Dorian was still a bit rough around the edges, and no one would ever turn him into the kind of wuss who would roll over for people, but with Jansen, it was always TLC and perfect gentleness. Dorian went from a raging grizzly to a sweet-as-can-be teddy—like zero to sixty—where Jansen was concerned.

Jansen shook off his sorrow as best he could. After all, he had one major reason to be happy right now. Dorian was coming home, and Jansen needed to get his butt in gear and make it happen.

He reached out, and grabbed Dorian's phone, then sat back in his hubby's comfy chair. He scrolled through name after name, hoping one of them would be annotated as a bail bondsman.

Dorian had been to jail a few times in his life, though not for anything serious. He'd gotten picked up for fighting with a guy in the parking lot of the sporting goods store once, and another time, he'd gotten mouthy with a cop after being pulled over for reckless driving. For the most part, Dorian had done a good job of staying out of trouble... until this.

And dammit if Jansen couldn't find a number for anything that looked remotely close to a bail bondsman. He expected some corny, movie-type, Mafioso name like Johnny the Finger or Clyde the Rat. Not a single name in Dorian's phone screamed "I work with criminals."

Sighing, he set the phone down on the laptop and flopped back in the chair. His stare bounced around the room—at the row of file drawers, at the closet Dorian kept God only knew what in. Jansen rarely came into the office, save for the occasional romp and naughty play, so he didn't know his way around. Just the desk with the permanent mark of one of their many trysts.

He looked down at the narrow drawer that would've hovered right above his husband's lap and he thought, if Dorian had any business cards... for a bail bondsman maybe... then they might be in there. He wrenched the drawer open, and a myriad of office supplies slid around against the wood, but off to the right was a single gray card that read "Andrew Lister, Bail Bondsman."

Holding the card in his hand, he fished his cell phone out of the twist of flopping flannel pocket, and with more than a hint of ferocity, he pounded the number into the screen. Then he parked the phone between his ear and his shoulder and he waited and waited and waited for Mr. Lister's greeting.

"Andy here," the guy on the other end finally said.

He sounded winded, as if he'd had to dart across a great expanse of whatever to get to the phone. His voice was gravelly, like a smoker's would be, and the sound immediately conjured images of an overweight man with a round face and a big nose, with thick black hair and huge golden rings on nubby fingers... just like in the movies.

"Mr. Lister, this is Jansen Gr—"

Jansen stopped himself. He didn't know how many of Dorian's associates knew about their nuptials two years ago. If Jansen hadn't met them at the wedding, he'd always assumed they didn't know and assumed Dorian wanted it kept that way.

"I'm calling on behalf of Dorian Grant. He needs your services."

"I was waitin' for this call. Saw 'em on the news takin' him in. I told him the long arm of the law would catch up to him soon," the guy said with a hint of laughter. "So, what can I do ya for?"

"Dorian was locked up in Orleans Parish Prison. They denied him bail at first, but now—in light of new evidence—they're giving him a new bail hearing."

"Can't do nothin' 'til I know the amount."

"A million dollars," Jansen said grimly, hoping the hefty figure didn't turn the man away.

"Whoo-wee, boy," the man caterwauled. "You got the ten percent down?"

"As soon as I go to the bank, I will."

"You willin' to take responsibility for him?"

"If it gets him back home, absolutely."

"Guess I'll be seein' ya at OPP."

With that, Jansen ended the call but kept the phone clenched between both hands. He sat back in his husband's chair, relaxed, and for the first time in what was starting to feel like an eternity, Jansen breathed easy. He inhaled a deep breath, let it fill his lungs and expand his chest. He savored it and savored the welcomed feeling of hope, welcomed the warmth and light he could now see, and then he exhaled.

8

THE TODDLER cooed from the seat next to Brad's spot at the dinner table. Jason sat on the other side of her, only half-aware of the child and half-aware of his partner. His mind had turned into a typhoon of thoughts and concerns, some pinging harder than others, all colliding. This had been going on since he'd woken up that morning, just like it had every morning for the past week.

Nothing had changed—unless he considered his situation becoming more grim a change. He'd met with the owners earlier in the evening, and they'd dumped more bad news in his lap. The last investor they'd had their sights on rejected the offer and the two counteroffers that had come after. No one wanted the place. The club was still closing.

Needless to say, this had absolutely ruined the mood of the evening. He'd planned on coming home and making love to Brad until neither one of them could hold their eyes open anymore. Melody was going to come and get Hope and said she would keep her until the morning, so everything had been perfectly arranged and ready to go. Then *boom!* Bad news of the nuclear kind. To make matters worse, Melody had to cancel because of work, so Jason didn't even get his husband all to himself when he wanted Brad most.

God, they'd needed the intimate time too. Jason couldn't remember the last time they'd made love and both men had been so on edge, not only with each other but with the people in their professional lives.

"Jason," a distant voice he very much recognized said.

From the banging of a fork against a hard plastic surface, he knew Hope hadn't been given her plate yet, which meant Brad hadn't joined them. He knew by the smell of garlic and rosemary a plate of food had been set in front of his face, but that was all he really processed with the rampant churning inside his head. The noise and the smells and the presence of his loved ones were fodder for an overactive mind, a mind that needed a good distraction from the worries of business and responsibilities, and the things that came with being an adult.

"Jason?"

He raised his head and stared blindly at his partner, blinked a few times, then finally opened his mouth. "Yeah?"

"I have to keep Hope this weekend. Melody is going out of town with her boyfriend."

That was important. Jason's logic didn't fail him there, but the significance was completely lost on him. All the backtracking through the memory train wouldn't get him to the final destination of *a-ha!*

"Okay?" Jason responded. Confusion filled his voice in a very, very harsh way.

"Sooooo…," Brad drawled. "I won't be able to come to the club for the promo shoot."

Oh yeah. That. How could I forget that?

The promo shoot was meant to help Jason kinda, sorta, *try* to drum up some business, at least for the closing show. Though Brad thought they could use the video in a commercial for the club, and maybe in a packet for potential investors… *if* they somehow managed to find more potential investors.

It was probably way too late to do any good now, but he swore to his guys he would be the best manager he could be and he would do everything he could to help the situation.

"Jason?"

"Sorry. I…." He paused to process. "Someone will still do the shoot, right?"

"Of course, baby. I told you I wanted to help."

"And the station is going to run the ad, right?"

"Yes. So are a few affiliates."

"Okay." Jason nodded slowly as if the English he'd been speaking his entire life took more than a few minutes to comprehend. "Okay. Good."

Brad frowned. "Are you okay?"

"Yeah. Yeah. Absolutely." Jason took a sip of his iced tea, licked his lips, then set it back down. "I'm fine."

"You haven't touched your dinner."

"I…."

Jason looked down and sure enough, only a few bites were missing from the grilled ahi and sautéed green beans. A tiny chunk was missing from the whole wheat roll, and condensation dripped from his tea glass, leaving a wet ring on the tablecloth. When the hell did he miss the entire meal?

"I guess I haven't really eaten much," he admitted. He wasn't even aware of Brad holding his hand until he felt fingers squeeze around his.

"The club closing is really getting to you, huh?" Brad asked, stroking his thumb back and forth across Jason's knuckles.

"It is. The guys are acting like everything is okay and I've been lying to them all this whole time. I have Lance up my ass to do something. Plus, I have to plan this big finale show that's supposed to happen New Year's Eve and I have no clue what to do."

Jason exhaled sharply, shoulders slumping, head lowering. He hated not knowing what to do, hated feeling helpless and insecure. In the past, he'd always had a plan. He'd always been the one who knew how to handle anything and everything. Not in this case. This time, he was in over his head, drowning and grasping for the water's surface, sucking for air and failing miserably.

For a moment, he stared at his partner—the man he loved with every ounce of his soul—as if he'd never seen him before. Jason couldn't remember the last time he felt so lost and unsure of himself, like a blundering, nervous boy.

Wait. Yes, he could. He hadn't felt that way since Brad had come into his life. In fact, he'd been waltzing through the days and months without a care in the world because everything had been so perfect. And just like that, one random night at work made all that tranquility and euphoria come crashing down.

His voice lowered significantly when he said, "I don't know. I don't... know what to do."

"Then ask for help," Brad said. "You have friends. You have... me. Ask for help." He brushed his thumb over Jason's knuckles, looked him right in the eyes, and without so much as blinking, Brad said, "Ask *me* for help."

They laced their fingers together and Jason took a deep breath. This was his support system, his family, and his heart. This was everything right in a fucked-up world.

He closed his eyes and pressed his forehead to Brad's. Every single breath his partner took brushed along Jason's lips. Every little happy sound Brad's daughter made reminded Jason that nothing else in the world mattered as much as the people he loved. So no matter what happened with the club, those people would stand by him and support him and love him.

"I should get to work," Jason whispered before gently kissing the bridge of his partner's nose. Pulling back, he reached up and brushed his fingertips through the soft hairs just above Brad's ear. "I love you."

"I love you too," Brad said in an equally airy voice. "Be careful, and Jason?"

"Yeah?"

"Have fun tonight. Enjoy your job... like you used to."

"I will. I promise." Or so he hoped.

He stood from his chair and kissed Hope right over the swirl of her soft blonde hair. She giggled happily as she bounced in her chair.

Part of him would've killed to stay home and play family man, which was weird considering he'd never wanted that life prior to meeting Brad. Or maybe he just didn't know he wanted that life. Either way, now that he had it, he wouldn't trade it for the world. But then the other part of him—the responsible adult who cared about the people he worked with—insisted he go take care of his other family, and do his best to save their jobs.

He padded back to the bedroom he'd been sharing with Brad after they had decided to take the next step. They'd rented a house together right outside the French Quarter a year into their relationship. It was one of those cute old New Orleans homes that were scattered all around—the ones that were way out of his price range, but Brad had insisted on renting for them. Jason had immediately sold his car and traded it for a really cool ten-speed that pretty much carried him everywhere he needed to be. In the ten months of riding a bike to get around, he'd toned up well and found himself in damn good shape... save for that little issue with his back. Brad loved it. It seemed as though every time they were alone, Brad had his hands all over Jason's body.

Jason wasn't complaining.

Unfortunately, they didn't get a whole lot of time alone anymore.

After closing the bedroom door behind him, he slid out of the nylon basketball shorts and ratty T-shirt he'd been hanging out in all day. Then he changed into a pair of faded jeans and a slightly nicer T-shirt. He tousled his auburn hair enough to give it that cool messy look the guys thought worked so well for him, sprayed on some cologne, then grabbed his backpack from the edge of the bed.

Tonight, when he met with the guys he would have a plan for them... somehow. Even if the plan didn't save their jobs and their income, he would come up with something. He would help them all out. Either way, he wasn't going to let them down.

He *couldn't* let them down.

9

HERE IT was, an entire week after they'd found out the club was closing and Davi had laid one wildly unexpected kiss on Lance, and for some stupid-ass reason, Lance hadn't stopped thinking about the way those sultry lips had felt against his. He hadn't stopped thinking about how his heart had skipped a beat, how his breath had been stolen, and how, for the first time since his teenage years, he'd felt butterflies when his mouth had touched someone else's.

It sort of went without saying, that unexpected kiss screwed up Lance's entire freakin' world. And it wasn't even a big kiss, nothing more than an innocent touch of lips that lingered a lot longer than it maybe should have. They didn't even twist tongues or swap spit or anything. It was the kind of high school kiss stolen at lockers or in between classes before the last bell rang. Seriously. It was nothing. Still, Lance couldn't deny the fact he felt a hell of a lot more after that one little kiss than he had after fucking any of the handful of other men he'd been with in his past.

And the fact a week hadn't made a difference in the way he felt made Davi a problem.

Squaring his shoulders, Lance lifted his chin and headed into the club's side door. He had it in his head he could be all cool and shit, and play like nothing had ever happened between them. Really, nothing *did* happen. The kiss was purely innocent, but still the feel of their lips gently touching and the soft caresses as Davi opened and closed his mouth remained with him. The memory remained so strong, in fact, occasionally, Lance could still feel his mouth tingling.

So not good.

As soon as he crossed the threshold, the scents of the dressing room railed him hard. It was the combined smells of sweaty men and damp concrete walls, of booze and sex, and an ambrosia of all the different colognes. It might've been nauseating if it hadn't been so welcomed. The smell in the air reminded Lance of what he was and what he did—a borderline stripper who fucked men with money. It reminded him not to get wrapped up in pretty Portuguese boys because being with one person never suited him well. Love was just a game... a sweet little lie that made people feel better about themselves.

Yeah, well, Lance wasn't the loving kind of guy.

Keep lying to yourself.

He kept his eyes straight forward and kept heading down the hallway, past Jason's locked office and the couch where Lance had held Davi in his arms while he had cried over being disowned by the only two people who were supposed to love him unconditionally. How could anyone not love him or want him? The kid had the kind of personality that caused people to have mad crushes on him, the kind of caring soul that made people warm from the inside out. He had beauty and brains and heart and a smile that could chase the rain away, and if Davi kept going the way he was, he'd be a star.

And if Lance kept thinking the way he was, he would turn into a lovesick fool.

Shaking his head, he dropped his backpack down at one of the many vanities lining the dressing room wall. The music coming off the stage permeated the concrete. It wasn't time for the club to be open, but routine was routine, and every night before the doors opened, the DJ ran through the club mix to make sure everything was still kosher—something about mids and lows and the sound distorting. Lance had listened to him talk technicalities once or twice because the DJ had a smoking-hot body, but his techno-jargon had gone in one ear and out the other. Lance had just wanted to watch his plump lips move. He had a habit of rolling his wonderfully thick tongue over his mouth when he spoke. It was one of the hottest things Lance had ever seen, but they never went any further than talking. Apparently, Mr. DJ liked the fairer sex.

By the hard pounding in Lance's skull, either the bass was just right or he'd talked himself into one massively annoying headache.

Lance had just started settling in—iPod and earbuds front and center, sapphire blue hoodie hanging on the back of his chair—when the sound of sneakers squeaking up beside him made him lift his head. When he saw who'd joined him, he wished he hadn't.

His stare immediately trained on a set of very, very kissable pinkish-bronze lips he'd barely tasted less than a week ago. No matter how badly he wanted to, he couldn't make himself look away. Those lips represented things he couldn't accept wanting, things that almost always led to heartbreak and misery, and an absolutely complicated life.

Talk to him, idiot. If nothing else, tell him you never want to kiss him again.

Oh, but wasn't that a lie? As soon as his sights landed on Davi's lips, kissing him was all Lance could think about, all he *wanted* to think about, and it didn't even have anything to do with sex. Lance wanted the intimacy and the closeness. He wanted things he'd never really dreamed of with anyone else.

Oh, God.

Lance's mouth dried and his breath caught. He needed to say something fast, anything to take the attention off his stupid staring, but he had no voice. He opened his mouth and closed it again, like a starving fish fighting for food. Nothing. No sound. Hell, he wasn't even sure he was still breathing.

Panic in five… four… three—

"I'm glad you are alone," Davi drawled, and God help Lance, his voice sounded a hell of a lot more seductive than Davi probably meant it to. "I wanted to talk to you about—"

"The kiss?" Lance said for him.

"Sim."

"It never happened." *What are you saying, man?*

"Sim, it did."

"No, it didn't."

Davi frowned, head tilting to the side. "How do you mean?"

Finally, Lance's stare got with the program and obeyed the commands his brain had been yelling. He looked back to the mirror and those horrible globe-shaped lights that showed off every single blemish and imperfection in harsh, blinding reality. He brushed his fingers over his cheeks, his lips, his brows, as though he were preparing his face for makeup when he really only wanted something else to focus on.

"We didn't kiss," Lance said very pointedly, keeping his focus on his reflection because it was the safest place for his eyes to go. He knew as long as he didn't look at Davi, he could fight whatever ridiculous draw his body had to the kid.

"But… we did."

"Whatever." Lance shrugged. It was his way of dismissing Davi and *trying* to dismiss the chaste little kiss that had thrown his world completely off-kilter.

Suddenly, his chair was being swung around, spinning so fast the force tore his fingertips from his face and sent the world into a pattern of blurring images and melding colors. He had to blink a few times before he could focus on Davi's very irritated expression.

"Do not 'whatever' me," Davi growled. The sound was unexpected, forceful as hell, and the sexiest fucking thing Lance had heard in a long damn time. "We kissed. I wanted it. And you… you…."

"I didn't want it," Lance finished for him. *Lies.* "I'm good with what I have." *More lies.* "So yeah, don't… don't kiss me again." *Please kiss me again.*

Davi clenched his jaw tight, flesh rippling over rigid bone. There was something incredibly sexy about a man who had a jawline fierce enough to pull of something so damn... manly. Was that the first time Lance had looked at Davi as more of a man than a helpless, innocent kid?

Yes. Yes it was.

Now just what the hell did that epiphany mean? Did it mean Lance would find fucking Davi a little easier? Maybe not, but it sure made Davi sexier than Lance had ever imagined him being.

Davi's brow furrowed as his stare narrowed. He was now rocking one pissed-off expression, the kind that normally led to violent kissing and angry sex, and dammit all to hell if Lance wasn't getting hard just thinking about the ways Davi could nail him to the wall, the way that impressively thick cock would feel inside him, milking him and making him come undone.

Oh, God....

The thing was Davi never seemed like the kind of guy who wanted down and dirty in the back of a nightclub. He always played all soft and sweet, the innocent little import from Portugal who just wanted to be coddled and cared for, and for a moment—the briefest, most fleeting of moments—Lance thought he wanted to be the kind of guy who could take care of someone like that. He didn't. He was the loose cannon, the one who made bad mistakes, the one who jumped into everything feet first, the one who always found himself hip-deep and wading in shit. He couldn't take care of himself, let alone someone else.

But this side of Davi was something he'd never seen before. The power rolling off Davi's rigid body was something to be revered and maybe even feared. It demanded respect, and God help him, Lance's cock stood at full salute now.

"If I choose to kiss you again," Davi said, leaning those wonderfully muscled arms against the armrests of the chair Lance sat in, "then I *will* kiss you again. *Compreendes?*"

Lance couldn't do anything more than nod. His tightened throat squeezed off his voice. The only thing he could smell was the spicy scent of Davi's cologne and the only thing he was aware of feeling was Davi's warm breath brushing along his cheek.

"*Excelente,*" Davi said with the most devious grin Lance had ever seen.

For the measure of a few rapidly thudding heartbeats, they stared at each other with the kind of heat and desire that would've made Lance want to squirm if he hadn't been too afraid to move.

His budding erection pushed harder against his jeans. The tightened feel in his groin had him biting down on his bottom lip. Everything inside his body begged him to just go with it, to give in and see what Davi could do for him or to him or....

He grabbed Davi's hips and held on with the kind of ferociousness a lion might zero in on his prey with. He pulled Davi down to his lap, mouths inching closer and closer. Lance closed his eyes and gave everything over to the sense of feeling and touch and things that really made the body come alive when it didn't have the benefit of sight to get in the way.

First, he felt Davi's strong thighs pinching his legs together. He felt the restraint of denim on denim, and the weight of another body pressing down on his stiffened cock. Then he felt lips he'd briefly tasted only once before caressing his. Lance opened his mouth and kept his eyes sealed tight. He felt Davi nipping teasingly along his bottom lip. Then suddenly all that playfulness stopped and Lance's mouth was being utterly devoured.

A set of hands gripped his neck tight, not tight enough to cause alarm, but tight enough to make a rush of adrenaline surge through Lance's body. Davi licked across Lance's lips, then licked against the roof of his mouth, and his tongue kept going deeper, reaching toward Lance's throat. He was being controlled and dominated and loving every single second of it. Maybe because it was new and exciting. Maybe because he'd always been the one to take charge and now it was his body being commanded. Whatever. He didn't care. He just wanted to give in to the moment.

Bucking his hips, Lance raised his ass off the seat and Davi had no other choice but to follow through with the motion and plant his feet on the concrete floor or land on his ass in a not-so-sexy sort of way. Lance didn't let go of his hips, though, and damn sure didn't let any sort of space come between their mouths. In fact, he took over the kiss *and* the movement of their bodies as he walked them backward toward the racks of costumes and out of sight.

Davi's back hit the wall hard enough an "umf" sound wedged between their lips, but didn't break their kiss. He reached down between their bodies and made great haste with removing Davi's jeans. The denim pooled at Davi's feet, and Lance was more than pleased to find Davi didn't have a stitch of fabric on beyond his pants. His thick, olive-colored cock sprang free with the kind of tenacity that made Lance's mouth water, and as Lance did with every other man he intended on laying, he dropped to his knees and opened his mouth wide.

He was just about to swallow Davi whole when a hand locked in his hair and restrained him from pleasuring in the taste of swollen, ready cock.

"No," Davi said. "I please you."

"You want to or insist on?"

"I insist."

Well now, wasn't that a pleasant surprise?

Raising his hands, Lance lifted back to his feet and gave Davi a go-ahead-and-do-your-best kind of smirk. He watched as that beautiful boy knelt down on the concrete floor in front of him, wrenching Lance's jeans down with him. The rough fabric burned Lance's skin as it quickly rode down his body. He hissed, but damn if that hint of pain didn't turn him on more.

Davi circled one hand around the base of his erection. He cradled his sac with the other. Lance closed his eyes and let his head rest against the wall. The coolness of concrete chilled his bare ass, but he didn't care. He didn't even flinch. And within a matter of a few agonizing seconds, a warm mouth sheathed his cock completely, swallowing it down until the head hit the back of Davi's throat.

From the slight part in the costumes, Lance caught a glimpse of his reflection in one of the vanity mirrors. Why it caught his eye right then, he wasn't sure, but he noticed the difference in his posture—the way he was the one being serviced, not some filthy whore on his knees for some rich old man who didn't care. He was the one being worshipped and pleased and he was the one with all the power for a change. Oddly enough, the idea made him feel ten times worse. That was when he realized this wasn't about *just* getting off.

He more than cared about Davi.

He more than respected Davi.

And sex wasn't the way to show it.

10

"SO HOW is Dorian?" Jason asked into the tiny white hands-free mic attached to his earbuds. He gripped the handles of his bike, pumping his legs hard against the pedals, fighting the bright sun of a Friday afternoon as he made his way down Decatur.

On the other end of the line, he could hear the wind whipping in through a car window, as if Jansen suddenly needed the fresh air. That was the first time Jason had asked about Dorian since his best friend's husband had been thrown in the slammer. Every time they'd talked—which hadn't been often—Jason had been intent on raising Jansen's spirits, so he never brought up Dorian. They talked about other things, like Jansen's dancing in a real theater instead of a nightclub, or he would invite Jansen out to lunch. Granted, conversation only happened if Jansen actually answered the phone. When they did finally talk, the last thing on Jason's mind was Dorian. He'd never liked Dorian, and that hadn't changed. Honestly, if it wasn't for Jansen's state of well-being, Jason wouldn't have given two shits about Dorian.

"He's... well, he's Dorian." Jansen inhaled so deeply Jason could hear it over the wind and the miles between them. "He's surviving, but he's ready to come home."

"Who wouldn't be?"

"Exactly."

"But he'll be home soon, right?"

"We hope so."

Jason pulled his ten-speed up to the bike rack behind the club, rolled the back wheel up between the bars, and put the kickstand down. He then reached in his backpack and pulled out a lock and chain to fasten it into place.

For a long moment, he stood there in the back parking lot of Sin & Seduction, staring at the broken-down fence as his best friend in the entire world went on about the man he'd married.

"So...," Jansen cautiously continued. The hesitation in his voice pulled Jason's focus away from his surroundings. "I haven't talked to you in forever. How's the family? How's the club."

"The family is great. Brad and I get Hope every other week, and weekends when his ex-wife wants to get away with her new boyfriend. She's being really great about him seeing his kid, and Hope is growing so damn fast." Jason smiled, though Jansen couldn't see him. The dreamy-eyed grin just kind of happened every time he talked about his new little family. "Brad's doing great at work. He just got a major promotion. He's managing people now, not just doing live spots. He loves it."

"And the club?"

The smile faded almost as quickly as it had made an appearance. A sigh pushed through Jason's lips before he could stop it. He hadn't told Jansen about the club. A) because Jansen had other shit on his mind, and B) Jansen would want to help, and—well, see point A.

"What's wrong, Jason?"

Oh, the silence must've given him away. Or maybe it was that stupid telltale sigh.

"The club's closing, man," he finally said.

Jansen gasped so hard that it came across the information superhighway so clearly he could've been standing right in front of Jason's face.

"That's insane. It can't close. What will everyone do for work? What...? Why...? Jason, what happened?" Jansen rambled, asking his twenty questions before Jason could interrupt. His questioning finally stopped long enough for Jansen to breathe. "Are you going to tell me what happened?"

"Jeez, you gonna give me a chance to?"

"Sorry, I... I couldn't help it."

"It's okay. I sort of had the same reaction." Jason raked his fingers through his messy auburn hair, all the way back until his hand landed at the nape of his neck.

He hitched his backpack up on his shoulder, then headed toward the back door of the venue, silently remembering everything Hank had told him in the office on Thanksgiving. Funny, it felt like only yesterday, and somehow a part of a past he wanted to forget.

"The owners are just over it," Jason said as he fished his keys from his pocket. He jingled the ring until the one to the back door sprung free. "They're not making the money they want to make and they're bitching about getting old. They're just... over it."

"Damn. That really sucks. That place was like a home for me."

"Then you got married."

"Yeah," Jansen said softly.

"And you left."

"Jason—"

"Don't. It's cool. I understand why you left. Hell, I would give it up for Brad in a heartbeat. I just can't live with him paying my way. I can't be that guy."

"What are you saying?" Jansen sounded genuinely offended. "What kind of guy—"

"Look, bro, don't even go there with me. I didn't mean the shit that way." Jason wrenched open the heavy, rusted metal door, then slammed it behind him. "Dorian's got loads of money. He has plenty to cover the two of you. Brad doesn't. Plus, he has a kid and an ex-wife to take care of. It would be wrong of me to take from their pockets. You know?"

"I guess."

"Don't get your panties in a twist, 'kay?"

It was Jansen's turn to sigh. "I'm sorry. I guess I'm being a little more sensitive than normal. It's been more than six months since I slept in the same bed with Dorian. Six. Freakin'. Months! I'm going crazy. I want him home so bad."

"Yeah, I can imagine."

"I'm on my way to the prison now." The tone of Jansen's voice changed. It went from borderline whining to lilting with enthusiasm. "They're giving him a new bail hearing."

"That's a good thing, though, right?" Jason asked with a frown. He didn't know shit about the legal system, never really had a need for it.

"Yeah. They're going to let him come home until the trial."

"What the hell took them so long?"

"They said he had enough money to be a flight risk. Apparently, though, new evidence proves his innocence."

"That's great."

The sound of someone moaning pulled Jason's attention away from the conversation he'd been having. He distantly heard Jansen talking, but wasn't paying any attention. There was something more important than locked-up criminals and bail hearings going on in the backstage of the club. As he got closer, the moans got louder. He caught a glimpse of glistening skin through a part in the costume racks, and he immediately knew what the hell was going down.

"Let me call you back," he said into the phone.

They both said a quick good-bye, and then Jason slipped the device into his back pocket. He took slow, careful steps until he cleared the rack. He found Lance pressed against the wall, butt-ass naked for anyone to catch him, and Davi was kneeling down in front of him, sucking so hard his cheeks hollowed.

He waited for the last wailing scream, waited while Lance jerked his hips. He was fucking Davi's mouth pretty damn hard, and no doubt the puffy, irritated evidence of their indiscretions would encircle Davi's lips for a few hours after they finished... if they ever finished.

"When you get a minute," Jason said, turning to head back toward his office. "I need to talk to you."

He didn't specify the *who* he needed to talk to, but he really didn't have to. While Jason loved all the guys pretty equally, Lance was the only one he ever really opened up to. They had history, after all. Lance had been there—in more ways than one—when Jason first started seeing Brad and things in the blossoming relationship had been rocky at best. Lance had wanted more than Jason had to give, but they still remained friends... good friends.

Jason sat down behind the old metal desk that had become like a throne to him over the years. He laid both hands, palms down, on either side of the clipboard holding the dancers' schedules. The plans he'd been jotting down for the grand finale show were just beneath the pages. They had less than a month left to get everything settled, and it seemed like the more time dwindled down, the faster it flew.

He settled into the old wooden chair that had often been the reason he'd gone home with a stiff back and a sore ass, tucked his arms behind his head, and closed his eyes. All the possibilities of life after Sin & Seduction passed through his mind—possibilities that had been appealing on those nights he hated his job and would've rather been at home with Brad and the kiddo, possibilities that, until now, he'd never really put a whole lot of thought into. He could pick up writing again or maybe get back into the photography he used to love. He could spend a little more time bonding with Brad's daughter since she was usually around while her daddy was at work. The possibilities seemed endless at this point.

A soft knocking at the door finally dragged him away from those thoughts.

"Come in," he said. The hinges whined as the door slowly opened. Lance's headful of blond hair appeared first. "Feel better?" Jason asked.

"Actually, I do," Lance said, dragging a T-shirt over his head.

"Sit down."

"Am I in trouble?"

"Trouble? For what?"

"Getting a blowjob backstage."

"Has anyone ever gotten in trouble for getting or giving blowjobs around here?"

"Well... no. I guess they haven't."

"So what makes you think we're gonna start today?"

Lance shrugged, and then he plopped down on the seat across from Jason's desk. Jason sat forward and leaned his arms across the cool metal surface, framing the clipboard he almost always carried around the club with him.

"You know I'm not the kind of guy who asks for help," he said.

"Who doesn't?" Lance smirked.

"Right." Jason swallowed, and then sat straight up in his chair, posture perfect. "Well, I need some help."

"Anything for you, boss."

The anything Lance said, he meant it wholeheartedly. Jason knew that without an inkling of doubt. Good thing too. If Jason was going to make a real effort to do something to save this place, he needed help and he knew it. So he decided to take his husband's advice and ask for it. Everyone would have their little parts to play. Everyone would have a role. Lance's role—help formulate a solid plan and stand behind Jason when he finally manned up enough to go to the owners with his ideas.

11

No, JASON absolutely wasn't the kind of man who asked for help, and the fact he'd asked Lance and no one else stroked Lance's ego in the best possible way. Well, almost best. Would've been a hell of a lot more awesome if there was a little down and dirty coming with the sweet stroking, but unfortunately, that would never happen. Jason was now a happily, practically married man.

And don't forget you're interested in someone too.

Shit.

"I'm going to do it. I'm going to talk to the bosses about letting me take over the club," Jason finally said. He had an intensity about him now, a sincere air of *do-or-die*. Oh, but Jason wore it well. He always wore determination well. It gave him the kind of palpable strength that commanded respect from everyone around him. It rallied the troops when the troops only wanted to roll over and surrender.

"And how do I fit in this equation?" Lance asked, crossing his legs high at his thighs and crossing his arms over his chest. He was very aware of the smirk he now wore.

"I'm thinking you can take over managing the dancers. I'll need help. I can't run the entire club by myself, and you're the only person I have here who I genuinely trust."

Aww. I feel genuinely honored.

"They all respect you," Jason added, as if the trust wasn't enough. "They talk to you and listen to you. I had that same relationship with them."

"*Had?*" Lance frowned. "You still have that relationship with them. Everything just got... crazy. You wanted a real life with a real family and this place didn't necessarily facilitate that so you took a step back. No one blames you. No one faults you. They still adore you."

"And they adore you too, hence the reason I think you would be great at this."

Lance sat back in the chair, arms dropping from his chest, hands folding in his lap. He eyed Jason hard, considering him and the offer presently on the table. It paid more money than dancing alone did, but Lance would lose his ten minutes of fame if he didn't grace that stage, and losing that fame meant losing the fans who not only fed his withering ego, but fed his light wallet.

"I'll only do it if I can keep dancing," he finally said.

"Why...?" Jason sighed and shook his head. "Never mind. I get it," he said, which was probably the truth.

It wasn't too many years ago Jason had been in the same position. Dancing. Fucking. Making bank. He'd hurt his back one night after work—the details of said incident were never shared with anyone—but he couldn't dance anymore, not without a major dose of pain the next day. So Jason didn't grace the stage, not unless he got a wild hair, and he always paid for that handsomely. Lance had once been fortunate enough to rub the kinks out for him—long before Jason knew how he felt, long before Jason felt something for someone else.

"So, can I keep dancing?" Lance asked, forcing his brain to shift gears.

"As long as it doesn't interfere with managing the dancers."

"Perfect."

He popped up from the chair with a huge grin on his face, ready to march right back into the dressing area and tell the boys who their new commander-in-chief was, when Jason saying "You have to go up and talk to the bosses with me" stopped him dead in his tracks. He spun back around to face his boss, expression completely deadpan, as if all the life had been sucked out of his body.

"I have to do what?"

"I need backup, Lance. You have to go up there with me."

"I'm just a stupid fucking dancer. What the hell do you think they'll want to talk to me for?"

"Hey."

Jason popped up to his feet, palms pressed against the surface of his desk. "I was a 'stupid fucking dancer' at one point too, but they put me in charge of the stage when I couldn't do anything else." He walked around to the front of the desk, gripped Lance by his shoulders, and gave him the kind of look that had Lance's knees knocking together.

God, that man still did it for him.

"I need to show them I have a plan in place," Jason said. "I think they'll be more willing to hand over the club if… if I have support and something mapped out."

So there it was. Lance couldn't say no to that, not after everything Jason had done for him… *been to* him. Christ, would he never forget those feelings? Sighing, he slumped his shoulders as he conceded. "Fine. When do I have to go? What do I need to do?"

"Tomorrow night. Dress like a businessman—a serious businessman. If you don't have a suit and tie, I'll borrow one from Bradley for you."

"A suit and tie?" Lance whined, nose curled. He swore he could feel hives erupting along his skin. The only silk he liked was against his bare ass, and frankly, *never* was a great time for wool or poly or any of that synthetic shit people liked to make suits out of.

"Lance. C'mon. Work with me here."

"Fine," he bitterly spat. "But you owe me."

The second time Lance spun around and headed for the door, Jason didn't stop him. He walked out into the hall with a heady combination of dread and excitement. Though he was really getting ahead of himself here. The owners still had to accept Jason's plan, which they could very well shoot down. Lance hoped they didn't. A lot was riding on Jason's success, not least of all the sexy new crush he found himself growing more and more fond of.

Speaking of sexy new crushes....

As soon as Lance rounded the corner back into the dressing area, he found himself almost nose-to-nose with Davi. He had the space of a single breath, a single heartbeat, to decide whether to run or stay, to take that step closer and go in for a kiss, or back away slowly and pretend nothing ever happened. Oh, but something had happened already. Something lewd. Something incredible. Something that had led to one toe-curling, heart-stopping orgasm.

"Hey," he rasped, dragging his fingers though his thick blond hair.

Davi grinned wickedly, as if he were daring Lance to move just an inch— one little inch.

Just. One. Little. Inch.

Lance took that last step forward and Davi didn't move, didn't so much as flinch. He had a steely composure, an unrelenting strength and surety. He was no longer their shy, quiet, *innocent* kiddo. He was hot and sexual and something to be craved. Someone to be devoured.

Davi leaned his head down and as softly as anyone possibly could, he brushed his lips over the hard edge of Lance's jaw, up, up, up to his earlobe where Davi whispered oh so carefully, "I want to fuck you."

Holy hard-on!

Without a moment of hesitation, Lance hooked his forefingers in the belt loop of Davi's jeans and tugged the kid out of the backstage dressing area. When they cleared the stage and hit the first step leading up to VIP, Lance let go and grabbed one of Davi's hands. He pulled him up to the balcony and over to the last booth on the end—the very same booth where Jason often hid away.

Fumbling fingers made a mess of his belt and jeans, and when Lance realized he wasn't getting anywhere with himself, he took to Davi's clothes. He silently coached himself to calm down, to go slow. To try fucking breathing for a change.

He inhaled, grinned up at Davi, and his hands found the kind of calm they needed to operate a zipper and button. As soon as the little metal teeth broke free and the denim slipped down Davi's bronze muscled legs and his thick cock sprang free, Lance gasped. He'd admired the impressive prick from afar, through very thin fabric, just as the patrons of the club had. The only up close and personal hadn't lasted very long because Davi had had something else in mind for them. Now, though....

Lord, have mercy! It was wide and long, veiny and rippling, and probably one of the prettiest dicks Lance had ever seen. And boy, if anyone was a good judge of gorgeous cock, it was he. Thick blue veins ran down to the tip. It didn't crook to the side, didn't hang low and slap against his perfectly proportioned balls. It stood erect and proud, just as it should. Every little wrinkle begged for a good, long, savoring lick.

I'm in love with a penis.

With the same lascivious grin he'd had before, Davi flipped a condom out onto the table. Lance looked down at the package and frowned, then turned his curious stare back up to Davi.

"Had it in my pocket. Pulled it out when I realized we were heading up here."

Ooooooohhhh. "You carry condoms around with you?" *Are you* that *kind of guy?*

Davi shrugged. "Don't you?"

Jesus, Lance was that *kind of guy.*

He smirked. "No. I make the men who fuck me provide them."

"Good I had one, sim?"

Very.

"Now, put it on me."

Ay, captain!

Without a single second of hesitation, Lance reached down and swiped the little foil wrapper from the table. He put one corner between his teeth. Rip. A purple rubber popped free just as Lance was taking Davi's cock into his hand. With the kind of accuracy gained from years of practice, Lance one-handed the condom, pinching the tip between his thumb and forefinger, then using a circle of fingers to roll it into place.

No sooner did he have the rubber situated than Davi spun him around and bent him over the side of the bench. The whirling motion stopped Lance's heart for a split second, but the moment he felt one slender finger plunge deep into his ass, his heart kicked in at double time. He let out a loud hiss and the sound rolled into a soft moan. Lance bit down on his lip and hugged the booth the best he could.

The tips of Lance's fingers bit into the leather seat as Davi added the second finger. As crude as it was, Lance was no stranger to the pain of being stretched. He always bottomed and loved nothing more than feeling a thick, hot cock drilling inside him, and though he understood Davi's need for slow and easy, Lance liked his fast and rough.

"Please, dear God, boy, fuck me already," he rasped, looking over his shoulder to see the vision of physical perfection standing behind him. His stare traced that beautiful V leading down to the glorious prick poking out from two very muscled thighs.

As soon as the words hit the air, Davi clamped his hands onto Lance's cheeks and spread him wide. Lance refused to look away as the first of many hard, thick inches pushed into his hole. The wickedness in the man's otherwise innocent face was a turn-on all on its own.

Lance finally turned back toward the bench and pressed his forehead to the leather. Davi fell into a hard, pumping, hammering rhythm that matched the music flowing over the club below. The tempo was fast and varying, just like Davi's thrusts, and when the bass dropped, Davi nailed Lance with a force that pushed him farther up the seat and brought him closer to orgasm.

Those strong hands moved up his ass to his waist, then tightened on his hips about the same time Davi's thrusts became more ferocious. The in and out, and in and out, and grazing just the right spot had Lance's sac tugging and his cock twitching. He held on to the seat as best as he could. He thought maybe he could last a little longer just to keep the connection going, but when Davi reached around and gripped his shaft, and the pulsing in Davi's hand met the pulsing in Lance's cock, the grand finale started its ascension up from his sac. Their heat combined and the pumping intensified, picking up speed and depth. The pressure grew strong and Lance's sac tightened to his body.

"I'm coming!" he warned, though the club music drowned the sound.

Apparently, so was Davi.

There were no more than ten or fifteen hard, quick pumps before the heat in his hole got twice as hot. He felt Davi slow, then felt pressure along his backside and warm breath gusting over his shoulder.

Lance raised his head and looked back. He found Davi curled against his back, eyes closed and sweat glistening on his bronze flesh. The innocence Lance had always known and adored had come back, replacing the lust and lewdness he'd seen in Davi's big brown eyes before. The transformation was just as dramatic and startling as it had been before they'd gone up to the VIP booth together, and now that Davi was back to his old self, Lance felt like shit for even taking him up there.

I'm so pathetic.

"Sweetheart," he said. Though his voice sounded soft, he'd spoken loud enough to be heard over the club music. He pulled Davi's hand up to his lips and kissed his palm. "Let's get you cleaned up and... and...."

Let me take you home and make you mine.

Lance's eyes widened. What the hell was he thinking? Why the hell was he thinking like *that*? This was not good, not good at all. Time to revise that "off-limits" list and firmly cement Davi's name there. And almost as if Davi knew Lance had been thinking about him, he raised his head and gave Lance the most serene, blissful smile.

Lance's heart melted.

12

SUNDAY. MONDAY. Tuesday. The days felt like they were bleeding into each other. Wednesday. It was already the middle of the week and though Jason had had his dancers in there eight hours a day, every day since Sunday, it didn't feel as though they'd gotten anything accomplished. Well, nothing save for a few shots for the video Brad promised him. The new routines—while amazing in theory—looked like shit in practice. Every missed beat, missed cue, or misplaced step made Jason's hope for the club's survival diminish.

"Stop. Just... stop," he yelled over the music, clapping his clipboard against his palm so hard it stung. It got their attention, though.

The music died down and seven dancers stood there staring at each other as if none of them knew where they'd gone so horribly wrong. Of course they didn't. How could they? Perspective changed from out in the audience. Sad thing was, two days ago, they'd looked a hell of a lot better than they did right now.

"Take a break, guys. In fact, go out and have dinner or whatever. Relax for a little while. Meet back here in about two hours."

Everyone grumbled and started to scatter.

He watched as the guys paired up in their normal cliques. The twins surrounded the newest addition, arms linked around his, and they disappeared. A few of the others went in the opposite direction, most likely up to VIP for God only knew what. The last two to head down the hall were Lance and Davi. They'd been inseparable lately, and no, that wasn't supposed to bother Jason, but it did... in a weird way. Maybe because he knew Lance and knew the guy wasn't the settling-down type, and Davi... well, he very much seemed like the settling-down type. That was not what really bothered Jason about the situation. If they were screwing and Davi got attached, and Lance broke his heart like Lance was so capable of doing, then there would be drama. Drama the club didn't need right now. Drama the dancers didn't need right now. More importantly, drama Jason didn't need right now.

Frowning, Jason absently planted his ass in a chair at a table to the right of the stage. He spread his legs wide and slumped his shoulders. The weight of exhaustion was heavier now that he had disastrous romances added to all the other stress.

The club lights were still changing colors—red, blue, green, and yellow. The spotlight flashed to the pulse of music that should've been there but wasn't.

He lost himself in the flashing lights and the diminishing fog, trying to work out the logistics of the routines and where the hell they were going wrong. Nothing immediately popped into his mind. The fact he couldn't work any of this mess out made him wonder what kind of stage manager he really was.

Stage manager. Not choreographer.

He scrubbed his hand down over his face and settled into his chair, lolling his head back as he closed his eyes. The tension in his shoulders made it almost painful to keep holding his head up. He could even feel the knots of muscle rolling around beneath his skin.

Doom. Utter doom. Nothing was going as planned. Nothing was going to end up the way he wanted.

A set of strong hands wrapped over his shoulders and Jason nearly bolted straight out of his seat. "Calm down, baby," the velvety voice attached to those hands said with a hint of laughter.

Jason's racing heart dialed back to a normal rhythm. He exhaled. "You scared the shit out of me," he said, leaning his head back enough to steal a quick kiss from his partner's delicious lips.

"I was hoping to surprise you."

"You did, but…." Jason frowned. "I thought you had the kiddo tonight."

"No, Melody's boyfriend got called into work, so…."

"So we have the house to ourselves and here I am slaving for nothing."

Brad squeezed his shoulders a little harder, rubbing his thumbs in a circular motion over Jason's tight muscles. The relief elicited a soft moan and made Jason's eyes roll back in their sockets.

"I thought maybe… well, if you're taking a break…."

"What?" Jason somehow managed to rasp out despite his mouth not wanting to move.

"I got us a room at the Bourbon Orleans. Thought maybe we could rekindle some of that old flame we used to have."

The old flame, huh?

Jason turned in the chair and he looked up at his partner. His beautiful, blond-haired, blue-eyed angel had the sweetest smile on his face—the very smile that had lured Jason in a little over two years ago. He'd fallen for that smile before he'd ever gotten to know the heart of the man behind it, but he wasn't disappointed in the least. The heart ended up being ten times more radiant.

He pushed up to his feet and took Brad's hand. "A room at the hotel sounds perfect."

"It's not just any room. It's *our* room."

"Even better," Jason said with a grin as he jotted a quick note to the dancers on his clipboard. It said he was stepping out but he'd be back in a few hours. Start the routines without him. Then he turned back to his partner with the widest grin on his face. "I'm all yours."

They laced their fingers together and headed out of the club, walking side by side. It brought back a lot of memories for Jason—mostly fond memories, but some not so fond. Their relationship had started with a lot of heartache, a lot of lying and sneaking around. Thankfully, though, it had blossomed into something beautiful, and Jason attributed their strength as a couple to the strife they'd endured early on.

As soon as they'd stepped around to the front of the nightclub, Jason spotted a taxi that had obviously been waiting there to pick them up. By early evening on Wednesday, the warehouse district was dead as a doornail, and taxis didn't randomly come through. It served no purpose because there were usually no patrons to pick up. Brad grabbed the door, and Jason slid in first. Brad joined him with a "Bourbon Orleans" called over the back of the seat.

The cab ride didn't take long at all. Wednesday was one of three dead nights in the French Quarter, so the crowds were sparse and navigating through traffic was a breeze. Cabbies always made it look easy, though. Their *move-or-die* mentality got them everywhere fast. Jason couldn't be more thankful. Time was limited, and the thought of being in their old room alone with Brad had his cock on the eager side of ready to go.

Brad slipped a twenty over the seat and told the driver to keep the change before tearing out of the cab and hauling Jason with him. They darted past the bellboy with nothing more than a two-finger wave and straight over to the elevator. Brad didn't let go of Jason's hand, even as he struggled to free the key card from the pocket of his gunmetal-gray slacks. The whole scene would've been comical to watch had Jason not had the same exact sense of urgency.

The elevator couldn't have been any slower, and the *ding* as the doors slid open felt a hell of a lot like the firing gun at a horse race. They both practically dove inside the elevator, lips crushing together. Their hands found each other's bodies with the kind of forceful fluidity of a starving man finding food.

Oh, but they *were* both starving, weren't they? Their bodies had needs. Their libidos screamed with frustration. Yes, they were most certainly starving.

The elevator chimed at their floor and the doors slowly ground open. They practically fell into the hallway, still wrestling each other's clothes. Brad's sage-colored dress shirt had lost a few buttons, one tail hanging out of his gray pants. The buckle of Jason's belt jingled as they stumbled down the hall, lips still locked together with no chance of breaking free.

"Key," Brad said against Jason's mouth as he held the card out, obviously searching for the door. It would've been so much easier to stop molesting each other and wait until they were in the room, but desire and the need to be intimate drove them both into a frenzy and there was no backing away.

The door swung open, and in the twist of each other's arms, they fell into the room, somehow keeping their footing even as they pinged off the edge of the couch and went waltzing toward the bed. Jason's legs hit the edge of the mattress, and he had no choice but to flop backward. Brad let him go.

"This isn't as sexy as I pictured it," Brad said with a laugh.

"Babe, this is plenty sexy." Jason hooked his thumbs on the waistband of his jeans and tugged down, legs flailing as he recklessly kicked out of his shoes. "This is the epitome of sexy, all things considered. Hell, I'm just happy to have you alone and we're not too tired to fool around. Oh yeah, this is sexy."

Brad laughed again. He reached out to help Jason relieve himself of the denim binding his legs. Their hands met at Jason's thighs. Their lips met above the fray. For the space of a few heartbeats, their mouths lingered and their stares remained steadfast. There was one thing in the entire world that made Jason not only happy, but alive in ways he couldn't put words to, and that was the man staring back at him. Brad made everything so much better, and God, Jason loved him like there was no tomorrow.

After stealing a slow kiss, Brad pulled back, taking Jason's jeans down to the floor with him. He tossed the pile of denim aside but stayed on his knees and reached up to take Jason's hand.

"What's wrong?" Jason asked as he sat up on the edge of the mattress. He intertwined his fingers with Brad's and frowned.

"Nothing, I…." Brad's lips curled into a smile, and with his free hand, he reached into his pocket. "I wanted to save this for something more romantic, but… but I think now is a perfect time." He had a little black box in his hand and when he popped it open, the low light of the hotel room glistened on something silvery. "Now that same-sex marriage is legal in so many states and DOMA is a nonissue, I um… I want to make this real, Jason. We've been playing house for a long time. I think it's time to commit, I mean *really* commit."

"Are you…."

"Yeah." Brad nodded, lips thinning into a tight smile. "I'm asking you to marry me."

Wow. Just…. Wow.

Jason hadn't spent a single second considering married life. It wasn't that he didn't love Brad enough to marry him, but commitment of any kind wasn't at the top of his to-do list. Damn, did he even want to be married?

"Jason?"

He exhaled, shaking off his daze. "Yeah?"

"Will you marry me?"

"I…." *Dude, don't do this to him. Think about what he gave up to be with you. Think about everything he's done for you. Think about how he makes you feel. You love him. Say yes.* "I…."

"It's too soon." Brad started to push up to his feet and Jason tugged him right back down. The hurt on Brad's kind, handsome face was too much to bear. It was tragic and heartbreaking, and Brad didn't deserve to feel the things that could make an expression like that find life. He deserved to be with someone who didn't have a single doubt, who didn't fumble and falter when asked to take that big leap. Brad deserved someone who was ready to commit and play house and be a father.

Could Jason be that guy?

"Jason?"

"It's not too soon," Jason blurted without thought. He inhaled deeply and exhaled raggedly. He couldn't believe he was really going to do this. "I want to marry you."

"So that's a yes?"

"Yes. It's a yes."

13

OUTSIDE THE club, at the back of the building, Lance held Davi's hand without panicking or really thinking about how intimate and meaningful simply holding someone's hand could be. The situation wasn't comfortable, and not exactly uncomfortable, either—more weird, but not necessarily in a bad way.

God, he sounded like a freakin' psychopath.

Even worse, they stood at the foot of the rusty steps leading up to Lance's apartment, and he wasn't sure he could take Davi up there. Not because he lived in a shithole or because his digs embarrassed him. Quite the contrary. The apartment above the club was plenty spacious for one person. He had a nice place with nice shit, a comfortable bed, and food in the fridge. Okay, the latter was questionable, but still, taking someone home meant something huge, right? He couldn't do huge. Not with Davi. Not with anyone. *Huge* was right smack in the middle of his strictly off-limits list, written in bright red.

"How about we just go for a walk?" he said, rubbing his forefinger over his crinkled brow. "The Riverwalk isn't too far from here. We could go down there and relax, then come back in a few hours."

"That sounds very nice." Davi flexed his fingers, making Lance very aware of the fact they were still holding hands. Ironically, he didn't want to let go despite his internal panic.

They headed east down Decatur, walking away from the dark, dank edge of the French Quarter. The closer they came to the Mississippi River, the moister the air became. He could now hear the water crashing against the shore and the sound of riverboats chugging along. The Riverwalk was one of Lance's favorite places to go and ponder or just chill out when life started running away on him— a dose of serenity among chaos and turmoil.

He led Davi down the cobblestones, as close as they could get to the water's edge without being dangerously close to the mighty Mississippi, and far away from any possible passersby. It wasn't for wanting to hide, but more for the peace and quiet of being away from the bustle of the Quarter.

Lance sat down first and Davi followed. Their bodies pressed together— arm-to-arm, leg-to-leg. Lance gave the beautiful object of his interest a sideways grin, a tight, faked smile for Davi's benefit because Lance never wanted him to feel unwanted.

Oh, he wanted Davi, wanted him a little too much.

Davi nudged Lance's leg with his knee. "Why are you so quiet?"

"Things on my mind."

"I could take your mind off… things."

Didn't that sound tempting?

Lance shifted where he sat, spreading his legs only slightly. He didn't mean it as an invitation, but Davi sure took the move that way. Before Lance could stop him, Davi rolled over and used his hips to spread Lance's legs wider. With his chest, Davi pushed him down until Lance's back lay against the cobblestone. Their mouths connected and Davi had his fingers knotted in Lance's hair. Their tongues twisted. Lance closed his eyes. He was just about to give in to the kiss and the feel of Davi's artful form on top of him when that switch in his brain controlling rational thought clicked away from the twitch in his groin. He pressed both palms to Davi's shoulders and gave a gentle shove.

"What are you doing?" he asked in a gasp.

"Kissing you," Davi all but purred, leaning into another kiss.

Lance stopped him again. "Let's not." *What are you doing?* "I didn't bring you here to kiss you and fuck you. I brought you here to"—*Don't say it*—"to hang out and talk…. To get to know you."

Davi quirked a brow, sitting back on his heels. He didn't move from between Lance's legs and didn't break his stare. The longer their gazes remained locked, the harder Lance had to fight the draw of those sweet, plump, kiss-reddened lips.

"What do you want to know about me?" Davi asked. He ran his hand down Lance's leg, then back up to his thigh, not really getting handsy, but a sensual touch nonetheless.

"Did you leave anyone important in Portugal?"

The next sound was Davi's harsh exhale. He did a good job of keeping his expression stoic until the look in his eyes became distant and almost empty, as if he were trying hard to put a lot of space between him and his feelings. His chin dropped and so did his gaze.

"Tell me. Please," Lance whispered. He touched the tip of his finger to the underside of Davi's chin and gently lifted his face until they were looking directly at each other again.

"His name is Paulo," Davi said. His voice lost all the strength and demand it once had. The innocence returned and he became the man Lance had been falling for. "When I decided to leave Portugal, I asked him to come with me. I wanted a new life in America, a life with him. We could be together here. We wouldn't have to hide our love here. But he refused. He said he wanted a family and he couldn't have that with me."

The few heartstrings Lance had tugged like a son of a bitch. Every instinct in his body screamed for him to pull that boy in his arms and never let go. He hated the pain and the heartbreak he saw, and wanted nothing more than to take it away.

"I told him in America, we could have a family," Davi continued, "but he said it was impossible. He said we had no future. He would marry a good Catholic girl and they would have many babies. It broke me."

"I can only imagine."

"I took every cent I had and left. Here I am."

"If it's any consolation"—Lance wrapped his hand around Davi's and held on with unwavering tenacity—"I'm glad you're here."

The smile Davi returned was less than warm, but as genuine as Lance had ever seen—genuinely sorrowful, genuinely sad, though genuinely trying to be strong. Lance admired him for trying. The effort won him a hell of a lot of respect.

"So…," Davi cautiously proceeded, "what is your story? Is there someone important in your life?"

Someone in Lance's life? That was laughable. After losing his first true love, and his second and his third, and not getting his fourth, Lance stayed far, far away from the big L-word.

"Is that a no?" Davi asked.

"I haven't had a 'someone special' since high school," Lance admitted.

The confession elicited a frown from Davi, a frown meaning Lance needed to explain. Could he, though? Could he lay out his first big experience with heartbreak to someone who might as well have been a complete stranger? He'd kept the story well guarded in the vault of his mind for so long he swore it would never be set free.

"You can talk to me," Davi said. "Your secrets are mine."

The idea of having someone Lance could unload on sounded utterly amazing, but he'd never been quick to trust, not since Nathaniel.

He tightened his fingers around Davi's hand, holding on because he needed to feel anchored. If any of his past spilled from his lips, he needed the kind of warmth and care and accompaniment he could only get from someone as sweet and kind as Davi. He would never in a million years share any of his past with the other guys from the club—Jason, maybe, but no one else. And hadn't the time come to get this shit off his chest?

"His name was Nathaniel," Lance said with a sigh. "We met in third grade and became best friends because we were both odd and lanky, and didn't like the same things boys our age liked. We ended up at the same junior high school."

There was a certain fondness in that memory. It came with the remembering how Lance had been such an outcast and a loner until Natty came along. He'd had someone to play with, someone who wouldn't throw stones and poke fun, someone who wouldn't call him names. He'd no longer been lonely on the playground at school. While the other kids had been jumping rope and playing dodge ball, Natty and Lance had hidden beneath the canopy of the largest weeping willow tree and pretended they had a castle all to themselves. They'd both been kings and both ruled their realm. No one else had mattered to them.

Lance exhaled a sharp breath, more like blowing out the burn in his throat. It came from fighting to hold back his feelings and the sadness that came with the next round of memories.

"Somewhere around the ninth grade," he slowly began again, voice wavering slightly, "I noticed him in a way I hadn't noticed him before. We kept catching each other staring. We always wanted to spend the night together. I started getting bold and sleeping with very little clothes on. He started doing the same. During the night we would end up close to each other. It all happened very gradually. Then one day, we kissed. It was weird when it happened, but probably one of the most amazing things I'd ever experienced. It was like discovering a new book and instantly falling in love. You can't stop reading and don't want to put it down. I was so curious. I wanted to kiss him again and again and again. But I was so overwhelmed with everything I felt, I panicked and so did he, but we never left each other's side. We sat on my bedroom floor, staring at each other without making a sound. Then we tried it one more time, and again. Before I knew it, we were naked and under my covers, touching and kissing. All that time, I'd been head over heels for that boy and I didn't know what it was until we kissed."

"You really smile when you talk about him," Davi said, reaching up to run his finger over Lance's dimple. "What happened to him?"

"He tried to kill himself our junior year." The floodgate broke right then and there. Lance couldn't hold back his tears anymore. They welled in his eyes, clung to his lashes, then spilled down his cheeks. They were hot compared to the cool of his skin, and the cold December breeze rolling off the Mississippi made the tears feel like tiny pins poking into his flesh.

With the back of his hand, Lance wiped the tears away and sniffled back the rest as best as he could. He inhaled sharply and swallowed hard, cleared his throat, and said, "The bullies got to be too bad. His coming out to his parents didn't go so well. My parents found out about me and weren't happy. Things got really ugly for a while. We weren't allowed to see each other. Mom and Dad threatened to send me off to one of those pray-away-the-gay places. Nathaniel's parents pulled him out of school. We had to sneak around to see each other. When we finally got caught, he got in so much trouble I guess he just broke. He tried hanging himself in his closet. When that didn't work, he tried a bottle of aspirin." Lance shook his head. "He just didn't want to be alive anymore."

"That's horrible."

Davi looked genuinely sad for him, but afraid to say much or touch or comfort, as though he was afraid Lance's very fragile will would shatter if he did. It very well could have.

"What happened to him?" Davi carefully asked.

"Nathaniel was shipped away. His parents had him locked up. No one would tell me where he was. I left home thinking I could find him and start a life wherever he was, but I never did. Eventually, I made my way south and landed in New Orleans. I loved it so much I never left."

"And you never forgot him?"

"Nope."

"He is a part of your soul." Davi splayed his free hand over Lance's heart. "He's in here."

"Yeah, I... I suppose he is," Lance whispered as he laid his hand over Davi's.

As soon as Davi eased back up on his knees, Lance leaned forward. Their lips met in the middle, a chaste kiss to seal their secrets. The sentiment meant they would never bring it back up again unless Lance wanted to talk about his past. Oddly enough, now that he'd gotten it off his chest, he was almost ready to move on. Not necessarily fall in love or open his heart to anyone else, but let go and take the first step out of his past and into his future.

Closing his eyes, Lance hugged Davi tight, and this time when they lay back on the cobblestone, there was nothing sexual in the way they held each other. Davi snuggled against Lance's chest. Lance wrapped himself in Davi's warmth. It was innocent and absolutely everything Lance needed after spilling his guts the way he had.

Even though the two hours of freedom they'd been granted was coming to an end, they didn't move from that spot on the river's shore. They stayed for the sunset—the first of many, Lance hoped. They stayed as the golden halo of the sun descended on the horizon, leaving a trail of pink, purple, and deep blue in the sky.

14

AFTER JANSEN'S last visit to OPP, he really didn't think going back was such a great idea. Dorian had been all happy and smiles, hopeful from the good news Rebecca had given him. It seemed better to give Dorian a little space, considering he had said on more than one occasion he hated Jansen seeing him locked up. But there Jansen sat, waiting to see Dorian despite his gut telling him to run back home until they finally set Dorian free.

The last phone call they'd shared had Jansen more on edge than anything else. Dorian's voice had been flat and lifeless, his words curt and as straightforward as Dorian had ever been. There was no sweet "I love you" before he hung up. Only a simple "Watch your back, babe. Always watch your back."

Those had probably been the oddest words Dorian had ever spoken to him, made stranger by the tone and seriousness in his voice rather than what he'd said. It left Jansen with a foreboding feeling, but he did his very best to put a smile on his face and pretend everything was all hunky-dory. It created the kind of false façade that let people know they didn't have to worry and didn't have to ask questions. It kept him from having to talk about the situation.

Talking about the situation ad nauseam was utterly exhausting.

"Grant," the guard on Jansen's side of the windowed wall called out.

Jansen jerked his head up in time to see Dorian walking down the row. He passed behind a pane of glass, disappeared behind the partition for a second, then reappeared. Jansen held his breath each time the partition wall blocked his view. He genuinely feared something bad might happen in that second.

Rubbing his sweaty hands down his thighs, he stood from the hard chair, then hesitantly approached the window. Dorian looked bad; he was healing well, but he was thinner than he'd been before. The rings around his eyes were darker. Cheeks hollow. Lips dry and wrinkled. His facial hair had gotten out of control.

I'm so sorry....

Tears knotted Jansen's throat. They were determined to well up in his eyes, but he tooth-and-nailed them back, swearing to himself he wouldn't cry in front of Dorian. Clearly, he needed to put up a strong front. Dorian needed to see everything would be okay, that this would all end very soon and they could get back to their lives.

Jansen sat down and reached for the receiver. He curled its handle in his fist, keeping his eyes on Dorian as they both lifted the device to their ears.

"Hi," Jansen said. Awkward. Tense. Everything he'd never wanted their relationship to be.

"Hey."

Jesus, say something more than one syllable words.

"Angelo says hello."

"Is he here?"

"Yeah. Well, he's at the car."

Dorian squared his jaw, now sitting a little more rigidly. The expression on his face darkened, exactly how it had once appeared when Dorian was still considered one of the bad guys, sort of like it had the first time they'd ever fought over something.

"Good," he finally said. "I don't want you goin' nowhere alone."

"Dorian, that's unreason—"

"I mean it. People are fucked up. Nobody out there's gonna care 'bout you and won't hesitate to hurt you. I can't do nothin' 'bout that in here."

Oh wow. Okay. Um…

"Dorian, what's going on?" Jansen hunkered down behind the partition, close to the glass. He held the phone tightly to his ear, and when he spoke, he whispered, "I love you. Talk to me, please. This isn't you. Please, talk to me."

The pleading, almost whining, sound of his own voice made him withdraw again. He sat straight up, as posture perfect as he usually did. He reached inside himself for the best lie to make him feel better and plastered on the most stoic expression he could muster. God, he hoped it turned out to be more believable than it felt.

THERE WAS no way in hell Dorian would tell Jansen about the shit he'd seen and been through since arriving at OPP. He didn't want to talk about the nights spent with one eye open because his cellmate was a violent maniac who spent all night blabbering on about how voodoo drove him to murder and ways to hide bodies. Not to mention the fact the guy might've been bigger than Angelo and as black as night. He could hide in the shadow of his bottom bunk and no one would know he was there. Dorian half expected to wake up to a shank being plunged into his back.

Then there were the groups. Depending on ethnicity, a convict might have a whole lot of backup from some pretty powerful gangs. Dorian didn't fit into none of that shit. He could've been confused for mafia, but he wasn't Italian, and besides, the Italians didn't really run OPP. Their numbers were too small. He was as white as they came but didn't want to have anything to do with the Aryans. They were crazier and more screwed up than any of the others. That left the street gangs. They all did their recruiting, and Dorian had politely declined each time. Being classy about a "fuck off" didn't mean he didn't have hell to pay for saying no to any of them. They all had their points to prove, and for two weeks straight, Dorian found himself in flash fights, some right under the guards' noses while they pretended not to see anything.

Yeah, Jansen didn't need to know about any of that shit.

"Don't you worry about me," he said, tone completely void of emotion. "Just take care of yourself. I want something to come home to, ya know?"

Jansen nodded. The rims of his eyes were turning red, as if he wanted to cry but was doing everything in his power not to. Dorian could certainly appreciate that. He'd spent a time or two fighting not to cry himself.

"Look, I'll be outta here soon, 'kay? So don't you worry. Everything'll be all right."

"Two days," Jansen said. "The trial's in two days. Then you'll be mine again, right?"

"That's the plan."

"Dorian, I—"

"I love you." Dorian knew Jansen needed to hear him say those three important words. It'd been a while since he'd been able to say them, mainly because he hadn't had the privacy, and frankly, he didn't like the idea of anyone in OPP knowing his sexuality. He had a feeling something like that might be more trouble than he wanted to deal with. But when he saw Jansen smile again, it made him feel good. It made the bad stuff pale in comparison.

"I love you too," Jansen said so softly all Dorian really heard was static. Didn't matter. He watched Jansen's mouth as he formed each syllable.

"I gotta go now. Be careful going home."

"I will. I promise."

Even with the guard calling time behind him, Dorian didn't want to get up from that uncomfortable metal stool. He wasn't ready to walk away from Jansen again. He wasn't prepared to say good-bye. Jansen stood first. Dorian followed, and he backed away from the glass. The lonely, miserable, hopeless feeling rushed through him, like cold water sliding down his body to break him from the trance he'd found himself in. It made him shiver.

I miss you.

15

"YES?" BRAD asked for the third or fourth or maybe tenth time. Jason couldn't help laughing. The precious dose of surprise on his partner's—no, his fiancé's—face was priceless. To think, he would be the only man to enjoy that smile and Brad's incredible body, and all the love he had to give for... forever.

Oh, if that thought didn't make the smile on Jason's face widen.

They lay in the hotel bed, all naked and draped in soft white linens, still glowing from the quick orgasms they'd given each other, still glowing from the bliss of being so in love. Every possible inch of their bodies was as intertwined as they could be. The white gold bands from the box were now on their ring fingers, nestled together as they held each other's hands.

Admittedly, Jason loved the view. To think the perfect someone existed for him. At one point, the idea had been so outside his realm of serious thought he'd been content to ignore it with meaningless sex with random men. Now he had an amazing man and they had a family of their own. This was absolutely the life he wanted now that he had it. How could he not say yes?

"Yes," Jason said again as he rolled into Brad's arms.

They pressed their lips together and Jason ground himself against Brad's body. The move had been meant to get a little closer, but the nakedness and the kiss of flesh, the newly rousing erections, and the bliss of the moment turned it into something much, much more.

His lover's thick, firm cock brushed along Jason's inner thigh and sent ripples of heat travelling over every inch of Jason's flesh. He loved that feeling and Brad was the only person who'd ever elicited it in him.

"Let me make love to you," Brad whispered as he slipped one long, slender finger down between Jason's cheeks, applying a teasing amount of pressure to his hole.

Jason straddled Brad's legs and rolled his hips, dragging his hard-on down the length of his lover's thick shaft. He moaned against Brad's lips, and when they parted, he plunged his tongue inside.

He lost himself in the kiss, in the connection he had with Brad. It ran so much deeper than the flesh, deeper than anything he'd ever felt with anyone else. It filled his body with the kind of warmth that came from being madly and utterly in love with someone, someone who made his soul come alive. He smiled against

Brad's mouth and the two of them rolled together. Jason lay on his back now, with his fiancé between his legs.

"I love you so much," Brad said, staring down at Jason with nothing but true adoration in his eyes.

With a wicked grin, Jason reached back and grabbed the lube Brad had set out on the nightstand after the proposal and before they'd climbed into bed together. He squeezed a generous amount onto his hand, then slid down enough for him to reach his lover's cock. When his slick palm made contact, Brad hissed and pushed his shaft deep into Jason's fist.

"I love the way you touch me," Brad purred.

Jason tightened his grip as he slid his fingers down his fiancé's cock. It pulsed against his palm, thickening, ready to feel the warmth of Jason's channel sheathing it. He raised his legs and hooked them around Brad's waist, pulling him down until the blunt tip grazed his hole. The feel of the slight pressure and the promise of being filled with Brad's girth tugged his sac. Then the pressure grew stronger. A slight burn followed, and Brad had slid all the way inside.

"I love the way you feel," Brad said in a moan.

A small laugh slipped through Jason's lips. He tightened his legs, holding Brad in place just so he could relish the feeling of having his body filled, relish the physical connection to someone he'd bonded with on a much deeper level. He reached up and cradled his lover's neck, urging Brad down for another kiss.

"You love everything about me," Jason said, voice husky with desire. "And I love everything about you. Now stop talking and make love to me."

Brad let out a subtle laugh.

Their lips connected again, and Brad rolled his hips, pulling out until the head of his cock kissed Jason's pucker. He hesitated a moment, then plunged back in, tearing a moan from Jason's lips. The sensation of being emptied then filled all over again was nearly enough to make Jason come, and God, the rhythm his lover kept made music of its own. He growled against Brad's mouth, thrusting his tongue as deep inside as he could, brushing his thumbs along the ridge of Brad's jaw as their kiss climaxed.

Fingertips bit into his ass cheeks as Brad lifted and repositioned Jason, angling him so Brad could dive deep inside him. Brad brushed across his spot and Jason tore away from his mouth, sending a long stream of full-bodied moans into the air. The pressure in his sac pushed into his cock and pulsed down his shaft. He moved his hands up to Brad's hair, knotted his fingers, and let everything go. The pearly evidence of his bliss exploded onto his lover's chest.

"Oh, God, I'm… I'm…." Brad's eyes rolled back and his pumping became more diligent, more frenzied. The smooth glide felt like sliding over silk. The sound of skin slapping against skin was a symphony of carnal beauty, and damn if it didn't turn Jason on all over again. "I'm coming."

Heat burst into Jason's hole. Brad's body became a little heavier and his movement slowed but didn't stop. He stroked Jason's nub once, twice.

"Me too," he rasped, his second orgasm railroading through him like a freight train. His already racing heart felt as though it was about to rip right out of his chest, and every breath felt like fire.

Brad lay on top of him, ear pressed to Jason's chest, spent cock still inside Jason's body. Their ragged breathing mingled. Their hearts slowed as they relaxed into each other. Jason wrapped his arms around Brad's shoulders and held him there.

"I never want to move," Brad said.

"Neither do I."

"You don't have to."

The idea of staying there all night sounded so heavenly. They could talk about where they would go to get married, which of the many states had legalized same-sex marriage. They could lie in each other's arms and discuss a small ceremony for their friends and a party somewhere special. They could talk about their future and where they wanted to go in life, but he couldn't. There was another, more immediate future he needed to tend to right now—the future of seven dancers and a place they called home.

"I *do* have to," Jason begrudgingly said. "I have to get back to work. People are counting on me."

"We have the room until tomorrow afternoon," Brad whispered as he lifted Jason's hand to his lips. He pressed a soft, lingering kiss to his palm. "I'll wait here. In this bed. Completely naked. You come back as soon as you're finished at the club."

Who in their right mind would turn down such an offer?

"Oh, I will." Jason kissed the tip of his nose. "I'll be back as fast as I can."

He extracted himself from his fiancé's body and the mess of soft linens, padded across the room, and pulled on his clothes. When he spun around, he caught sight of his future husband lying on his stomach with the sheets tangled around his muscled thighs. Brad had the most beautiful dimpled ass, a perfect slender waist, and broad shoulders. Jason's mouth watered. He had to fight the urge to climb right back into the bed and make love again.

Pulling his shirt over his head, he crossed the space of their hotel room and stole a quick kiss. Brad's lips tasted as delicious as they had every other time their mouths had touched, and Jason would've given anything to stay there forever, but responsibilities came first. Taking care of his responsibilities made him a man worthy of someone like Brad.

"I'll be back as soon as I can," he said with a sorrowful smile. "I promise. I love you."

"I love you too. Be careful."

"Always am."

Outside the double doors, he flagged down the first cab he saw and caught it back to the club. A glint of light coming from his lap pulled his attention from the New Orleans streets, and when he looked down, he found the white gold band still on his finger. He'd forgotten to take it off before leaving the hotel. They weren't going to wear them until they made it official, but it appeared as though the secret would be getting out pretty damn soon.

The sight of it painted a smile across his face. Nothing in the world could've made him happier. Nothing else in the world could've made him feel like he could do anything, conquer anything… achieve anything. And he hoped when the euphoria of multiple orgasms and the happiness of saying yes wore off, he wasn't too afraid to go through with making the ultimate commitment.

When the cab pulled up in front of Sin & Seduction, the flashing red neon hanging over the front door pulled him away from the ring he wasn't supposed to have on his very important finger. Everything he felt in that moment contradicted so badly it made his head spin. He couldn't be happier about where he and Brad found themselves, and yet, the idea of the club closing broke his warm, cheerfully thumping heart.

He stepped out of the cab after passing a twenty over the seat, and he stood before the two-story converted warehouse, staring up at a place he'd been calling home since the beginning of adulthood. The façade was still dingy, just like every other building on that side of Esplanade. Litter scattered the streets. Velvet ropes hung from golden posts that normally lined the walkway, but were now corralled by the front door and chained to the wall so no one would steal them. The neighborhood was shitty, sure. Crime ran rampant in that part of New Orleans, but people still loved that place. Sin & Seduction still had class. It was still a nice place to have a good time. It was still home.

There was no way he could let the club close. No. Possible. Way.

Spinning on his heel, Jason started in the direction of the employee entrance—the only doors unlocked on a Wednesday night. He was in his own world, a place hidden deep in the far recesses of his mind, lost to the real world and on a mission. Ideas, be they good or bad, formed in quick bursts. He was so lost in his thoughts he almost collided with Davi and Lance.

"Sorry," he said, running his hand down his shirt.

Lance and Davi held hands like lovers would, which wasn't exactly Lance's style. After the blowjob behind the costume rack, Jason assumed Lance would have no use for the kid and send him packing as he did everyone else. Apparently, Jason was wrong. Not that it was any of his business what Lance did with his sex or love life.

"Never mind apologies. Is that…?" Lance reached for Jason's left hand. He locked eyes on the ring. "Get married on the break?"

"No. Engaged."

"Engaged, huh?" Lance stiffened.

"Yeah, Brad proposed. I said yes."

"Well, then." Lance tugged Davi a little closer to his side, never once taking his eyes off Jason. Whatever that was about. Surely, Lance didn't still have feelings for him. Hadn't they worked past that? "Congrats," Lance continued with a smirk before ducking back into the club, tugging Davi right along with him.

Jason tilted his head, watching in complete confusion as Lance abruptly disappeared. He wasn't sure what had just happened. Weren't he and Lance over the complicated and unreciprocated feelings crap? Hadn't Lance moved on to younger, and more single… things? Drama. He appeared to have it in spades now.

16

HANDS LOCKED together, Lance dragged Davi back into the building as fast as he could, far away from the man he'd once thought he could fall for and the shiny white-gold evidence of the relationship Lance had known was serious for a long time already. And this was the relationship he'd wanted but never had. Jason was the last heartbreak Lance had allowed himself. Seeing that band on his finger reminded Lance why he didn't let people get close and never let himself care anymore.

The soles of his tennis shoes frantically slapped against the concrete, a fainter thudding sound followed. Was it his racing heart or the person being dragged behind him?

Lance was back inside the hallway and far away from Jason and the ring, and he had someone so much more important than a long-lost crush by his side. That someone looked curious. Rightfully so. Lance had spent the last few hours getting close and personal with Davi, the way someone would if they cared for another someone. This little display of shock and jealousy obviously didn't look good.

Exhaling, he let go of Davi's hand, frowned, and said, "I'll be right back," and he left the man he'd been getting so cozy with standing in the middle of the room, probably watching every single step Lance took as he walked away. Lance couldn't do anything for Davi right now. As selfish as it sounded, his own emotions were plowing through him much faster than he was ready for. This was much too much reality crashing down on him all at once, and he hadn't been ready to deal with any of it.

He stepped back out into the New Orleans night, crossing paths with Jason in passing. Lance didn't stop, and didn't acknowledge his boss's presence, at least not verbally or physically. Emotionally, though, the acknowledgement came in the crushing truth that no matter how much fighting Lance once planned on doing, Brad and Jason were and always would be a very real thing. He couldn't come between them now if he wanted to.

What the hell am I doing?

Lance leaned against the cool brick wall just beside the employee entrance. Freaking out like this didn't make a whole lot of sense. Seriously. He considered himself of fairly sound mind, and while he'd had a crush on Jason for ten forevers, he'd known for a few years now that nothing would ever happen between them. Brad made Jason happy. Brad gave him a life Lance hadn't been able to offer.

"What about him?"

The voice belonged to Davi. Lance would've recognized that sexy, sultry accent anywhere. What he didn't recognize was the flatness, the distance and emptiness. As though all the progress they'd made at the Riverwalk was undone with a stupid, uncontrolled freak-out brought about by the sight of something that had nothing to do with him.

Jesus Christ, why couldn't he rewind time right now? He would take that whole mess back. In fact, he would take back ever caring about Jason that much.

Swallowing hard, Lance raised his head, but couldn't make himself meet Davi's stare. He feared feeling the heartbreak bound to be in his dark eyes. "He's nothing," Lance muttered.

He heard the soles of Davi's shoes scrape the concrete just before the scuffed tips came into view. Lance forced himself to lift his head, gaze slowly winding up Davi's body. One deep breath—inhaled, exhaled, inhaled again. He finally met Davi's stare.

"That didn't look like nothing," Davi said.

"I can't talk about it right now."

"Fine." Davi shrugged. "You know where I'll be when you're ready."

Silence lingered between them for a few heartbeats before Davi turned and walked away from Lance. Lance stood there, waiting for his heart to burst through his chest and take off after the man it really wanted. Yes, that was right. His heart wanted Davi. He could feel it just like he'd felt it with Nathanial and Jason, but because of those failed encounters, his brain happily flipped his heart the bird.

So, dumbass, how do you plan on fixing this mess?

17

THE METAL door slammed so loudly Jason could hear it in his office all the way down the hall. Jason's head bolted straight up. He had just sat down to settle in with business affairs when the commotion derailed his train of thought.

"What the hell is going on now?"

He popped up and hopped out from behind his desk and he poked his head out the door in time to catch the wind rolling off Davi's back as he charged down the hall. Clearly something had happened, and since he wasn't hand-in-hand with Lance anymore, Jason assumed the other shoe had finally fallen and Lance had given Davi a heaping dose of the real him.

With a groan, Jason stepped out of his office. He looked toward the huge metal door, then toward the backstage area. What to do first? Console the kid or chew Lance out for putting an unneeded wrinkle in the delicate world of Sin & Seduction?

Jason furrowed his brows and spun toward the door. He had it in his head he was going to give Lance a stern talking to, maybe even make him go apologize to Davi.

He stormed all the way down the hall, slammed both palms against the metal door, and shoved it wide open. The parking lot out back was dark, and for the most part empty, but there was no sign of Lance. Jason headed around to the front where he'd run into them when he'd gotten back from being with Brad. Nothing. The street was like a ghost town. The only other place Lance would've been was his apartment.

Jason spun back around and headed toward the rear of the parking lot where a rusted old fire escape led up to the second floor.

As soon as he rounded the corner, he saw a darkened figure sitting at the foot of the steps, head buried against his palms. The coppery lights at the edge of the parking lot gave his hair an orange glow. He knew it had to be Lance. What he didn't know was why Golden Boy was sulking behind the building.

Lance raised his head. Apparently, he'd heard the scuff of Jason's shoes on the pavement. "Hey," he said flatly, before turning his face back toward the ground again.

"What the hell is going on?" Jason asked, a whole lot of demand filling his voice. He hadn't meant to sound so harsh, but... well, some things couldn't be helped.

"Going on?" Lance pinched his lips together and gave a subtle shake of the head, as though he planned on shrugging off everything Jason had just seen. "Why would you think something's going on?"

"Hm... well—" Jason crossed his arms over his chest, shifting all his weight onto one foot. A whole lot of *I-don't-think-so* was written on his face. "You're back here sulking like a brat and Davi is slamming doors when we're all supposed to be in the main showroom practicing. So, I'll ask again. What the hell is going on?"

Lance didn't immediately speak. Jason couldn't tell if he was arranging his thoughts or coming up with a viable story, or maybe he didn't want to talk about what had gone down with Davi. Not that he had much choice in the matter as far as Jason was concerned. If it was serious....

"Oh shit, you care about him, don't you?" Jason said with a gasp. He moved over to sit down on the step next to Lance—not touching or sitting too close, just being there like Lance had been there for him back when he and Brad had first started dating. "Talk to me."

"I don't care about him," Lance blurted a little too quickly, completely giving away the fact those words were a lie. Besides, Jason knew Lance well enough to read through the tall tales he told. Just as Lance could say the same for him.

"Try again."

"What?" Lance frowned.

"You're lying through your teeth. Now, tell me what's going on?"

"Jason, you know yourself I'm a pushover for boys with drama," Lance said all nonchalantly, as though he planned on playing that whole scene up as no big deal. "Look how I fell for you."

"That was a long time ago."

"And I'm over you."

"Ha!" Jason snorted. "I saw the way you looked at my ring."

"So did Davi...," Lance muttered

Of course he did. Davi had been right out front with Lance when Jason had pulled up. If Jason hadn't missed the knee-jerk reaction to the announcement of his pending nuptials, it stood a damn good chance Davi didn't, either.

"You care about him," Jason said. It wasn't a question.

Lance raised his head again. He finally looked Jason in the eyes, but Jason knew good and damn well Lance wouldn't own up to any kind of feelings. He hadn't since that night more than two years ago when he'd told Jason how much he cared about him. Jason doubted very seriously Lance would be so quick to dive back into *feelings* again.

"I'm not going to push." Jason stood from the step. "But I will say you need to make this right somehow. I have a show to put on and all of us have a club to save." Jason licked his lips. He really hated doing this part, but knew shock factor would make Lance take responsibility for whatever was going on. "If you guys can't work together, I'll have to fire you both."

It was probably Jason's imagination, but he would've sworn all the color drained from Lance's face. He definitely gaped. His eyes definitely widened. If he hated any part of being a manager, it was moments like this.

"You're not serious, right?" Lance asked.

"Completely."

"My personal life has nothing to do with my job."

"It does when it affects the club and the other employees."

"It won't affect anyone. I promise."

"C'mon, Lance. What if you *do* end up managing the dancers? You gonna show favoritism to the one you're fucking? When you two get in a fight, are you gonna tiptoe around each other at work?

Lance jerked straight up off the step. He silently paced back and forth, keeping his eyes on the ground the entire time. When he finally did say something, a quiet "That's bullshit" was all he had to offer.

Jason shrugged. "No, it really isn't, and I'm not changing my mind." He turned and started back toward the dark side of the parking lot. Without stopping and without turning around, he said, "Make it right, Lance. Just… make it right."

AS IF he hadn't beaten himself up enough over this already.

Lance let out a growl as he plopped back down on the steps. He spent the next twenty minutes silently conjuring new and creative four-lettered, foul-mouthed nicknames for the man he once had a crush on. Or maybe *still* had a crush on. Regardless about how he felt for either man, he had to get his ass inside the club and at least *try* to make amends with Davi before he was the reason they both became unemployed.

Back inside, the dancers were lined up in front of the stage, all in their respective spots with a gaping hole in the very center where Lance should've been. The music blared. Bodies twisted and turned. No one seemed to notice him missing. No one seemed to notice him there.

He hung back in the shadows, watching each dancer move. Obviously, some were more graceful than others, some more beautiful. Most of those men Lance had known for years. A few he'd never really said more than a few words to, and only in passing. Still, he considered them all family and he knew he had to bite the bullet and make things right for all of their sakes.

His gaze immediately landed on the one who twirled his way to the front. In this particular scene, Davi was the one all the boys fawned over, the one everyone wanted, which actually wasn't far from true off the stage. Lance wanted him, had even made an ass of himself because of his attraction toward the bronze-skinned beauty. How could anyone blame him, though? Davi was the epitome of the perfect man in Lance's eyes. He had the kindness and warmth so many men lacked. He had the innocence of a child, which was only a façade for the wickedly sexual creature hiding inside. That alone was a total turn-on. He had everything Lance dreamed of in a fantasy man—all the way down to the sultry foreign accent.

You've already established how much you want him, idiot.

Right.

All the dancers circled around Davi, all hands reaching out for a touch. This was the big climax, and Davi was supposed to emerge from the circle of men in nothing but a Speedo, ready to dance his way into their hearts, or their pants, depending on the patron. Well, Davi had certainly wormed his way into Lance's… everything.

Crossing his arms, Lance stepped out of the shadows and into the edge of spotlight raining down over his colleagues. Most of the dancers continued on as if he wasn't there, but one—the only one who mattered—looked his way. When Davi did, he missed a few critical steps and blundered the whole last part of the routine.

"Okay. All right," Jason said, clapping his hand to the clipboard. "Take ten, then we'll do it again."

Instead of walking toward him, Davi went to the opposite side of the room, closer to the bar and the grand front entrance, as though he was doing his best to avoid Lance. Had it really gotten that bad? Were they really reduced to acting like children?

Apparently so.

He crossed the room and sidled up to the bar right beside Davi. Davi didn't bother looking over. In fact, he didn't move an inch. He didn't pretend not to see Lance, but didn't act as though he wanted him to be there, either.

"We need to talk," Lance said.

Davi finally looked over at him. "I am only interested in talking if you talk the truth."

"I'll tell you whatever you want to know, okay? Just… give me a chance."

Whoa. Did Lance really just say that?

"Fine."

"Good."

"So let's talk," Davi said with a smirk, as if Lance wasn't man enough to bare his soul.

Pft... of course he was. "Not here. I would like a little privacy."

"Where? When?"

"You don't think I want to talk about this, do you?"

Davi turned toward him, leaning one arm on the bar, looking Lance right in the eyes. Without so much as blinking or missing a breath, Davi said, "I think you do want to talk. I don't think you want to be honest with me or yourself. I think you're too scared. Somewhere inside, you believe that opening up to me is going to hurt you. I'm not going to turn out like Nathaniel and Jason."

"I never said that."

"You didn't have to."

Lance cut his eyes away in shame. He really hated when people got the better of him, and right now, Davi was getting the best of him.

18

FRIDAY MORNING, at the crack of dawn, the alarm went off and Jansen bolted straight up in bed. It wasn't for being startled awake, but more from the excitement the day brought with it. Today was the hearing, the day the judge either allowed Dorian to come home or decided to keep Jansen's husband locked up in a cell like an animal.

Like all the nights and weeks and months before, Jansen hadn't gotten any sleep. He might've dozed here and there, but that didn't count because his body and his mind never truly rested—only his eyes, which were rocking some pretty heavy baggage these days. Too bad he couldn't make the dark circles go away.

A light tapping at the door pulled him from the bed. He padded across the room, opened the door, and found Maria on the other side with a smile on her face and an oversized cup of piping-hot java in her hand.

"I make for you," she said as she passed the mug over. "Your friends, they wait downstairs to go get Meester Dorian."

"Thanks, Maria." He popped his head out of the crack and kissed her cheek. "Please tell them I'll be down as soon as I have a shower."

"Yes, Meester Jansen." She bowed her head slightly, then spun on her heel. He watched her waddle back down the hall before closing the door.

If it wasn't for wanting to be clean when he finally saw his husband again, he would've skipped the damn shower and gone to the prison in his flannel pants and wrinkled shirt. No one would notice. Hell, he would still look better than half the riffraff meandering about that place. He couldn't do it, though. He couldn't bring himself to stoop so low, to be seen in public that way.

He peeled away his clothes, leaving a trail between him and the bathroom. He popped open the opaque shower door, and as soon as he looked at the rails and the tiles, he pictured Dorian's lean, muscled, tattooed body and the hot water flowing over the expanse of all that skin. He pictured Dorian gripping the rails and giving him that lust-filled look that always led to some really, *really* hot sex.

The thought made Jansen's cock jump. He could almost feel Dorian guiding him into the shower, and if that wasn't a testament to how far-gone his mind was, nothing else would be.

He climbed into the shower stall and turned the knobs, waiting for the temperature to even out before climbing under the water. He closed his eyes and leaned back against the tiles, picturing Dorian's full, thick lips covering his. "I love you," he could hear Dorian whisper in that low, husky voice that always sent chills rippling up and down Jansen's arms.

"I love you too," Jansen whispered back.

As long as he didn't open his eyes, he could imagine Dorian in that shower with him. The scent of his husband's soap and shampoo filled the space and Jansen breathed in deeply. He rubbed his hand up and down the patch of coarse hairs surrounding the base of his cock, and moaned as little flutters of excitement scattered through him.

He moved his fingers up, encircled his shaft, and started to slowly pull, eyes still clenched shut. In his mind's eye, he saw his husband as clear as day—leaning in for a kiss, lowering his head until their mouths connected. Jansen could see himself reaching up to hold the nape of Dorian's neck just to keep him in that kiss.

"Make love to me," he whispered, pumping his hand a little faster, squeezing just a little tighter. The only thing missing was the strength of Dorian's grip and the rough slivers of scars he only noticed when Dorian was touching him so intimately.

His shaft swelled against his palm and his sac tightened. He pumped against his hand, hips jacking faster and faster. He could feel Dorian's lips moving along his neck and the warmth of his husband's breath gusting across his skin. And before he knew it, pearly ropes shot out of his cock and painted the tile wall across from him.

As he sucked air and his heart raced, he hung his head under the spray, washing away a night of restlessness and a solid fifteen minutes of pure desperation. He turned under the water to clean off the little bit of jizz that had hit his hand and his stomach and his thigh.

Watching the water swirl down the drain, he thought about what he'd done and why he did it. No one ever knocked masturbation. Hell, sometimes they did it for mutual gratification. Dorian liked to watch Jansen get himself off and vice versa, but this time…. Well, it wasn't the same. In his mind, Dorian had actually been there with him. Dorian had been the one kissing and touching him. Jansen was losing his shit. His mind had a one-way ticket out of there. The second foot had finally pulled back from reality. Dorian had to come back before Jansen found himself in a padded cell of his own.

After cleaning his body and changing into his clothes, he headed downstairs, where he found Andy Lister, Rebecca Chambers, and Angelo the gentle giant, all sitting at the table. He took a seat among them, and immediately a cup of hot coffee and a plate of food were shoved in front of his face.

"So what are we doing?" he asked, scooping up a heaping forkful of scrambled eggs. With the other hand, Jansen hugged a steeping cup of java. Hopefully, no one noticed his fingers shaking so badly. Hopefully, he didn't have *crazy* printed across his forehead.

"We're facing the judge today," Rebecca said.

"And hopefully getting Dorian out of jail," Angelo added.

Hopefully.

Jansen's right leg bounced ninety-to-nothing beneath the table. He couldn't stop it if he wanted to. Not with that not-so-reassuring *hopefully* lingering in the air. Nervous didn't even begin to cover the way he felt right now. Nervous just barely scratched the surface of the shit going on in his head.

Jeez, what I wouldn't give for a smoke right now.

As soon as he stood and turned to head for the coffeemaker again, he damn near collided with Maria. "I'm so sorry," he said as he gripped her forearm. "I wasn't paying—"

"Is okay, Meester Jansen," she said, patting his arm.

She moved out of his way and let him finish his original course to the fountain of caffeinated bliss… as if he needed any more of that shit. He poured some into his cup, foregoing the sugar and creamer, and downed it straight up like an alcoholic with a bottle of cheap whiskey. He hissed as it burned its way down his throat.

With one hand, he gripped the edge of the counter as tight as he could, listening to the group behind him talk about Dorian, the bail hearing, the trial, and how they were going to get Dorian home. God help them all if Jansen didn't get to see his husband soon. They had yet to see crazy.

"We leavin' finally?" he asked, returning to face them all again.

"Whenever you're ready, boss," Angelo said.

He still hadn't gotten used to that. Angelo the gentle giant—as long as you didn't piss him off—calling him "boss" like he always did Dorian. The guy kind of acted like he might possibly, in a roundabout sort of way have a little bit of respect for Jansen now. Though why, Jansen wasn't exactly sure.

"I'm ready," Jansen declared, setting his empty coffee cup in the sink. "I want Dorian out of that zoo."

"We all do, kiddo," Angelo said. He laid his heavy, meaty hand on Jansen's shoulder.

Together, the four of them headed out to Dorian's sedan. The driver stood patiently by the back door, as if he'd been there forever and then some. Angelo climbed in the front. The lawyer, the bail bondsman, and the impatient husband all squeezed into the back.

"If they let Dorian go, how the hell are we all going to ride back to the mansion?" Jansen asked. How his mind was clear enough to think that far ahead was anyone's guess.

"It's okay," Rebecca said, patting his leg. "Andy's car is still at OPP and we both have work to do. He can give me a ride back, right Andy?"

"Sure, can do," the bail bondsman said with a huge toothy grin.

"Then what are we waiting for?" Jansen asked.

The driver closed the back door. No one said a word. Though the mood should've been lighter than it had been in months, the tension in the air was thick enough to strangle.

Closing his eyes, Jansen laid his head against the back of the seat and started with the slow, easy-breathing routine. He let his mind become filled with images of his husband—Dorian's smile, the tenderness he reserved for only Jansen, how sexy he was when he went into all-business mode. He thought about Dorian's strong body and the way he held Jansen every night when they slept. He thought about the way his husband smelled after he climbed out of the shower and sprayed on a bit of Armani cologne.

God, his mouth was already watering.

Soon. Very, very soon. He would have Dorian back home before the sun rose tomorrow morning… hopefully.

Keep that hope alive, guy.

"So, the judge can still deny bail," the lawyer said.

The words instantly sucked every ounce of life and hope out of the cramped space. Jansen bolted straight up in his seat, eyes flying wide open. "What?" he all but growled.

Rebecca jerked to the side, away from Jansen and into Mr. Lister's rib cage. Her eyes widened and she held up one hand. "Let me finish."

"Do it quickly, please." Jansen sat back but didn't relax.

"The judge *can* deny bail. That being said, I doubt he will. I just wanted you to know the possibility was there."

"Why do you doubt he will?"

"It wouldn't be smart." Rebecca turned as much as she could, what with being wedged between Jansen's slender frame and the much larger Andrew Lister. She laid her hand on Jansen's thigh in the way a mother might comfort her child. "The DA is going to recommend bail, and normally, the judge will take that recommendation and run with it. Ultimately, it's the judge's decision. Williams isn't a hard one to work with. He's retiring soon, so he's suffering from short timers. That's the good news."

"And let me guess," Jansen said, folding his arms over his chest. "There's bad news."

"Sweetie, there's always going to be bad news."

"Don't placate me. I don't want to be handled with kid gloves." Jansen stiffened. "Just tell me everything."

"Well, Dorian has a reputation. He has friends in high places, but he also has enemies in high places. Just... be ready for it to go either way. Chances are, he'll be released until trial, but be aware of the possibilities, just in case it doesn't work out that way."

"Perfect," he grumbled as he settled back in his seat next to the window.

Bye-bye, hope.

Bye-bye, sanity.

19

"HERE. I ironed it for you," Brad said, holding up a crisp, sleek, cobalt-colored dress shirt and a slightly lighter blue tie. "The slacks are hanging on the back of the bathroom door."

From the edge of the bed they shared, Jason shook his head at the shirt. "I can't do this."

He'd been sitting there for the last two hours, staring over the proposal Brad had helped him come up with the night before. He'd read through the freakin' thing a hundred or more times and it still didn't make any damn sense to him. There was no way in hell he would get through this without making an ass of himself.

"I don't know shit about business proposals or managing a nightclub. I can't do this."

"Yes, you can." Brad hung the shirt on the bedroom doorknob, then sat down on the edge of the bed. "You can and you will, because you're smart and you have what it takes to make this thing a success."

"If the owners have any sense at all, they'll see right through this ridiculous charade and sell the club anyway," he said in defeat—voice low, head hanging.

He set the proposal aside, then braced his elbows against his knees. The throbbing in his temples had been growing stronger by the minute. It seemed like the best thing he could do for himself right now was give up on reading and fighting to comprehend things he didn't get and apply a heavy dose of pressure to his head.

"If you tell yourself this will never work, then you're setting yourself up to fail and you might as well not even try." Brad softly spoke, pulling Jason against his side.

"That's what I've been saying. What's the sense in trying?"

"That's not what I meant and you know it."

"I know, but I'm seriously asking. This'll never work, and even if it does, I can't run that place. So, what's the point?"

"So you can say you did something. At the end of the day, when it's time to pack up and go home, maybe even go separate ways from the family you made there, you can look them all in the eyes and say you did your best to save everything. You'll have a clear conscience because you tried." He rubbed his hand up and down Jason's upper arm, squeezing a little tighter. "I know you. You wouldn't be satisfied if you didn't at least try."

All great points, Jason wouldn't deny that, but Brad always had good points. He had calm and logic and perspective, and he knew Jason better than anyone else. Brad was the anchor who always kept a flighty Jason on solid ground, but he was wrong about this. Jason could feel it in his gut. Going to the owners with any kind of hope would turn out to be a huge letdown. He didn't feel like being let down right now, not after Brad's utterly beautiful proposal and the talk of the new future they planned to make for each other.

He twisted the white gold ring around on his finger, smiling down at the sight of it. Brad believed in him enough—in them—to want to spend the rest of his life with him. So why the hell couldn't Jason have a little faith in himself?

With a sigh, Jason laid his head on Brad's shoulder. He closed his eyes and simply enjoyed the feel of having someone he loved so close to him, being so strong for him.

"So, what are you going to do?" Brad quietly asked.

"Well, I'm going to the club." He paused, giving one last thought to backing out. Brad was right about him, though. If he didn't do something, at least try, he would never forgive himself. "I guess I'm going to meet with the bosses."

"Glad to hear it."

Brad kissed Jason's forehead, then pushed up from the bed. He snatched a gray-and-blue tie from the dresser and tucked it under the collar of his pale yellow dress shirt. The color made his tan look twice as dark, which made his blond hair twice as light. He was a vision of pure beauty, and Jason would've given anything to rip his partner's clothes off and pull him back into bed. But as adult life went, they both had responsibilities, jobs to go to. Not to mention the toddler sleeping right down the hall from their room.

Brad held out his hand. "You coming with me?"

The *with* his partner referred to was a little routine they'd had since the first time Hope had stayed overnight with them. They'd been so excited about it, the next morning when it'd been time to wake her up, they'd gone to her room together and stood over her crib until she'd opened her little blue eyes. They hadn't missed a morning since.

"Yes. Wouldn't miss it for the world," he said with the sincerest smile.

Hand in hand, they walked down the hall to the pastel-pink-colored room where Hope slept when Brad kept her. All the furniture was white and expensive and the best of the best—the Mercedes of kid's bedroom furniture because nothing was too good for that little girl. Jason concurred 150 percent.

She curled around her little pink pillow, blanket twisted around her body. She'd been sleeping in a toddler bed for a few months now without incident. Thankfully. The first few nights had damn near driven Jason crazy. All the ups and downs Brad had spent the better part of the evening doing had left Jason with hardly any sleep. Every time the bed had moved, Jason had bolted straight up out of dreamland thinking something bad had happened. It'd left him a grumpy mess for a few weeks.

Now, everything was great.

Her little eyes slowly fluttered open when her daddy softly spoke her name. She reached her arms around to him, tiny fingers making a grabbing motion. He picked her up and she nestled into his chest as he cradled her head to his shoulder. Her soft blonde ringlets trickled down around his fingers. She was such a beautiful little girl, beautiful just like her daddy.

"I need to get going," Jason whispered. He kissed her warm, chubby cheek. Then kissed Brad's plump, tender lips. "I love you. I'll see you in the morning."

"Good luck today," Brad whispered back. "And I love you too, with all my heart."

It never failed. Every time Brad said those words to him, Jason got all warm and fuzzy inside. It made him feel as if nothing was out of his reach and there was nothing he couldn't conquer. By God, with Brad's love, he felt as if he could move mountains and lasso the moon, and that was exactly the kind of courage he needed going into work today.

"Hey," Brad softly called back.

Jason stopped in the doorway. "Yeah?"

"Are we keeping our rings on or putting them away?"

Jason looked down at his hand again. That ring had garnered the illustrious role of being the replacement rock for him to lean on since Brad couldn't go into the meeting with him. Jason made a fist and held it up to his heart.

"Keep it on for today," Brad said. "We'll put them back in the box tomorrow."

A thankful, tight-lipped smile tugged at Jason's mouth as he ducked out the bedroom door.

He felt utterly ridiculous climbing onto a ten-speed bicycle wearing dress slacks and a business shirt, with a ratty backpack attached to his backside, but he did it anyway. He prayed he didn't have sweat rings dripping from his pits by the time he got to the club. December in the Big Easy didn't always mean cold weather. In fact, just the other day he'd lounged in the backyard in shorts and T-shirt, but today, the weather cooperated and kept things nice and cool.

He took his time, not pedaling too fast so he didn't exert himself. The leisurely ride allowed him to enjoy sights of New Orleans he'd seen a million times but never really took the time to pay much attention to. That part of the Big Easy, the houses and landscaping, the old French feel, was incredible, and some of the many reasons he'd fallen in love with the place.

All that beautiful scenery came to an abrupt end when he reached the warehouse district.

Behind the club, he chained up his bicycle as usual, but the one thing out of place was Hank's white Mercedes-Benz already parked in the back lot. Normally, the owners didn't show up until later in the evening, long after normal people called it a night. The sight of the car struck a chord of fear in Jason. If they were there already, did that mean they were moving ahead with the business of shutting down the club?

No. They couldn't. He hadn't had his chance yet.

He took off in a jog, then broke into the fastest run of his life. His dress shoes pounded against the asphalt. The temperature under his collar started to rise. The rusty metal door on the side of the club didn't want to open no matter how hard Jason tugged on it. His heart started racing, hands shaking.

No. No. No.

"C'mon," he growled, yanking it hard enough the door flew open and slammed against the brick wall behind it.

After wrenching the door shut again, he charged up the hallway and through the backstage dressing area, up the stairs and down the walkway overlooking the barren nightclub. The office door was shut, but even over his panting, and the thudding of his heart in his eardrums, he could hear the low murmur of a building conversation.

Doubled over, Jason gripped his knees and sucked in short stabs of air. It burned going down, and God, what he wouldn't give for a big-ass bottle of water right now. He swallowed, closed his eyes, and tried to breathe as quietly as he could so he could eavesdrop on the goings-on behind the office door.

He couldn't distinguish voices. Both owners had the same raspy, gravelly tone from smoking for too many years. They were both older, heavier-set men with deep, rich Cajun accents. The only unfamiliar voice in the room was a younger man who didn't sound 100 percent sure of himself. He had a bit of a stutter and his voice wavered when he spoke.

"I'll um... b-bring over the documents from the um... Realtor for you to sign. They'll list the building as is. As f-for the LLC—"

No, they can't!

Jason flung the door open and every face in the room turned in his direction. They all stared at him as if he'd lost his mind. Yeah, yeah, he knew he was a few eggs shy of a dozen, knew it when he'd tucked the proposal in his backpack and climbed on his bike.

"You can't sell the club," he demanded.

One thick, hairy, salt-and-pepper eyebrow cocked at him. The owner it belonged to sat back in his chair and crossed his arms over his rotund belly. "And just why in the hell can't I, son?"

Again, Jason swallowed. This time the lump got caught in his throat.

He inhaled, squared his shoulders, and lifted his chin. "Because I have a plan to save it," he said with unbreakable resolve. He almost sounded as though he believed his own crap. "And if you're willing to try, I'll run the place so you don't have to be here. It's exactly what you guys want, and what we... the employees want too."

"Son—" Hank had a lot kinder demeanor than boss number one.

"No. Listen to me. Please."

Jason held up one forefinger as he slipped his backpack off his shoulders, distinctly aware of the fact that every single soul in the room had their eyes locked on him. He felt like an innocent little deer with a giant bull's-eye tattooed on his ass. They were probably waiting for him to royally screw up, and he fully expected to.

Hands shaking harder now, he dug past his change of clothes and the few toiletries he carried with him, a book he'd been meaning to finish months ago, and the iPod he carried everywhere. Beyond all that mess was the file folder stuffed with papers Brad had spent all night helping him put together.

"It's all there," Jason said, righting himself and handing the folder across the desk. "Cost plans. Promotion plans. Earnings. Payback. Everything."

Hank took the folder, eyeing Jason hard enough to make him squirm. His boss sat back in the chair and started thumbing through the papers, only occasionally looking up. Every time he did, he had a stifled smile. As though he was proud of Jason but didn't want to let on to the fact so no one else would know.

Hank handed the folder over to the other owner, who perused the pages with the skinny, twitchy younger guy reading over his shoulder. Jason waited with bated breath for them to either approve of his plans or tell him he'd lost his damn mind. Suddenly the room felt hotter and smaller, the tie around his neck felt tighter, and the air became thick and suffocating.

As soon as the guy closed the file and handed it back over, Jason's stomach knotted. He watched the two of them exchange looks as if they were telepathically discussing his fate. They'd been in business together so long they probably knew each other's expressions better than anyone else... hence the silent stare down.

"This is what we're gonna do, kid," Hank finally said. "New Year's Eve is the big finale show. I want ya to double the average Friday headcount. If ya can pull that off, we'll give ya one more month to pull in the kinda dough we need to stay in business. Got it?"

"I got it," Jason said with an excited lilt, nodding a little too eagerly. "I got it, and I swear I won't let you down."

"Okay then, son." Hank waved his thick finger toward the door, signaling for Jason to get a move on it. "Sounds like you got work to do."

"Yes, sir. I do. I... I do."

Jason backed toward the door, keeping the excited grin on his face. Hank gave him a wink and a smile, as though he expected and possibly wanted Jason to pull this shit off. It became clear then that Smitty, the grumpier of the two and the owner people would rather not speak to, wanted the club shut down. The friendlier one, the beloved Hank, wanted to keep it around. Well, Jason planned to do his best and save the home the guys had all grown to love.

He charged back down to the dressing room full throttle, feet galloping against the concrete flooring. Only problem was, he didn't have anyone to celebrate his good news with. The late-morning hour meant none of the dancers had shown up yet, and Brad was working, and who the hell knew where Jansen was right now. Jason had this excited little bubble around him, and if he didn't share it with someone soon, the damn thing was going to explode.

No sooner than the thought crossed his mind, the back door squealed and whined. He saw Lance's head of golden-blond hair, then Davi strutting in behind him. Two more dancers followed. Jason clapped both hands together and his smile widened.

"They're giving me a chance to save the club," he said.

Every face erupted in a full-on grin. The kind that made eyes glisten and birthed deep dimples. But out of all those faces, the one that looked the happiest was Davi. His bronze cheeks shone and his eyes sparkled. He looked as though he might've been on the verge of shedding the happiest tears of his life.

"You met with them without me?" Lance frowned.

"Yeah. I'm sorry. It just happened. We were going to lose the club if I didn't go in there."

"It's okay. I'm not upset. I'm just glad you did it."

"With Brad's help. He did the paperwork. But I still need you guys for the rest."

"What do we need to do?" Davi asked.

And there was the hard part....

20

JANSEN SAT in the first row behind the defense table, wringing his hands and tapping his foot fast enough to generate some major kinetic energy. Hell, his whole body shook with the movement. He was probably vibrating the whole wooden bench beneath his ass. Rebecca Chambers sat up front with Dorian. Angelo and Lister sat on either side of Jansen, towering over him.

"Dorian Grant," the judge's loud voice boomed through the quiet courtroom. It tugged Jansen's already knotted stomach up into his throat. In unison, his and his husband's heads darted straight up. "Please stand."

Dorian popped up from his seat, and Jansen was about to pull a lost-puppy move and follow, but Angelo arm-barred him across the chest. "Relax, kid," the behemoth whispered from the corner of his mouth.

Relax? You're kidding, right?

"Your honor, in light of new evidence," the prosecutor drawled in a thick, swampy accent. The guy was about a hundred pounds too heavy for his height. His solid white hair and wrinkles meant he was probably on the upper side of fifty… or he'd lived a very rough life. He even wheezed a little when he spoke. "The state of Louisiana is willin' to allow Mr. Grant bail until the hearin', if your honor would so oblige."

"Mr. Wheeler, now"—the judge sat back, crossing his arms and arching his brow—"didn't ya stand in this here courtroom not six months ago and tell me Dorian Grant was a flight risk?"

"Well, I—"

"Did ya not say it would be easy for a man with his means to flee the country to avoid bein' incarcerated for murder?"

"I—"

Jansen's stomach pushed its way up to his tonsils. All the food he'd eaten that morning threatened to paint the tiled floor beneath his rapidly pounding foot.

"Now you want me to give him bail?"

"As I said, your honor—"

"Shut it, Wheeler. This is the second time this month your office has reneged and come back for a new rulin'. I'm gettin' damn tired of it." The judge looked down over his glasses, licked his thick thumb, then flipped back a few pages. His dark, baggy eyes darted over the black and white. "A million dollars, huh? Ya think he can afford to get the hell outta Dodge, but can't afford a million dollar bond?"

"I—"

The gavel pounded and it was like a jolt to Jansen's already fragile nerves. He jumped in his seat, heart rushing a little too long, then gradually slowing to a dull thud. His temples started to pound as adrenaline surged and receded. He exhaled a breath he hadn't been aware of holding.

"In the case of the State of Louisiana versus Dorian Grant, I hereby grant bail in the amount of one million dollars. Mr. Grant, you will remain within the boundaries of the state of Louisiana and in the custody of the indemnitor until you are to return to this court for your hearin'. Understood?"

"Yes, sir, your honor," Dorian said, folding his hands behind his back.

"Bail is set for one million dollars," the judge said, striking the gavel again.

And one more time, Jansen exhaled. He expunged that bated breath so hard his shoulders slumped and he almost fell into the wall of Angelo right beside him.

Lister stood first, made his way down to the end of the bench, and stopped. He eyed Jansen for a moment before giving a nod—a signal to get his ass in motion so they could get the paperwork started to get his hubby back home where he belonged.

The clacking of heels and the thumping of loafers against linoleum echoed through the virtually empty hall just outside the courtroom. For whatever reason, Jansen was hypersensitive to the sound, and every footfall gave his wrecked nerves a pinch they really didn't need.

It took the sound of metal slamming against metal to shock Jansen out of the tunnel he'd been careening through. He looked back to find a heavy door settling into place and Angelo's wide body sauntering down the hall behind him. Andrew Lister led the parade, guiding them down to yet another room lined with chairs and people waiting for God only knew what.

"Sit," Lister said, indicating the first chair on the first row. "Ya got shit to sign, my friend."

We're not friends, Jansen thought as he took a seat as he'd been told.

Angelo plopped down across the two seats directly behind them and leaned up enough to read over Jansen's shoulder. Jansen could feel every hot breath Angelo breathed brush across his face, smelled the bacon, eggs, and coffee he'd devoured earlier that morning.

God, please make this end soon.

"Sign here, here, and here," Lister said, indicating each blue X he'd made on the page.

Jansen didn't bother reading the contract. Dorian couldn't get out of jail without it and he damn sure wasn't going to let a little thing like a refused signature keep him away from his husband another night.

"Now, fill this part out, and I'll go post the bond. Cool?"

Jansen nodded slowly, then turned his stare back to the page. It asked a bunch of questions about Dorian's build. Jansen wanted to answer "eyes like milk chocolate and the body of a god." He went with "brown hair, brown eyes, weight two-twenty, height six-foot...." Jansen frowned. How could he not remember how tall Dorian was?

Shaking his head, he went back to the questions.

Tattoos? God, yes. Beautifully colored tattoos trailing over Dorian's muscled arms.

Scars? Unfortunately. Thanks to the life Dorian had been living.

He continued to fill in all the pertinent details, trying not to let the low hum of surrounding conversation distract him... until he heard Angelo talking on the phone. He raised his head at the sound of Dorian's name being whispered. The moment he locked eyes with Angelo, the big guy paced over toward the edge of the room, as though he was trying not to make it obvious he was aiming for out-of-earshot range with Jansen.

Well if that didn't sound any alarms....

Dorian might've trusted Angelo with every single secret he had, but Jansen didn't know the guy from Adam. For all he knew, Angelo could've been plotting to kill Dorian, or plotting to pin the murder of Leo Cabrezzi on the man Jansen loved with all his heart. And boy, that shit wouldn't fly at all.

"All right, kiddo," Lister called from across the room. The grating sound of his voice made Jansen jerk his head back. "The paperwork's bein' processed. You can either wait here until they release him, or wait at the office with me. What's your choice?"

"I'm not leaving," Jansen said with unbreakable resolve.

"It could be hours before they let him go."

"I don't care."

"Like... twelve of 'em."

"I don't care."

"Maybe even a day."

"I don't care."

Lister sighed. "Kiddo—"

"Stop calling me 'kiddo'! I'm not a fucking child," Jansen insisted with a growl.

"Whoa." Lister held up both hands. "I didn't mean anything by it."

Clenching his jaw, Jansen closed his eyes and sucked in the deepest breath he could. His chest expanded, growing much broader than it was naturally. He held on to that breath, let it seep into his lungs and into his blood, let the breath wind through him and relieve him. He let it relax him before exhaling sharply. His shoulders rounded, and then he opened his eyes again.

"Sorry," he said. "I'm on edge."

"I know, ki—man." Lister patted his shoulder. "I'd try to get some rest somewhere. Even if ya don't go home, go somewhere else. They ain't gonna have Dorian ready to be released for a good six hours at the very least. I'm betting on closer to twelve. That gives ya plenty a time to go… somewhere."

There was no place in New Orleans close enough to OPP for Jansen's taste. While the waiting area left a hell of a lot to be desired, and the idea of sitting down anywhere that hadn't been Lysoled turned his stomach, there was nowhere else he wanted to be right now. He wanted to be standing right there, front and center, when Dorian walked through those doors again.

"Go," Lister said softly.

"No."

"Look, tell ya what I'll do. They gotta call me before they release him anyway. Usually takes about forty-five minutes to an hour after that. I'll call ya."

Truth be told, he could live with that arrangement. Truth be told, there was somewhere he could go, and not be alone, and not dwell on the passing seconds, minutes, and hours until they finally set Dorian free. If nothing else, he knew he could go sit at Sin & Seduction and talk with Jason or just watch the dancers warm up for the Friday night show. It had been so long since Jansen had been on that stage—he sort of looked forward to a visit now that he thought about it.

"Okay," he said with a nod. "I'll go, but please be sure to call me."

"Scout's honor," he said, holding up three fingers.

Jansen doubted Andrew Lister, bail bondsman, had ever been a Scout.

21

SITTING BACK on the outer edge of the circle, Lance tried like hell to listen to every word Jason said. They were discussing the big closing show—the one that had to be more spectacular than all the rest, the one that had to draw in the huge numbers to impress the bosses, the one everything hinged on. As concerned as Lance was about saving the club, however, he couldn't take his eyes off Davi. He kept thinking of what they'd done behind the coat racks, then on the padded leather of the VIP booth, how he'd bared his soul when they'd held each other at the Riverwalk, the way he enjoyed having Davi in his arms more than he enjoyed the sexual stuff with him. And that wasn't a slight against Davi's talent at all. It simply spoke deafening volumes of what was going on inside the mushy red complication beating inside his chest.

Christ, what a mindfuck this is.

He imagined having Davi lying in bed behind him, spooned against his back, arms threaded around his body, one hand splayed over his stomach, one over his heart, plump lips against the nape of his neck. He could hear Davi's voice whispering sweet nothings just before they both drifted to sleep. It was magical, romantic, and something Lance hadn't wanted since his last heartbreak.

Again, his mind was going to places he wouldn't have chosen for himself. Relationship soup so wasn't on his preferred menu, but sure as he sat there, staring straight at Davi's long, lean body, he thought he could actually give it a go. He could hold hands and walk through the park. He could cuddle by a fire and watch those corny romantic comedies he hated so much. Breakfast in bed. Dinners by candlelight. Sharing a bed and a bathroom. Racing to get the last cup of coffee. The whole nine damn yards.

Shit.

Being in a relationship, though, would not only bankrupt his conscience, but bankrupt his wallet too. No way could he keep servicing those well-paying customers of his if he messed around and stepped in a big ol' pile of teeming, stinky love. It would ruin him. Destroy. Demolish. Wreck. Kill. End....

With a loud clapping of someone's hands, Lance jumped where he sat. The pulsing in his temples and the fluttering in his chest were no longer annoying little reminders that he was in fact very human, but a man who could find an early grave if he wasn't careful. He scrubbed his hand over his face, shifting his eyes about to see if anyone else had noticed his daydreaming.

No one had.

Not that he could tell.

His focus snapped back to the man in charge of the show. Jason stood among those eager dancers, making plans for a brighter future and a long, happy relationship together as long as everyone pulled their weight. Lance sincerely hoped Jason could deliver on this one. Jason was sweet, and a big-eyed dreamer. He had these great ideas and the follow-through to be a success, but as with any new venture, the potential to fail still remained.

Hopefully not this time.

Apparently their little get-together was over now, and somehow, Lance had managed to daydream through the whole thing. Sure, he'd caught bits and pieces, buzzwords and catchphrases that any good corporate manager would use to rally the troops. The rest of it, though, was background noise to the striptease Davi had been doing in his head. And with the clap of those two slender hands of Jason's, Davi didn't stop dancing. Not even for a second. Not even when Lance felt himself getting turned on by the view.

He pushed up from the metal folding chair where he'd been sitting, then stalked away from the crowd of people he wasn't interested in talking to right now. Heading down the hall toward the back exit, he thought he could get a little air and maybe clear his head, get back in the game and forget about his utterly inappropriate thoughts about Davi. The door slammed behind him a few seconds later than it should have, and when he spun around, the object of his daydreams stood right behind him with his arms crossed over his chest.

Through the thin white cotton shirt, Lance could make out almost every glorious mound, curve, and valley of Davi's chest. It hugged his waist and faded into a pair of tight, dark denims. Even though Davi was still fully clothed, Lance could still picture that perfect V and those thick veins pointing down to the most beautiful cock he'd ever laid eyes on. But the thing that tightened his throat and hitched his breath was the pure hurt in Davi's stare.

"Why you no talk to me?" he asked, voice soft and sad, just like his eyes. "We had one little disagreement and now... now, you avoid me. Why?" Davi laid his hand on Lance's forearm. The look in his eyes softened, turned almost pleading. "You said we would talk, Lance."

"We...." Lance shook his head. While he'd told himself many, many times he needed to face the truth and he'd come damn close to spilling his guts to the kid, now that he had the privacy and the opportunity, he didn't think he could go through with it. "Never mind."

"Please talk to me," Davi murmured. Even at a whisper, his exotic accent had the power to whisk Lance away from mundane New Orleans life off to paradise. He carefully eased his fingers down to Lance's palm, then whispered, "Please."

Lance curled his hand into a fist, forcing Davi's gentle touch away. He closed his eyes and turned his head because he knew if he kept looking into those big brown puppy-dog eyes, and staring at those delicious lips, he would want to kiss Davi again, and wouldn't that lead to nothing good?

"I can't," Lance admitted, trying for a strong, commanding voice and failing miserably.

"We talked at the Riverwalk. You opened up to me. Why can't you talk to me now?"

"Davi." He finally looked up again and found the heartbreaking hurt he'd heard in Davi's voice staring back at him. "I can't do this." He waffled his hand between their bodies. "Whatever this is, I can't do it."

A long moment of silence followed. Lance waited for Davi to say something, anything—an agreement or an argument in support of all the reasons Lance could do this—but Davi didn't say a word. His stare travelled up and down the length of Lance's body, then ping-ponged across his face. His lips parted as if he were going to say something, but all he did was take a breath. His chest rose, held for a second, then deflated much like Lance's willpower. Davi tucked both hands in his pockets, then turned and headed back toward the door.

The wave of sadness that hit Lance as Davi walked away from him made him stagger back toward the fence. He had to lean against the chain links for support, because God knew his legs weren't up for the job. He hung his head and stared down at the hand Davi had touched so tenderly. That empty, but very-touched hand became a metaphor for his heart and his feelings.

Davi had touched him, not just in a physical way, but in a very deep emotional way, and Lance couldn't handle it. He wasn't equipped to deal with feelings like this. Not since he'd had his heart completely broken in high school. Sure, he'd had the hots for Jason and cared about his boss very much—so much he'd wished Jason would've picked him over Brad. But at the end of the night, when the sex and romance ended, Lance knew he couldn't offer Jason half of what Brad could. Yet, with Davi, even if he had a hard time opening up and letting himself truly feel, he almost wanted to give it a try.

Didn't they both deserve that much?

Of course….

22

IN THE low light of his office, Jason reviewed the numbers for the past month and came to an average headcount. The number of patrons he needed to walk through the doors wasn't astronomical and still well beneath the maximum occupancy for the building, so this should've been a breeze. Funny, it didn't feel easy at all. In fact, the more he thought about it, the more monumental the task seemed to be.

People had stopped coming to Sin & Seduction. The place had a bad reputation now. Back in the day, people came and knew they could escape the pressures of life with whatever kind of pleasure their little hearts desired and no one would mess with them. They let loose and had fun. Everything was great. Then something changed, and secrets became public knowledge. The goings-on in VIP were asked about at the front door by red-rope dwellers and people who had never seen the inside of the club. Sex became dangerous. Drugs became dangerous. Life inside the club became dangerous. It wasn't all harmless fun within four secure walls anymore. People were scared to come. They were afraid of their dark sides spilling into their day-to-day, so they didn't come anymore.

Now how the hell was he supposed to get them back?

Only something huge would pull those people back in, something epic and grand, something they would talk about for days and months and even years after the night came to an end. But what could possibly be so amazing? He thought about theme nights and drink specials, parties, and the plans he had for the big show. Taking inspiration from little quips tossed back and forth between the guys, Jason even considered throwing a little bit of kink into the mix. But while all those ideas sounded fabulous, past experience led him to believe none of them would work, not on the grand scale he needed. All those corny hat tricks wouldn't bring the old regulars back and wouldn't drag new people in. They wouldn't double the numbers and the ship would finally sink.

"Shit," he sighed as he leaned back in his chair. He pressed a thumb to either temple and slowly rubbed, applying enough pressure to deaden the thumping in his head.

A knock at the door sent another wave of curses rolling through him. He really didn't want to face anyone right now, not with imminent failure on the cusp of his being. Regardless, he softly muttered his favorite flagrant four-lettered words as he stalked around his desk to open the door.

Surprise nailed him in the chest and pulled a hard gasp from his throat when Jansen—the man he'd once loved and lost to someone else, the best friend he missed, the man whose suffering was so much worse than his right now—appeared in his doorway. Poor guy looked like he'd been run over by a freight train, and without bothering to utter the first word, Jason stepped out and threw his arms around his best friend's body.

The hug was a "glad to see you" and a "hope you're okay" and a "thank God you're here" all rolled up into a quiet, hard embrace. He didn't immediately let go, because right now, he needed a good solid hug from the kind of friend Jason knew he could rely on. And Jansen threaded his arms around Jason's body, holding him as if he needed Jason in the same way.

"Are you okay?" Jansen softly asked, pulling away enough to look Jason in the eyes while still keeping a death grip on his waist.

"I should be asking you that question." Jason gave him a sad, sympathetic smile.

Jansen sighed.

"Come in. I'll brew a pot of coffee." Jason took his hand and led him into the office and closed the door behind them so the eavesdroppers mingling about backstage wouldn't be able to spy so easily. Jansen sat down in the chair across from Jason's desk. Jason went straight to the minifridge and pulled out a bottle of water, then went to making a pot of coffee.

"I'm waiting for them to release Dorian," Jansen finally said. The sound of his voice and the nervousness in his words made Jason raise his head. Jansen softly continued, "They're letting him out on bail until we go to trial."

"Well, that's good news, right?"

"Oh yeah. Absolutely. Great news."

Jansen smiled, but it didn't fill his eyes with the gleam of genuine happiness. There was still worry or something similar there. Jason must've been frowning, because Jansen forced his smile to widen.

"I'm tired of waiting," Jansen explained. "I want him home now."

"What's the holdup?"

"Processing the paperwork. I came here to kill some time."

"You look like you could use some sleep. Why don't you kick back on the couch and see if you can—"

"Won't do any good," Jansen interrupted. "I haven't been able to sleep worth a shit since Dorian got locked up. When I have him back home and in our bed again, then I'll sleep." There was a long pause. Jansen frowned, eyeing Jason as though he didn't recognize his best friend anymore. "Speaking of looking like hell," he said. "What's up with you?"

Without immediately answering, Jason padded back around the desk and to the chair he'd spent way too many hours sulking in. He sat down and propped his elbows on the desk's neat surface, framing the pages he'd been staring at right before Jansen's arrival.

"The bosses are giving me a chance to save the club," he said without the kind of excited inflection that normally came with good news.

"That's awesome!"

"Awesome. Right." Jason snorted.

Jansen frowned. "What am I missing here?"

"I have to double the numbers at the door. I have to pull in more money. I have to put on this amazing fucking show, and I have no idea how." Frustration dripped from his voice. "I have to... I have to learn how to run a club and.... Jesus. Fuck. Jansen, I have no idea what I'm doing. I was excited at first. Brad helped me come up with this great plan. I presented it to the bosses and they were cool with it, but after looking at the figures...."

"You don't think you can pull it off?"

"No." Jason sat back in his chair, dropping his hands to his lap. "I don't."

Another long moment of silence pushed tension up through the room. It seeped from rigid bodies and unspoken words, making the air too thick to breathe.

"Talk to me, please," Jansen said softly. "You know I'm still here for you. No matter what, I'll always be here for you."

"I know." Jason's shoulders slumped. "I just don't think I can do it. I don't see how I can. What's so badass that it'll bring all the old crowd back in?"

Silence. Then Jansen said, "What about bringing some of the old stars back?"

"Like who?"

"Me and you. Maybe some of the dancers we used to look up to before we got on the main stage. Don't you remember how people went crazy over us?"

Jason grinned crookedly, running his fingers through the thick, hard-gelled coiffure Brad had fixed him up with this morning. The pasted sprigs didn't budge much, and when Jason pulled his hand back, he had an intense need to wash it, but he let it go.

Jansen had a point. People loved them, but they were both married—or rather, practically married—men now. Jesus, Jason had been dealing with diapers and pureed food for so long he wasn't sure he knew how to be sexy anymore.

"Dude, I don't know," he said, shaking his head and rubbing his hand over his brow. "I don't know if I can even move like that anymore. My body isn't as flexible as it used to be." He paused and frowned. "I didn't think Dorian wanted you onstage anyway."

Sighing, Jansen relaxed back in his chair as if all the pizzazz, all the fight, and the get-up-and-go had been kicked right out of him. "Don't worry about Dorian," he said. "I can handle Dor. He'll be okay with it because we're trying to save a place he and I both love."

"If you say so."

"I do."

Now what?

They both sat there silently staring at each other. Jason knew they both had ideas flittering about in their heads. That was just the way they operated, always had been, ever since they'd first met. They had always been the kind of friends who could quietly sit in a room together and not need to talk to pass the time. Thank God, even though they were both tied down to other men, nothing had changed.

"I miss this," Jansen finally said.

Those three words made Jason raise his head. He looked over at his best friend who still stared down at his folded hands, probably at the ring Dorian had slipped onto his finger after vowing to love him until they took their last breaths. Jason really didn't know what to say, and didn't plan on responding until Jansen looked over at him.

"This." He waffled his hand between them. "The comfortable quiet. We were always really good at comfortable quiet."

"Then we got attached to other people."

Jansen chuckled. "Yeah, we did. Who knew that would happen... to us of all people?"

The thing was, Jason had always been *that* type. He wanted love. He wanted companionship, but the one he'd wanted it with never reciprocated those feelings, so he'd given up. When that someone married someone else, he'd moved on and found a someone of his very own.

"I knew we would both settle down," he finally said. "I just thought I would be the one to climb out of the dating pool first."

"Dorian was totally unexpected."

"So was Brad."

Jansen glanced back up and their eyes locked. He looked like a deer in headlights and Jason was the big-ass 4x4 about to drag him down the road. It wasn't like that. This wasn't *that* kind of conversation.

"I love Dorian," Jansen said.

"I love Brad." Jason paused. "He proposed. We're getting married."

"Congrats. You deserve to be happy."

"Thanks."

Silence again. Jason was the one who finally had the decency to look away. He stood from his desk, then went over to the file cabinets, fished around until he found a schedule, then grabbed his trusty clipboard. He pulled a pen from the holder on the edge of the desk and started scribbling names into the various slots. It was normal routine. Safe. Normal. Routine.

"I guess I should be going," Jansen finally said.

"Yeah, I, um… have work to do."

23

"DAVI, WAIT!" Lance yelled down the hallway right before the big metal door slammed behind him. The sound echoed against the cinder-block walls and rattled every single nerve in Lance's body. The piercing sound made his heart skip.

When Davi finally turned around and Lance caught a glimpse of his shiny cheeks in the hall's low light, it crushed him. He'd made the kid cry. His stupid fears and insecurities had made that poor, innocent guy shed fucking tears. Damn, that made Lance feel like a bastard, but boy, didn't he deserve it?

"What do you want?" Davi asked, voice soft and quivering, much like a scolded child.

"I'm sorry," Lance blurted. The words surprised him. He couldn't remember the last time he sincerely apologized for anything. He took a step closer and offered a hand. "Maybe I can try to do… this."

"This?" Davi frowned.

Again, Lance took another step, and this time, he actually reached for Davi's hand. Their fingers intertwined, giving Lance a serious case of cold feet. They were now joined at the digits like a real couple, and didn't that rock Lance's world?

Hang in there, tiger. You can do this.

"Yes. This." Lance swallowed and drew Davi closer. "Can we go upstairs and talk?"

"Jus' talk?"

"Yes. Just talk. I promise."

"Sim," Davi said, giving Lance a tight nod.

Lance held on to Davi's hand, guiding him to the employees-only stairs leading up to the VIP section. The front part of the club was a ghost town, save for the few workers who'd already begun their shifts. The same was true up on the balcony—just a lonely bartender wiping everything down before the club opened. He wouldn't pay them any attention. The staff had learned long ago never to mind the things that happened up in those booths.

"After you," Lance said, holding out a hand. He watched as Davi climbed in and settled on the bend where the two benches met each other. The backdrop of stage lights cast a soft rainbow on his curious face. He stared up at Lance with those huge, adoring eyes and Lance wanted to melt right there.

"Do you, um"—Lance swallowed—"want something to drink?"

"If you... ah, go to... get something for you." Davi stumbled through his English in the most adorable way.

Lance smiled. "I'll be right back."

He went straight to the bar and waited for the fair-haired cutie in nothing but a bowtie and a Speedo to come back. The kid had the greatest abs, and with so little on, Lance could see the very defined V shape dipping down behind thin black fabric.

Stop it, he told himself as he glanced over his shoulder to find Davi staring out at the stage. Lance almost felt guilty for checking out another man when he was about to have "the talk" with someone else. Strike that. He felt guilty as hell.

Grimacing, he asked Blondie for two bottles of water and tried not to watch as the kid turned and seductively bent down to reach in the cooler. He had the perfect rounded ass, but was soooo terribly submissive and flamboyant that instead of being turned on, Lance was actually a bit put off.

He thanked the kid and took the bottles, then returned to Davi, struggling not to give the bartender a second thought. He did, however. Lance spent a good, long moment wondering if the kid had been more... oh, manly, maybe... if Lance would've found him attractive enough to forget Davi and chase a date. Was he really *that* kind of guy?

Lance eased into the booth beside Davi and for a long while, he couldn't bring himself to say anything. He only stared at those plump pink lips and huge brown eyes, the way the cutest little dimples framed Davi's mouth when he smiled and how he was utterly trusting of everyone he'd met since he'd come to the States. He was amazingly independent, for someone so lost and scared. So brave for someone so far from everything he knew. Lance envied him in that way. Bravery just didn't come so naturally for him.

Funny though, when it came to keeping Davi safe and happy, Lance swore he could do brave all day long.

"You're not talking, Lance," Davi said matter-of-factly. "What is wrong?"

"Nothing. Nothing at all," Lance said, quickly bringing the water bottle up to his dry lips.

"Then we talk? Sim?"

"Sim." Lance sighed. "Look, I, um... I suck at this." Davi frowned. "What I mean is, I don't do emotional shit very well. I'm a fuck-'em-and-go type."

"'Fuck 'em and go'?" Davi's frown deepened.

"Yeah. I mean, I don't get involved with men because they'll always, *always* screw you over. They make you fall in love with them, then go back home to the people they claim to love. Love is bullshit."

"Love is not bullshit, Lance. Love is...." A dreamy-eyed daze came over Davi, and his expression softened into something wistful, as though he was remembering being in love or remembering how awesome it obviously felt. Good for him. "Love is wonderful."

"Not to spoil your fantasy, but I have to disagree."

"Then what is it you want from me?" Davi clenched his jaw, brow furrowed. The power Lance had seen the other day came back with startling quickness. If Lance had a little more Cowardly Lion in him, he might've begun to fidget and stutter and think of ways to backpedal his ass right outta there.

"I um...." What exactly did Lance want from him? If he didn't believe in love or relationships, and he liked sticking to straight-up fucking but wanted more than that with Davi, then what the hell were they doing there?

Those stupid feelings of yours, remember, jackass? Admit them.

"You're different," he finally said.

"Different?" Davi tilted his head.

"Yeah, different."

Sighing, Lance rubbed both hands over his face. His palms were wet from the condensation on the water bottles, and no doubt left glistening trails down his cheeks. He was wading into uncharted territory here. Maybe not completely uncharted, but territory he'd avoided since the last major heartbreak he'd experienced.

"How so?" Davi asked in a voice so soft Lance would've dismissed it as nothing more than whistling air had he not seen Davi's lips moving. The kid reached out and laid his hand over the knotted fingers now resting in Lance's lap. Lance's stare followed. "Please, tell me."

"I don't want just sex with you," Lance finally admitted, and as soon as the words left his mouth, he would've sworn he'd blanched. He could feel the color leaving his face. "I actually care. Honestly. I worry about you. I think about you. I don't imagine us fucking. I imagine us in bed or on the couch, just holding each other. When I think about being intimate with you, I don't think of the costume rack. I think about the Riverwalk and the sunset and the way you looked at me like I wasn't screwed in the head."

Davi's subtle smile widened to the point Lance could see his pearly whites. It was a heart-melting sight if ever he'd seen one, as if his heart could melt any more than it had already. In that second, in those deep dimples and shimmering brown eyes, Lance knew he'd found home. He knew his heart had made the decision his mind didn't want to make.

"Come home with me tonight," Lance whispered, pulling Davi's hand to his mouth. "Not for sex. Just... come home with me. Sleep in the bed beside me. Let's share a meal and—"

"Yes."

"Yes? Seriously?"

Davi nodded and kept his smile as wide as ever. His cheeks gleamed with sheer happiness, and it filled his dark eyes with a glow that could've lightened all the darkness in the world.

24

JANSEN HAD spent hours wandering around Sin & Seduction, trying like hell to pass the time until Lister called and said Dorian was free to go. A few of those hours had been spent reflecting on the relationship Jansen had once had with his best friend, the love Jason had confessed only after Jansen had announced his pending nuptial to Dorian Grant—a man Jason was very clear about hating with every breath in his body. It had been Jason's confession of feelings that had led to Jansen's realization of where that hatred stemmed from. Now, what did they have? An awkward friendship? Regret that things hadn't worked out differently?

No. No. Absolutely not. Jansen loved Dorian with every ounce of his being. That man was the sun and moon and stars. He was everything Jansen ever wanted or needed. He made Jansen happy.

But what if….

The sudden ringing coming from his pocket made him belt out a startled scream. It was a sound he'd been waiting for but not expecting.

It's time, the text said—meaning the moment Jansen had spent the last six months waiting for had finally come. Now Jansen didn't know what to do. He stood in the middle of the room, eyes wide, heart fluttering wildly. It was as if his mind had checked out of the race too early. He wasn't sure if the *thump thump thump* he heard came from his pulse or someone charging into the room behind him. When he swung around, he nearly ran right into Angelo.

"Hey," Angelo said, slapping his big-ass palm against Jansen's shoulder.

Jansen stumbled forward. "Jesus Christ, Ang."

"Sorry, man. You ready? Lister just texted."

"Yeah, I'm ready."

The length of the time and the motions it took to get them all back out to the sedan were a total blur. Jansen knew he'd been shoved in the backseat. He could feel the car moving and see the blurring of city life passing outside the window. Other than that, he was pretty much on autopilot.

Finally back at OPP, Jansen paced the prisoner-release area, back and forth, back and forth, worrying his bottom lip between his thumb and forefinger because his nerves were playing hell on him right now. He hadn't paid any attention to the vagrants loitering outside the prison as he'd made his way in. In fact, he'd practically been shoved out of the car because he'd been too lost in his thoughts to know they'd arrived.

He heard a door open, then slam behind him, and Jansen whipped around. There stood Dorian—full beard and mustache, hair longer than Jansen had ever seen it, eyes dark with bags, but still looking as handsome as ever. Dorian moved with every bit of the raw power he'd always had, as if being in jail for so long hadn't broken him in the least. He held his head high, shoulders squared. Every single step he took thudded against the worn linoleum and echoed sheer superiority against the walls.

A crooked smile tugged one corner of Jansen's mouth as soon as their stares locked. It took all the willpower he had not to sprint across that room and throw himself at his husband's body. It took every ounce of his strength not to throw his arms around Dorian's neck and kiss him so deep his tongue tickled the back of Dorian's throat.

Dorian sauntered toward him, checking his left side, then his right side, as if his six-month stint in OPP had turned him into the kind of hardened convict who always watched their back. Jansen didn't get it. He wanted to ask what had happened, what had changed in Dorian, but he didn't. He wouldn't. He had to believe Dorian wouldn't keep anything from him.

"I've never been so damn happy to see someone in my entire life," Dorian whispered as he hooked his arm around Jansen's waist and tugged him closer. The old lilt returned to his voice. It was no longer flat and lifeless and to the point.

He lowered his head and stole a kiss—not deep and passionate, but lingering and meaningful. It sort of felt like Dorian was daring anyone in that room to say a word about what he was doing, while still showing Jansen the kind of attention he normally would have. And through the kiss they both kept their eyes wide open, staring at each other with unbreakable resolve.

Jansen slowly pulled away, and he took quick stock of the people around him. A few were watching with their noses curled in disgust. Some didn't notice. Some didn't care. He laced his fingers with Dorian's and said a soft, "Let's get you home and into a hot bath. Maria's making a special dinner for us."

"God damn, that sounds good." Dorian rubbed his hand over his stomach.

They headed out to the car. Dorian's driver waited with the door wide open and a smile on his face. The man never really spoke, but in this situation, he chose to. "Mr. Grant, we're all very excited to have you home."

Color me shocked.

Dorian grinned and clapped his hand on the driver's shoulder. "It's good to be back, my man. Hopefully, it'll stay that way for a long damn time."

Ain't that the truth?

The door shut behind them, and before too long, the car was jostling over the broken pavement of Orleans Parish Prison's worn and weathered parking lot and back into traffic.

Neither one of them spoke much in the first few minutes of finally being alone together again. Dorian held Jansen's hand, clinging with the kind of strength that meant he was probably terrified of being ripped away again. It was awkward, not just the silence, but having a man as strong and unbreakable look like a scared child who'd finally found his way home again. Jansen should've expected as much, though. He'd witnessed Dorian's decline during once a week sessions at the prison, especially during the last few visits.

"You okay?" Jansen asked.

"Yeah, I...." Dorian's focus had been targeted straight ahead, but when he paused, he turned his stare on Jansen, and that fear shone in his dark eyes, in the furrow of his brow, and in the purse of his lips. "I don't wanna ever, *ever* go back to that place."

Jesus, did Jansen just step into an episode of *Scared Straight*?

"Well," Jansen cautiously began, "the plan is to keep you out of *that place*. Your attorney feels very good about the case and, baby"—he reached up and touched the side of Dorian's face, stroking his thumb over Dorian's dry lips—"you're innocent. You weren't there. You didn't do it. So the way I see it, you've got nothing to worry about."

"Solicitation to commit murder."

"Excuse me?"

"*That* is the crime they can put me away for. Even if they find me innocent on the murder charge, they can still come back with that."

"Dorian." Jansen sighed and dropped his hand. He settled back in his seat and looked straight ahead. "Why don't you just enjoy being free for right now, and let Rebecca deal with those bridges *if* we come to them?"

Silence. Dorian didn't bother responding and Jansen didn't bother looking over to see why. This wasn't supposed to happen this way. Dorian was supposed to get out of jail and be so overwhelmed with joy he couldn't stop hugging and kissing, and possibly fucking Jansen until they passed out. They were supposed to be smiling and laughing and having a good time. Not this... this tension.

When they arrived back at the mansion, Dorian headed inside and spent a few minutes receiving the warm welcomes from people who'd missed him—namely, the staff who'd been around since his childhood. He hugged Maria and hugged her husband, who kept the mansion's grounds in tip-top shape. He didn't spend a lot of time socializing and they all seemed to understand him being short with them. None of them innocently insisted on holding him up with idle chitchat. He'd said he wanted a shower more than anything. "I can't remember what a real shower feels like."

"We'll take one together... if that's okay with you," Jansen said, closing the bedroom door behind them.

Dorian didn't immediately speak. His eyes shifted from Jansen to the bathroom and back again. Clearly, he didn't want Jansen in there, though why, Jansen wasn't sure. After seven months of being apart, one would've thought Dorian wouldn't want to spend another second away from him.

"It's okay," Jansen finally said. "You take a shower. I'll be right out here."

"Thanks," Dorian mumbled before ducking into the bathroom.

For a few precious minutes, Jansen stood alone in their bedroom, watching the backside of the bathroom door, listening as eight showerheads pounded water against a tiled wall. He wasn't sure what to do. Dorian not wanting him in there confused him. It almost felt as though Dorian had lost something in prison, as though he didn't want Jansen like he used to.

He stripped out of his clothes and changed into a thin pair of sleep pants, no shirt, hoping maybe if Dorian saw a hint of his body the old flame would spark again. He sat down on the edge of the bed, stare focused hard on the back of the bathroom door. Confusion and worry seeped into his mind.

After a few minutes, the water finally stopped. Jansen waited for Dorian to strut his naked, tattooed ass into their bedroom and have his way with him. He waited and waited and waited some more. About a minute and a half later, he heard the low hum of the clippers buzzing. Jansen frowned.

He cautiously approached the door, cracked it open, and peeked inside. Half of Dorian's beard had fallen into the sink. He had the other half locked in his fist. Jansen couldn't keep himself from pouting. He'd loved that beard.

"What are you doing?" he asked in a soft voice.

"I'm teachin' monkeys to fly," Dorian responded as he dragged the clippers along his jaw. More thick hair fell into the basin. "I'm shavin'."

"But why?"

"I hate all the hair."

"I thought it looked nice on you."

"It was fuckin' filthy," Dorian barked.

Jansen jerked with surprise. It wasn't like Dorian to snap at him like that. "Whatever," he muttered, and he immediately left the bathroom and the mess Dorian was making of his face and for that matter, the mess their relationship seemed to be in now.

He grabbed the iPad from the nightstand and headed downstairs, thinking he would sit on the couch and read until Dorian was ready to deal with him, or better yet, deal with them. Though honestly, he'd been waiting so long to be near Dorian again, the distance killed him. But he wouldn't press. If Dorian needed to reacclimate himself to being in the world again, Jansen supposed he had no choice but to give him the space... even if it was painful to do.

Jansen heard a door open then close, and he half expected to see Dorian at the top of the steps. He watched and waited. Nothing. Dorian never appeared. The longer Jansen sat there staring, the more his heart ached. He set the iPad on the coffee table and settled down into the couch, pillow curled into his chest. He didn't raise his head until he heard the thumping of Angelo's shoes along the marble.

"You going up to see him?" Jansen asked.

"Yeah." Angelo stopped long enough to frown. "Why ain't you up there?"

Jansen shrugged.

Angelo arched a brow.

"He's... I don't know. In a mood."

"Ah. Gotcha."

"Be careful."

"Sure thing, boss... ah, Jansen."

25

Rubbing his thumb in a circular motion at his temple, Dorian propped both elbows on his desk. In the other hand was one deliciously fat Cuban cigar. The smoke wafted up and filled the room with a scent he'd been missing for a long damn time. The ledger from one of his businesses filled the too-bright screen of his laptop. Before going to jail, he'd hated dealing with them, but now he welcomed the little columns of numbers that didn't make a whole lot of sense to someone who wasn't an accountant. It gave Dorian something to look at, to think about, something other than the possible doom awaiting him and how he knew he'd been an ass to Jansen, yet couldn't help the way he'd acted.

Dorian absolutely hated feeling so out of control of his life. He wasn't the sit-around-and-wait-for-things-to-happen kind of guy. Frankly, he believed that fact had saved his ass more than once. Plus, he didn't plan to rely on sworn statements from hospital staff to keep him out of jail. No, he needed to come up with something. Somehow. Because he damn sure wasn't going back to jail. He'd die in a blaze of glory before that happened.

Tap. Tap. "Boss?"

"Yeah, Angelo. Come in."

He closed the laptop's lid and sat back in his chair. Angelo slipped his big ass through the door and padded over to the couch. The cushions had a permanent indention from all the hours Dorian and Angelo had spent in that office together. It had been a long damn time since they'd had quiet little powwows over a cigar and a joint.

"What's on ya mind, brotha?" Dorian asked.

"Nada, boss," Angelo said with a shake of his head.

Bullshit. Dorian wasn't buying that for one second. If there was one thing Angelo couldn't do well, it was hide behind a blank face and pretend like he didn't have a care in the world. No, something was bothering him. He needed to get something off his chest.

Dorian turned in his chair, now facing the couch. He sat forward and rested his elbows on his knees, fingers locked together, arms steepled, chin held up by two extended thumbs. For a minute or two, he simply sat there staring, staring a big-ass hole right into his best friend. He could tell the exact moment he began to get under Angelo's skin because the big guy looked away, shifted in his seat, then looked back.

"Talk," Dorian said. The one little word held a hell of a lot of power.

Angelo licked his lips. "I didn't do it, boss."

"Come again?"

"Cabrezzi. I didn't bump him off, Dorian."

It took a second for that news to completely register with Dorian. It processed in stages—shock, anger, relief, then back to anger. Though Dorian wouldn't consider it rage, just a healthy dose of pissed off.

"What do ya mean ya didn't bump him off?" The tension in Dorian's jaw muffled his words. "He's fuckin' dead, right?"

"Oh, yeah. Absolutely. Doornail dead. Ice cube and shit."

"What happened? And I swear to all that is holy, Angelo, ya better give it to me straight. 'Cause I gotta tell ya, I'm pretty fuckin' mad right now."

"I know, Dorian." Angelo held up both hands. "Trust me, I know."

Angelo sat forward, reaching a long arm all the way to the corner of the desk where the ashtray sat. The yellowing tip of a half-smoked joint peeked up from the edge of the glass dish. As he brought the joint to his lips, he rolled onto one cheek to fish a lighter from his pocket. Then he lifted the flame to the tip.

Every second that passed without Angelo explaining what the hell happened put Dorian a little more on edge. If Wide Ass didn't start talking soon, Dorian felt pretty certain nine kinds of hell was going to break loose in that office.

"As soon as I left the hospital," Angelo said as he exhaled a thick white cloud of smoke, "I called my guy. You know the one...."

Dorian nodded. The guy Angelo referred to was a low-life waste of space, but he always had the goods. He was one of those genius types who could manipulate computers and hack into every aspect of someone's life. For that reason alone, Dorian remained neutral. Since his tolerance for the guy ran thin more often than not, Angelo dealt with the geek.

"He knew exactly where Leo was. Had the info ready and waiting... like someone else had asked for it. I knew something was up. I almost asked, but...."

"Angelo."

"Right. Anyway. I got the goods, then headed on over to Cabrezzi's place. His car was in the driveway, but the house was dark. I kept going. Parked around the corner, then slipped through a few backyards."

Dorian tried to imagine Angelo hefting himself over a chain-link fence. The mental image wasn't exactly working for him. It even bordered on humorous.

"When I got to Cabrezzi's place, the back door was unlocked, but I didn't really think anything of it. I figured some people left their shit unlocked." Angelo shrugged. "So, I go inside and everything's quiet, boss. Like freakishly quiet."

"And that didn't clue ya in to somethin' bein' wrong?" Dorian interrupted.

"Nah. It was late, man, like close to three in the morning. I figured the guy liked to conserve energy while he slept. That's the big thing now, ya know?"

"Yeah. Yeah. Everybody's goin' fuckin' green." Dorian spun his forefinger in a tight circle. "Can ya get on with it already?"

Angelo took another long pull from the joint. His eyelids were already getting droopy. The thing about Angelo was, when he got stoned, his stories became longer and wordier. The important points were lost to little details. Oddly enough, Angelo probably could've been a writer. He was one hell of a storyteller when Dorian was in the mood to listen while he dragged on. Now wasn't one of those times.

"Boss, I shit you not, the smell coming down the hallway could've put ya right on your ass. You know how the alleys get 'round here sometimes? Like... after Mardi Gras or if the trash guy decided to skip a bin or two? Yeah"—Angelo made a nauseated face—"not good. That was the smell coming out of Cabrezzi's room when I got there."

"So he was probably dead close to a day, huh?"

"Yeah, boss."

"Meaning whoever killed him got to him right after he shot Jansen."

"Might've even been in the car when Cabrezzi pulled the trigger."

Foot relentlessly tapping, Dorian licked along his bottom lip. His mind was all over the place now. Scenarios flew at him faster than he could make sense of them. The one resounding idea was to find out who was with Cabrezzi that night. But this time, Dorian's first instinct wasn't to kill. If he could find out who really offed Leo Cabrezzi, then he could definitely clear his name and put this whole murder business behind him.

"Gimme that," he said as he reached out and swiped the smoldering joint from Angelo's lips. He snuffed it out in the ashtray. "This is what you're gonna do." He now had Angelo's complete attention. "You're gonna go to the geek and find out who wanted Cabrezzi's info. You're gonna find out who the hell did him in, and you're gonna get me proof. Got it?"

Angelo frowned. "You don't want me to *handle* 'em?"

"Did I say handle 'em?"

"No...."

"Then no, I don't. Listen to what the hell I'm tellin' ya. This is important."

"Sure, boss."

"I need to get proof to Rebecca Chambers. We're gonna clear my fuckin' name. I'm done with this stupid shit. It ends now." Dorian stabbed his meaty forefinger against the desk.

26

THE LAST of the Friday night crowd straggled out of the club and off to God only knew where. Some might've gone home with their dates. Some might've picked up new friends. Some might've even gone home to the families who loved them. Wherever they went, it didn't really matter. They were gone from Sin & Seduction, and the early-morning hours now belonged to the dancers who'd spent an entire night sweating and slaving just to give those gracious money-spending fools some entertainment.

Lance pitched the towel he'd been using to dry his drenched body into the cloth laundry bin at the rear of the dressing room. He grabbed a T-shirt and a fresh pair of gym shorts from his backpack and changed, even though he didn't need to. He could've been home in a matter of minutes, showered and changed there. Tonight, however, he wanted to be as fresh as possible, because tonight, he intended to take Davi home with him, and being naked with that man so close would've led to the one thing he wanted to avoid—sex.

"I am ready when you are," Davi said.

That smooth, exotic voice startled Lance. He thought he'd been alone this whole time. Apparently not.

He swung around and greeted Davi with a smile, not expecting to find himself so utterly entranced the way he was. Something about the low light raining down from the rafters or the sweat glistening on Davi's brow, or maybe it was the softness in his dark eyes and the way he looked eager but a little scared. Whatever attracted Lance to the kid, it held on. The attraction wasn't fleeting. This wasn't a *fuck-me, pay-me, watch-me-leave* situation at all. Dare he say he actually wanted to romance Davi?

"I'm, um… I'm ready too." Lance swallowed so hard it made his ears pop.

Davi moved in beside him as if they'd been dating forever and were very comfortable with being a couple. The kid reached down between their sides and wrapped his hand around Lance's.

"You look scared," Davi said, head tilting to the side, a confused, childlike expression on his face as if he didn't get it. "Are you scared of me, Lance?"

Oh no, that wasn't confusion and nothing close to childlike. The teasing lilt in his voice and the arch of brow read totally different. That was pure, unadulterated wickedness.

"I'm not scared of *you*," Lance said as he squared his shoulders and set his jaw. "I'm scared of me."

"There's nothing to fear." Davi turned so he now stood directly in front of Lance, mere inches from his face, close enough to feel the warmth of each other's breath. "Nothing to fear at all."

The world froze right there. No one breathed. No one moved. Lance pictured the devil on his shoulder telling him to take Davi home and let the kid fuck the shit out of him, just like all those horny old rich guys did. The angel on the opposite shoulder told him to think about his heart and how he wanted better, how Davi deserved better because he wasn't a whore. The angel wanted to save both their hearts and souls. Lance just wanted all the mixed, contradictory feelings to go away.

Do the right thing.

Do the wrong thing.

Think with your heart.

Think with your cock.

Lance wanted to scream.

He took only one step back, keeping his stare trained on Davi, not daring to break the lock of their eyes, not breaking the knot of their fingers. Lance could feel himself grinning, but didn't know if it looked devious or sorrowful. He genuinely had the most innocent intentions.

"How about we go up to my place, and just... just see where the morning takes us?"

"I like that plan," Davi said.

"Good."

Keeping Davi's hand in his, he led the way down the long corridor and out into the back parking lot of Sin & Seduction. On the opposite end of the building, the second floor contained small, low-rent apartments for people who worked at the club but couldn't afford nicer digs in and around the greater New Orleans area. They weren't great, but they were clean. No rats. No bugs. Nothing caving in. Things rarely falling apart. It was home—the best home some of those guys could ask for.

Lance could've lived somewhere nicer had he wanted to. The money he made off the patrons gave him a hell of a lot of wiggle room, but he never was one for an extravagant lifestyle. He grew up living a modest life and figured he would die the same way. Great thing about being frugal was being able to set back a hell of a lot of dough. He had a nice nest egg, not enough to retire on, not enough to provide for two people if the club shut down, but getting there... provided he kept working.

The stairs creaked under the weight of both their bodies.

The railing whined beneath their grips.

The outside door groaned as Lance wrenched it open.

They made their way down another long, dark hall, past doors on either side that led to occupied apartments. His was on the corner—giving it more windows and more square footage than the rest—and when he reached the last door on the left, he slipped his key in the knob and led the way.

Inside, the apartment was much nicer than the building led one to believe it would be. It was a studio with an open floor plan. His bed was in the far corner, opposite a love seat and a cabinet with a modest flat-screen TV. They had to walk through a small kitchen and past the door leading to the bathroom before finding the comfort of the living area. The walls were bare cinder block, but the light fixtures were much more upscale. The appliances were black and the cabinets cheap, but again, it was home.

"Want a beer or something?" Lance asked as he made his way toward the fridge. His hand felt so empty without the warmth of Davi's fingers wrapped around it.

"Whatever you have," Davi said, setting his bag down on the mini island.

"Well, do you want alcohol or not?"

"A beer is fine."

Of course it is.

He pulled two bottles of Corona out of the fridge and popped the tops, pitched the caps into the trash, and headed back over to Davi, who hadn't stopped looking around. Judging by his stoic expression, the kid just wanted to take in his surroundings. He didn't look put off at all. Not that the place was a dump, but in Lance's experience, some people didn't approve.

He handed Davi the beer and watched the flex of muscle in his arm as he lifted the bottle to those beautiful lips of his. His mouth encircled the slender neck of glass, and God help him if Lance couldn't picture those same lips hugging his shaft just like that, riding down his cock and back again.

Swallowing hard, he turned away and gripped his groin, silently begging and praying for the shit to go back to sleep like it had been all damn night. He closed his eyes and took a deep breath. His chest expanded as far as it would go, and he held that breath for as long as he could before letting it go. He released the stranglehold he had on his crotch, slowly opened his eyes, and turned back toward Davi.

Big mistake.

Davi had his arms crossed over his chest—fingers locked around the hem of his shirt, far-from-innocent stare locked on Lance. The wickedness in Davi's eyes would've been enough to break anyone's willpower.

"What are you doing?" Lance softly rasped.

"Putting on a private show. Isn't that what we do?"

God, yes!

With each step, Davi lifted his shirt a little higher, slowly revealing his firm abs and carved six-pack, his toned pecs and bronze flesh, his dark nipples and the hollow of his throat. Lance wanted to run his tongue over every square inch, starting with the thick veins running along the perfect V at Davi's torso, then moving up to the rippling ridge of his jaw.

Damn, I have to have him.

"Don't," Lance said with little conviction.

"Why?"

"Because."

"That is no answer, Lance. Why do you want me to stop?"

"Because I can't say no anymore."

"Then don't say no," Davi said as he stepped forward.

27

AFTER ALL the dancers left, Jason grabbed his backpack and climbed on his bicycle to head home. Instead of whisking his way west through the French Quarter, he headed east toward the banks of the Mississippi River, toward the Riverwalk and the riverboats, toward the tourist traps and places he avoided during normal hours. He hated those places when the happy, ambling masses milled about with their cameras and pamphlets. They spoiled the sanctity of those quiet spots, but when those bubbly, excited tourists were gone and the wee hours of the morning crept in, places like the Riverwalk were Jason's favorite spots to sit and quietly reflect on where he was in life and what he had going on.

He laid his bike down on the cobblestones, then sat down beside it. Dew seeped into the fibers of his jeans and left a thin layer of moisture on his skin. He didn't mind, though. It wasn't like he would melt or anything, and he could always shower when he got home. Right now, he just wanted to sit and quietly think about the unexpected turns his life had taken.

The Mississippi River was calmer than usual. Even the wind gusting off the bank was nothing more than a faint, cold rustling of air. The normal noise from the city behind him faded into the low din of a few moving cars and happily chirping birds. In front of him, the sky had begun turning light blue, waiting for the golden glow of the sun ascending the horizon.

Do I still love Jansen?

He frowned the moment the question popped into his head. It came from out of nowhere, or maybe it had stayed in the back of his mind, patiently waiting for a quiet second of Jason's time. After all, it was a pretty weighty subject, not something to be tossed around with the normal day-to-day—between changing diapers and making out schedules.

Technically, a part of Jason still did love Jansen, very much loved him, but there were so many different flavors of love… not just vanilla. His feelings for Jansen were more sherbet—light and fun and refreshing, like best friends, not lovers, and nothing at all like what he felt for Brad. The sexy blue-eyed reporter definitely had a firm lock on Jason's heart. No doubt about it.

Then, why are you sitting here now? Why aren't you home with him?

Sighing, he pulled his bent knees up to his chest, spine bowing as he hugged his legs tight to his body. He picked up a tiny sliver of cobblestone and pitched it out into the water. It didn't skip along the surface, but he was never good at that, anyway. Not that it mattered. Skipping rocks was something to do with his hands while his mind raced ninety-to-nothing.

The timing for all this uncertainty was horrible, what with the stress of wanting to save the club and Brad's wonderful, romantic proposal. He'd known marrying Brad was the right thing to do until Jansen had showed up at his door. So, where the hell was it coming from? Nothing in his personal life had changed. He'd been playing family man with Brad for two years and everything had been going perfectly fine. So why now? Why question his heart after saying he would marry Brad?

Whoa. Maybe that was it. Maybe he'd said yes to the proposal but he wasn't really ready to commit on that level. Did he actually see his life and what was left of his youth slipping away from him now that his partner wanted to tie the knot?

"Jesus Christ, Jason, get your shit together."

He sat there for a few more minutes, skipping rocks and watching the faint rippling of water along the shore, before he decided it was time to go home and either tell Brad the wedding needed to wait or be the best possible partner Brad could hope for and go full steam ahead with their plans of becoming a married couple. Jason needed to face his worries and the possibility he still had very real feelings for Jansen he needed to address.

Heading west back toward the house he shared with his partner and the child they had part-time, Jason tried to keep his head screwed on as straight as he could. It took maybe forty-five minutes to get across the Quarter, and two and a half minutes to lock up his bike and head into the house.

In the living room, bins of toys were all set in their proper places. Brad had bought one of those bench things with the baskets underneath so Hope could have her things and the house would still look masculine and sleek. The lack of hard plastic to step on meant the baby was probably back with her mother, but Jason would check the nursery on the way to the bedroom just to be certain.

He was pleased to find the room dark and the bed empty. Not that he didn't adore that little girl and consider her a daughter, but he truly needed a little one-on-one time with his partner, unrestrained one-on-one time. He didn't want to be quiet because a kid was in the next room. He didn't want to hurry up because she might wake up. He wanted to let go and make love like they used to, like they had the night Brad proposed, like the spark was still very much alive and not fleeting, not sated in a few short hours spent in a hotel room.

Without bothering to turn on the lights, Jason began stripping out of his clothes. He tossed his damp jeans in a corner near the closet. His shirt and underwear promptly followed. He stood there naked, staring at the imprint of his sleeping lover's body in the comforter. Was Brad completely naked under there, or was the bare shoulder peeking out from the edge of the blanket just a tease?

As soon as he pressed his knee to the bed and the mattress dipped, Brad shifted and groaned. His long blond lashes fluttered and he slowly opened his eyes. He parted his lips, then curled them into a sleepy grin.

"You're home," he said quietly. "I was wondering when you'd get here."

"Were you waiting for me?"

"I'm always waiting for you."

Brad sat up in the bed and the comforter rolled down his chest. It settled across his lap. Unfortunately, though, he wasn't naked as Jason had hoped he would be. Once upon a time, he would've been. Probably would've been half-hard too.

Disappointment rolled through Jason. He hoped he managed to keep the feeling from showing in his expression. Whether he succeeded, he didn't know.

"So how did work go?" Brad asked.

Sigh.

"Can we not talk about work right now?"

"Okay...."

"I want to make love to you."

"Oh...."

Oh? Really? That's all you got?

Jason sat down on his side of the bed—the place where his pillows always waited for him, his side of the great divide, with his own nightstand and a book lying facedown and opened to the center. They had actually become *that* couple, and there was nothing sexy about it.

"What's wrong with us?" Jason finally asked.

"Wrong?" Brad frowned. "What do you mean?"

"I mean, we used to be this incredibly sexy couple that made love all the time. We used to go out together and we talked. When we got in bed, we couldn't keep our hands off each other. Besides that one night in the hotel room, we haven't made love in... in forever. What happened?"

Brad didn't immediately respond. He licked his pink lips and furrowed his blond brow. He was deep in thought already, and that question shouldn't have taken any thought. The answer should've been simple—absolutely nothing had happened, nothing had changed, they were still as in love with each other as they had always been.

"Brad?"

"I don't want to say the wrong thing here."

"Then how about you try just being honest?"

"Because it makes me sound like a tired old man," Brad said with a hint of nervous laughter. He turned toward Jason, reaching down to lock their hands. "Nothing has changed between us, I promise. I am still very in love with you and very attracted to you. I can't wait to call you my husband."

"Then why aren't we having sex anymore? Why does it seem like we never even hang out anymore? Why do I feel like a third wheel?"

"A third wheel to what? My kid?"

God, when he put it that way....

What the hell was Jason supposed to say to that? He felt like such an ass now.

"That's just great," Brad said as he clumsily hauled himself out of the bed.

The sheets were twisted around his legs and he stumbled a few times before he broke free, leaving a pile of white cotton on the floor behind him. He stormed out of the room, pounded through the house so hard his footfalls echoed along the wood floors and all the way back into the bedroom. Then the thudding stopped for a second. Two. Three. Four....

Jason was about to climb out of bed to go check on his partner when the thudding started coming his way again. The door flung open and Brad stood in the frame—arms crossed over his chest, face curled in a scowl. He looked angry, but not raging pissed. He looked hurt, but not devastated. He looked as though he was about to blow a gasket and Jason couldn't do much more than sit on the bed, stare and silently pray for... something.

Please don't let this be bad.

"You need to understand something," Brad said rather calmly. "My daughter is the most important person on this Earth to me. Not you. Not my ex-wife. I love you, but nothing... I mean *nothing* will ever change that. So if you feel like you're a third wheel, then maybe you should find someone who can make you a higher priority."

Brad spun on his heel and stormed right back out of the bedroom they'd been sharing every single night since they'd moved in together. The thunderous sound of the door clapping against the wood frame made Jason jump.

"Brad," he called out. Nothing. Not even the sound of angry stomping. The silent treatment hurt Jason's soul. His heart banged furiously against his rib cage, banging like an inmate on prison bars and begging to be set free because goddammit, his heart belonged to Brad. Always.

It was that moment when Jason realized how much he truly did love Brad, and how his life was made better just by having Brad in it. He might've loved Jansen. Hell, he might still love Jansen, but it wasn't the same. Jansen didn't have his heart. Jason had made the right decision in saying yes to Brad. He'd made the right decision in coming home. Brad was the one who made his heart pitter-patter, even if it had taken a fight to make him realize the grass was perfectly green right there in his own backyard.

"Brad," he said again, this time climbing down from the bed so he could find his partner, and he did. Brad was sitting on the couch with his elbows propped against his knees and his face buried in his palms. His shoulders were rounded in defeat.

"I'm sorry," Jason whispered. Brad raised his head. "I'm sorry for being an ass." He knelt down in front of Brad and took his partner's hands in his. "We just… we're not like we were. You tell me all the time how much you love me, and you proposed to me, but I…. Well, I guess I was afraid, you'd…." Jason lowered his head.

"Afraid I would what?" Brad asked. "Cheat on you?"

Damn, was that what this really boiled down to? Or was he afraid they would cheat on each other?

"I don't know what I thought, Brad. I want what we had. Is that so horrible?"

"No. It's not, but"—Brad pulled Jason's hands to his lips—"we have a kid with us all the time now. It's impractical to think we can fuck all over the house."

"And she's gone now…."

"And she's only been gone for about eight hours. I slept for three of those hours because I was hoping to be awake when you got home. I wanted to spend time with you."

Jason sighed and plopped back on his ass. He let Brad keep his hands, though. "I went down to the Riverwalk and just… sat for a little while. I've had a lot on my mind and I just needed a little peace." Now was the time to do the right thing and be perfectly honest. If he couldn't tell the man he planned on marrying the truth, that didn't say much for their relationship. Did it? "There was some… weirdness between me and Jansen when I saw him earlier."

"Weirdness?" Brad arched his brow.

"Yeah, I"—Jason licked his dry lip—"I think he still loves me."

"Oh."

While Brad might've managed to keep a stoic expression on his face, the waving of his throat when he swallowed gave away just how bad the hit felt.

Damn it all to hell.

"So um"—Brad swallowed again—"do you… still love Jansen?"'"

"In a purely friendly way." Jason tilted his head so he could lock on Brad's downcast gaze. "You have my heart. Completely. Any doubt I had about that was gone the minute you walked away from me and I hurt more than I ever have in my life."

"Yeah?" Brad's head rose again. There was something resembling relief in his cool blue eyes. As though he hadn't expected Jason to say those words, like he was waiting for the worst and hoping for the best.

"Yeah," Jason softly responded as he leaned in for a kiss.

28

"JUST FUCK me already," Lance rasped. Davi's lips were firmly planted at the side of his throat, toying and nipping, and making his skin raw. Davi had his hand wrapped tight around Lance's cock. The pumping and pulling had roused him to the point of subtle pain a long time ago, but apparently Davi was more into teasing than pleasing.

"How do you want this, Lance? Slow and tender? Hot and rough? Do you want me to make love to you or do you want me to fuck you?"

Christ Almighty, when he put it that way, and in that spicy accent....

Lance was just about to tell Davi every dirty damn thing he wanted when that pesky angel on his shoulder stopped him. This wasn't about getting off, it reminded him. This was about giving something to Davi he'd never been brave enough to give to anyone else—a piece of his heart.

He cupped Davi's cheek and the beautiful man raised his head. Their gazes met and Lance took a moment to pray to God this didn't end up hurting him. Another heartbreak, especially from Davi, Lance knew he wouldn't survive.

He licked his lips and softly said, "I want slow and tender. I want... I want to make love."

That must've been exactly what Davi wanted to hear, because he pulled back and wrapped his hands over Lance's hips. He walked Lance backward toward the bed and gently sat him down on the edge, still keeping their gazes locked. He knelt and dragged one soft hand down the outside of Lance's leg, lifted it, and placed his lips on the inside of Lance's ankle.

His kisses were slow and deliberate, hitting every single sensitive spot— the side of his calf, the side of his knee, his inner thigh. Davi exhaled a warm breath as he passed over Lance's groin, and the feel of it sent tingles rippling along Lance's spine. His back arched as he lay on the bed and spread his legs for whatever Davi wanted to do. He was surprisingly disappointed when the kisses picked back up on the other thigh. How he wished Davi would've lowered that sweet mouth of his over his cock. But the disappointment came to an abrupt end when he felt Davi's warm hand on his shaft again.

A low moan rippled up through his body. Every nerve came alive, completely aware and completely ready for the love they were about to make. Even his sac was ready to deliver a pearly white gift into Davi's delicate hand.

"God, this is the best kind of torture," Lance whispered.

"Torture?" Davi frowned. "Torture is no good, sim?"

"Oh no, not this kind of torture. It's incredible." Lance reached down and stroked his fingers through Davi's long black hair. "There's lube and condoms in the nightstand. Why don't you get that for us?"

Davi nodded and rose to his feet.

As he walked around the corner of the bed, Lance watched the movement of muscle and the dimpling of Davi's glorious ass. He couldn't remember ever seeing a set of cheeks so perfect, and the bronze of Davi's skin made the sight even more heavenly. It sure beat the hell out of the old men he'd been fucking for too many years to bother counting.

Yes, change is good... very good.

Far too soon, Davi turned back around and he had a bottle of lube in one hand, a little silver square in the other, and a pleased grin on his face. He tossed the bottle of lube onto the bed beside Lance; then he took his place between Lance's thighs again. Only this time, he stayed on his feet.

"Put this on me," he said, tone firm, as he placed the tiny package in Lance's palm.

There was something wicked in Davi's eyes, something hot and completely lewd. For whatever reason, in that split second of seeing the truth behind Davi's stare, something changed in Lance. Normally, he wouldn't have cared how much or how little someone wanted to use him. Normally, he would've gone with whatever was given, but he couldn't this time. The mere thought of Davi using him for sex hurt. Whether it was true or not. Even if Davi had been acting as though he wanted more with Lance for a while now. This still felt wrong.

He curled his fingers around the condom and averted his stare. It was too much to keep looking Davi in the eyes right now. "I can't do this," Lance said softly. "I can't pretend this is only sex. It's not for me."

"Who said it was just sex for me?"

Surprise. Lance arched his brow as his stare darted right back up to Davi's big brown puppy-dog eyes. "It's not?"

"No." Davi lifted Lance's chin ever so tenderly. He brushed his soft thumb over Lance's slightly parted lips. "I like you. You've been kind to me. People aren't kind to me. They're... I do not know the word." Davi frowned. "Crude?"

Lance waffled his head back and forth, weighing the word, considering the meaning. "Sounds about right," he finally said.

"So, let us make love, *meu lindo*."

That beautiful, pouty expression of his did Lance in. He would've given Davi anything he wanted right then and there. He brought the condom up to his mouth and put the tip between his teeth, ripped open the package, and set the rubber free. With one hand around the base of Davi's shaft, Lance pinched the tip of the condom and fit it over the head of Davi's thick, fully hard cock. He rolled the rubber down slowly, applying just enough pressure to make Davi feel the gentle stroking. When it was settled into place, Lance reached down beside him and grabbed the bottle of lube, then handed it over to Davi.

"Slide back for me," Davi whispered, and Lance did as he was told.

He felt Davi spreading his legs again. He heard the lube being squeezed out of the bottle. He felt fingertips brushing along the insides of his thighs and warm breaths flutter along his sac and his shaft. Then the fingers slid down the valley of his cheeks. Lance closed his eyes so his body could enjoy the feel of what Davi was doing without the temptation of actually watching.

There was now a slight pressure on his hole. One lubed finger slid inside him, then a second. Davi was the only lover he'd ever had to treat his body so tenderly. Sex had usually consisted of a whole lot of praying the lube did the job or the cock wasn't too big. He liked this change. He loved the fact Davi cared enough to do something so intimate.

Davi scissored his fingers open and closed, open and closed again. As if that didn't feel amazing enough, Lance felt something warm and moist glide down his shaft. The head of his cock hit the narrow opening in the back of Davi's throat. Then Davi's tongue swirled around and around, lapping at the sensitive vein, toying with the ridge, and tracing lines along the length of his cock. It took everything he had not to come in Davi's mouth. He even bit down on his own bottom lip, hoping the pain would take the focus off the tug in his sac. It didn't work.

"Davi, I'm about to…."

Obviously Davi knew exactly what those four words were a prelude to, because his tongue worked faster and his mouth pumped harder. He took Lance from head to hilt and back again, and on the last thrust, Lance lost his composure and his release filled Davi's mouth. He milked Lance for every single drop, and when he finished, Davi raised his head and moved up Lance's body with startling quickness.

Their mouths locked. Lance tasted the bitterness of release on Davi's lips and his tongue, and holy shit if that wasn't the hottest thing he'd ever experienced. And the moment they became caught up in the kiss, the moment Davi's tongue dipped deeper into Lance's mouth, he began easing his cock into Lance's hole, and the smooth glide of it felt like heaven on Earth.

He knotted his fingers in Davi's thick hair, keeping his hold loose enough so not to hurt him and tight enough to hold his lover to the kiss. Their tongues twisted and their bodies danced. Davi rolled his hips slowly, sliding inch after thick inch into Lance's channel, then pulling back until the ridge of his cock met the ring of muscle, then dipping back in again. Every single stroke was an art form. Davi's rhythm was unlike anything Lance had ever felt before.

His legs were locked around Davi's waist, heels pressed hard into his lover's firm cheeks. Lance used the hold to leverage himself, raising his ass just enough to give Davi more depth. The change in position drove Davi deeper into him, brought their bodies closer together, and put a hell of a lot more passion into the kiss.

"You feel so damn good," Lance rasped against Davi's mouth. "Don't stop. Please. Don't stop."

As soon as Davi's hips started moving faster, Lance's sac tightened and the pressure in the base of his cock became painful. He was so close, oh so close, and he wanted to paint his pleasure all over Davi's beautiful chest just so he could lick it all off when they were done. The idea of having that gorgeous body and that wonderful heart beneath him while he trailed kisses along Davi's dark flesh was an amazing fantasy—one he planned to make come true very soon.

"I'm about to… to…."

Lance's eyes rolled back in his head as the pressure rushed down his shaft. His fingers knotted in Davi's hair tighter. His legs gripped Davi's body, heels bearing down into that sweet ass. He threw his head back and growled into the air as his orgasm pulled up from his sac and shot straight through his cock, and when he finally had the wherewithal to open his eyes again, he found Davi mopping his pearly gift from one nipple with his finger.

"You taste?" Davi asked, holding his jizz-crowned forefinger up to Lance's lips.

"Oh, yeah, I'll taste," Lance said before pulling the whole damn digit into his mouth. He sucked away the bitter remnants of their sex, but kept it on his tongue so when he got that kiss, Davi would taste him too.

29

IN THE faint swirls on the ceiling above their bed, Jansen's mind painted many pictures, mostly of the time spent with Dorian before the cops had hauled him off to jail. But the moment he considered Dorian being under the same roof now and how he still felt alone, his mind went back to that dark and lonely place. He remembered all those agonizing nights he'd spent praying and begging and praying some more for his husband's return. Funny how his prayers had been answered but he didn't really feel any relief.

Occasionally, Jansen slipped into other thoughts. He briefly wondered what life would've been like had he hooked up with Jason rather than Dorian. Sure, the obvious would be different. They'd probably still be sharing a shitty apartment with shitty furniture and not have a dime to their names, but would the love be different? Would Jason have loved him more than Dorian? Would life have been easier? Would they have gone as far as settling down and marrying each other?

It didn't really matter now. Jason was the past and Dorian was the future. And hopefully the wall between them would come crumbling down and things would go back to being what they were.

He could hope anyway.

Holding on to hope seemed a hell of a lot easier said than done. Things felt so damn different now, though. Even the sex had been different. Not bad. Just different. There wasn't any love in it. It'd felt like fucking just for the sake of getting off, and not just because it was hot and rough and greedy, but because Dorian didn't seem to be there during the act itself. He was somewhere else, mind far away from their bedroom, heart....

Jesus Christ, don't think that way.

Jansen rolled over and found Dorian still sound asleep. He lay on his back with his arms crossed over his chest, just as he'd been when he'd lain down earlier that night. Even the way he slept was different now. He slept like a convict, as though he was waiting and ready to wake up and jump right into a fight. Jansen wondered when Dorian last slept—truly rested without fear of having his life taken from him, and with that thought, Jansen couldn't bring himself to disturb whatever sleep his husband might've found in those few hours since their sex together had ended.

He eased out of the bed, careful not to jostle the mattress so he wouldn't accidently wake Dorian. He sneaked out of the room, slowly closing the door behind him and he padded down the stairs and into the living room.

Now, what to do with himself?

It was still very dark outside—too dark for morning and too light for night. Jansen wondered about the time, but wasn't curious enough and didn't care enough to check it. By his guess, it was sometime just before dawn, and if he was lucky, he could sit out on the back patio and watch the sun come up over the line of trees.

He grabbed the shirt he'd left lazily hanging on the banister on the way up to their room last night and pulled it over his head, then tugged it down until it met the waistband of the silky sleep pants he'd put on after the sex he'd had. Then he headed out to the patio.

He took a seat on one of the plush chaise lounges at the edge of the patio and settled in to stare up at the sky. There would've been room for another body on that chair. Oh, how he wished another warm body was beside him, one to hold him and tell him all this shit was his imagination, that Dorian hadn't changed and they were just as happy as they'd always been.

As if God himself had been listening, a warm breath brushed over the crown of his head, and he looked up to find his husband leaning down behind him. Dorian had a kind but worried smile on his face, with the warmth in his eyes Jansen had missed so badly, as if those few hours of sleep had completely transformed him. He kissed the crown of Jansen's head.

"What are you doing out here?" he asked, reaching down and around to cradle Jansen's face with his thick, warm hand. He stroked his thumb over Jansen's cheek.

"I don't know." Jansen sighed. "I couldn't sleep. Thought I would watch the sunrise."

"Alone?"

"I didn't want to wake you up. You looked... peaceful." *Not really.*

"I wasn't." Dorian slipped around the lounger and eased down beside Jansen. Now the seat was good and cramped, like sardines in a tin can, but Jansen didn't mind it one bit. Dorian pulled him against his body, Jansen's back cradled in the curve of Dorian's chest. He held on tight, really tight, as though he was afraid of losing Jansen. "It's just... weird bein' back home again. I was beginnin' to think I'd never get outta that place. Not alive, anyway."

"Well, you *are* out of that place and you're alive, so...."

"I know. I know." Dorian pressed his lips to Jansen's temple. Jansen could hear him taking slow, deep breaths. It seemed as though Dorian could only breathe deeply if Jansen was in his arms. Any other time, his chest looked tense, constricted or... or something.

Jansen sighed. "Do you want me to come back to bed with you?"

"I wanna make love to you."

God, not again. It was so bad the first time.

"I wanna do it right," Dorian added. "I wanna *make love*, not... not what we did earlier."

Jansen hadn't known Dorian was aware of just how off everything had felt during their first romp after his release from OPP. He thought Dorian had become incapable of making the sweet, caring, tender love they'd always made before he'd become a hardened convict. Jansen had thought, at least for the near future, he wouldn't have the man he'd fallen so madly in love with.

A hand eased between Jansen's thighs, fingertips brushing soft fabric against his sac. His eyes fluttered and a soft purr rippled up through his body. Without thought, he opened his legs wide enough for Dorian's hand to have full access to whatever Dorian wanted. Already, *this* was different.

Dorian drew his hand upward, putting gentle pressure on Jansen's groin. The shift of soft fabric against his shaft and the slight weight of Dorian's hand felt incredible, much like being touched by a lover for the first time. It was exciting and curious, breath stealing even. Dorian slipped his hand inside Jansen's sleep pants, down farther, farther, farther until the tips of his fingers put pressure on his hole.

"Tell me ya want me to make love to ya," Dorian whispered. The spice in his bayou accent made his words so much sexier. And his warm breath against Jansen's jawline only added heat to the fire.

"I want you to make love to me," Jansen said, begging for whatever attention Dorian intended to give him. The words came out in an airy rush.

He felt one fingertip slip inside him. It moved in and out—oh so slowly, oh so teasingly. Jansen's head rolled back against the lounger, eyes closed but just barely, lips parted enough for Dorian to claim if he wanted to. His body was ready for Dorian, ready for the heat and the lust and the hunger, and whatever else Dorian had to give.

Dorian slowly moved his thick finger—in deep, out to the first knuckle, in again, out, in, out. He picked up the pace, but wasn't moving fast. He kept his eyes trained on Jansen as he pumped his finger a little deeper and a little faster. Genuine love filled his stare—nothing but adoration, reverence, and all the wonderful things that made love what it was. Jansen couldn't remember the last time Dorian had looked at him like that, and he hadn't known how badly he missed it until he saw that heartfelt expression again.

"I love you," Jansen whispered, or he thought he whispered because Dorian never responded. Maybe the words never left his lips. Maybe the sound had been nothing more than him taking a breath. Who knew? At this point,

Jansen was so far gone in the feel of Dorian's hands and fingers he couldn't distinguish a moan from a word.

The second finger slipped inside his hole and he parted his lips in a gasp. Dorian began gently pumping, scissoring, stretching, readying him in a much more loving, tender way than he had the first time around.

A small whimper escaped Jansen's lips as he curled against Dorian's chest. He closed his eyes and took slow, deep breaths. Sure, they'd had sex once already, but there was so much more in Dorian's touch—more care, more gentleness, more everything, and Jansen wanted it this time.

"How 'bout we go back inside," Dorian said, lips brushing against Jansen's jaw. "I wanna do this the right way."

Be still my beating heart.

Jansen nodded and Dorian retracted his fingers. He settled Jansen's sleep pants back into place, then stood from the chair and offered Jansen his hand. Without hesitating for even a second, Jansen took it and Dorian helped him to his feet.

Walking back into the mansion this time was like moving through a dream. Dorian had always been a hardass, and frugal as hell with his feelings. He didn't give away much and never really let anyone in—even Jansen, whom he'd been married to for a few years—but now Jansen was truly seeing the softer side of the man he'd fallen in love with. Yes, he'd seen the romantic lover, but not the tender man who held his hand, who guided him up the stairs and to the bedroom.

Had being in jail really broken Dorian Grant?

"Dorian?"

"Mhm," he mumbled as he closed the bedroom door behind them.

"Are you okay?"

"Sure. Why?" Dorian frowned, thick brows burrowing deep between his dark eyes.

"Just making sure." Jansen tried shrugging it off. "I worry. That's all."

"Stop worrying," Dorian said rather bluntly as he laid his flattened hand over Jansen's sternum. The web where his thumb met his forefinger rested at the hollow of Jansen's throat, and Dorian guided him back toward the bed. A wicked gleam filled his eyes.

The back of Jansen's knees hit the edge of the mattress and buckled him backward. His ass hit the billowing blankets first, but Dorian wasn't satisfied. He kept easing Jansen down, climbing onto one knee at a time until he had wedged himself between Jansen's thighs and practically pinned him to the mattress.

There was something very predatory in the way Dorian moved, something hungry and lustful, but when he lowered his head and pressed their mouths together, it was kind and giving, and one of their most passionate kisses. It brought back the fireworks and the things that made Jansen fall so hard for him. It erased the worry and the fear that maybe they were losing touch with each other.

Dorian's tongue delved deep inside Jansen's mouth and explored him thoroughly as their lips met in a dance much like the ebb and flow of an ocean current, caressing and teasing, pushing forward and pulling back. Every single sound they made, every moan and whimper, vibrated their lips.

"Make love to me," Jansen whispered into the kiss. "Please, make love to me."

Dorian ground himself into Jansen, hard cock to hard cock. The only thing separating them was thin sleep pants. Jansen reached out and tried to cop a feel, but Dorian stopped him with one strong hand locked around his wrist.

"No touching. I'm making love to you. I'm pleasing *you*."

Oh, that'll be easy. Not.

What could Jansen do, other than nod and comply?

That made Dorian a very happy man.

He rose to his feet and stood between Jansen's legs, looking down with the same cocky, pleased stare that was the signature of Dorian Grant, and God, what a turn-on. Jansen propped himself up on his elbows so he could watch Dorian's body move. He saw two big hands going for his hips, and the talented fingers attached hooked his pants. Dorian kept his gaze locked with his lover's as he slowly slipped the fabric down Jansen's thighs, down his legs, over his feet.

He assumed Dorian would reach for the lube and fucking would commence shortly. That was the way of things, routine, and somehow not completely routine. Dorian would change up location and position every now and again, but everything else remained pretty much the same.

Not now.

Dorian knelt at Jansen's feet and locked his hands around Jansen's legs. He gently pulled, easing his husband closer to the edge of the bed. Jansen was going to ask him what he was doing, but before he could utter a word, he felt a warm set of lips at his inner thigh.

Tingles rippled down his spine. Dorian's lips moved farther up his leg, farther, farther. His kisses caressed Jansen's sac, and with a hard moan, Jansen threw his head back. Dorian was giving him a blowjob. Dorian never, *ever* went down on him. Ever. It was almost too good to be true.

"Don't stop."

30

THIS SATURDAY morning wasn't spent watching cartoons or chasing after a toddler. Thank God. Not to say Jason didn't love family time, but he needed more intimate time with his partner. Quiet time. Romantic time. Something that didn't involve yelling over a screaming child or stepping on toys left on the floor.

They slept in as much as either of them could stand. The natural light spilling in through the bedroom window roused them, or maybe it had more to do with their bodies knowing they didn't need to sleep so late. Either way, they grumbled in unison and shifted in tandem, but instead of rolling away from each other to climb out of bed, they rolled toward each other to meet in a chaste kiss.

"Good morning, Mr. Britt," Jason said with a sleepy-eyed smile.

"Mmm...." Brad dragged his hand over his face. "What time is it?"

"Who knows? Who cares? We can stay here for a little while longer and it won't hurt a soul."

"We both have to work today."

"Yeah, later this afternoon."

"Then it's still morning?" Brad peeled open one eye. A playful grin tugged at his perfect pink lips.

Their mouths connected and for a moment, everything in the world just stopped. Only the two of them existed—no nightclub drama, no late-breaking news, no screaming toddler and no ex-wife, no beloved friend. He could've stayed lost in that kiss all damn day, could've skipped greeting the Earth and its dwellers just to keep that magical feeling alive a little longer. Responsibilities and everything that came with being an adult ended the serenity of the moment, and it came crashing down with the ringing of one of their phones from the nightstand

"Is it mine?" Brad hesitantly asked.

Jason looked over his shoulder and found the white iPhone with the dark blue case lit up like a Christmas tree. Upon closer look, he saw Brad's ex-wife's name on the screen. While she'd been really great about letting Brad see the baby, and the relationship her ex-husband had with Jason, right now, he wanted to strangle that woman. Could they not just have one day—one freaking day—to themselves?

"It's Melody." Jason rolled back toward Brad without bothering to pick up the phone. "If it's important, she'll leave a message."

Sighing, Brad reached across him and wrenched the device up in his grip. He had it to his ear before Jason could stop him.

"You want me to keep Hope today?"

Jason groaned and plopped back down against the pillows.

"I can't. Jason and I both have to work today. We just woke up and—" Brad abruptly stopped speaking. A sigh followed, and then he closed his eyes and scrubbed at his face again. "Okay. Okay. How about when I get off work? I'm covering this huge fundraiser for one of the parish churches today. I *have* to be there. This is my job, after all."

Jesus Christ, he's really standing up to her.

"Fine. Just meet me over in Marrero. I can call you when I'm done."

He ended the call and pitched the phone toward the end of the bed; then he fell back against the pillows but kept his stare on the ceiling.

"If I didn't love my daughter so much...."

Brad didn't finish the sentence, not that he needed to. Jason knew how much Brad loved his kid and couldn't—wouldn't—ever fault him for that, but sometimes that ex-wife of his....

"I'm taking a shower. Supposed to be meeting the guys at the club." Jason pushed up from the bed. "We're rehearsing our numbers for the closing show."

"Give me a minute and I'll join you," Brad said.

"No." Jason held up one hand. "Just... stay in bed for a while longer. Sounds like you're going to need your rest."

Jason turned back toward the bathroom, but Brad saying a soft, "I'm sorry," stopped him.

"Don't be. I knew what I was getting into when I fell in love with you. Nothing is going to make me stop loving you, I promise. Now, get some rest."

31

SUNLIGHT POURED in through the curtains. Lance couldn't believe he'd forgotten to close them. He never forgot. But if the warmth against his cheek was any indication of what had happened last night—or rather, the wee hours of the morning—he had a good reason to forget.

Davi's chest rose and fell as he took quiet little breaths. Light snores rumbled in his chest. Normally, Lance hated hearing people snore. It annoyed him so much that, even though the old men who fucked him invited him to stay the night, he never did and never wanted to. With Davi though, the sound was welcome, like a lullaby. He could listen to those light noises all night.

Swallowing back the lump pushing up in his throat, Lance slipped out from under the blankets draped over his waist, threw his legs over the edge of the mattress, and eased out of the bed, hopefully without shaking it enough to wake Davi. He stole a glance back. His beautiful lover was still sound asleep. Thank. God.

It wasn't that he didn't want to see Davi right now. Lance just abhorred postcoital anything—talking, cuddling, making out... *sleeping*. Even if a very, very small part of him would've loved staying in that bed with Davi, he refused to do it. He could own some of the feelings, like caring and wanting to take care, but anything more was strictly off-limits. *For now.*

Why the hell did he have to go and step into a teeming pile of complicated feelings?

Boy, he was a lucky SOB.

Not.

He padded over to the kitchen, more precisely, to the coffeemaker that had been on autopilot since the day he'd bought it. The tank was normally full and the grounds waiting patiently to serve up a big ol' pot of Community Coffee. Not today, though. Just like the curtains, he'd forgotten to handle this business last night as well.

He fumbled the filters and fumbled the grounds, fumbled the water and fumbled the buttons. Somehow, though, probably through divine intervention, he got the coffee going. He became so lost in the *drip drip drip,* he didn't hear the footsteps closing in behind him. In fact, it wasn't until two arms wrapped around him and two lips pressed to his shoulder that his attention was stolen from the fountain of liquid joy.

"Shit!" Lance nearly jumped out of his skin.

Davi chuckled softly. "I did not mean to scare you.'

Dearest God in heaven, that accent is just as hot filled with the gravely noise of sleep.

Lance turned his head enough to press a quick kiss to Davi's upper arm. "I'm making coffee," he muttered, relaxing in his lover's hold.

"Then I shall cook breakfast."

"But you—"

Before Lance had a chance to tell him he didn't need to cook, Davi had begun digging through the cabinets, looking for God only knew what, and frankly, Lance couldn't be certain the eggs and bacon in his fridge were still good.

With a sigh, he sat down on one of the barstools and propped his elbows on the tiny island. Davi moved through his kitchen—stark naked and as beautiful as a New Orleans sun rising over the Mississippi River—as though he'd been there before. He found the skillets and found the bakeware, not that there was much to choose from. Lance didn't fancy himself a cook and survived on fast food and booze more than anything. Surprisingly, though, Davi managed.

He lost himself in the thought of waking up to breakfast every morning, or going to bed with a man he cared about after devouring a home-cooked meal. The idea wasn't as horrifying as he thought it would be. In fact, if he was honest with himself, he would admit to liking the idea… as long as the man on the other end was Davi. He couldn't imagine wanting anyone else.

Eventually, Lance's cute little daydream came with a soundtrack and scents that hadn't been there before. The music he heard was his lover humming something foreign, something low and somber but somehow beautiful and romantic. The aroma reminded Lance of Sunday mornings from his childhood, waking up with his family to prepare for church.

"All finished."

Well *that* voice wasn't from his childhood.

A plate was slid in front of his face. Heat rose, filled with the smell of fried eggs and bacon, toast, and coffee. He wasn't used to being waited on but couldn't say he didn't like it. Davi scooped up a bite of egg and slipped it inside Lance's mouth. Lance moaned around the fork as the buttery eggs slid over his tongue. The sound elicited a wider smile from Davi's utterly kissable lips.

The look on Davi's face was one of pure joy, as if he lived to serve and nothing made him happier. That made Lance wonder if that was the life Davi had lived back in Portugal, if he missed it… if he missed something or someone else enough to hop a flight back home on a whim.

"Is good, sim?" he asked.

"Very good," Lance said. He reached out and locked his fingers over Davi's hand. "Come around to this side of the counter, please."

Davi did, and when he leaned against the stool and settled in between Lance's legs, Lance took his hand again.

He quietly held on, not sure what he was doing or why he was holding Davi's hand. He knew he had something to say, something that needed to be eloquently worded and immaculately delivered. In his heart, he knew he was doing the right thing, thinking the right thing, feeling the right thing. In his heart, he knew if there was any *one* person for him, that one person stood right in front of him, and if he didn't say something soon, if he didn't make a move he'd lose his chance.

Lance brushed his thumb over Davi's knuckles. He couldn't bring himself to look into those sweet, innocent eyes. Even though he knew deep down inside he would never do anything to hurt Davi, he couldn't do it. Not being able to meet his lover's gaze had more to do with Lance's fear of rejection than it did with Davi.

Davi cupped Lance's chin.

"What is wrong?" he quietly asked.

"Nothing. Actually." Lance smiled softly. "For the first time in my life, everything feels right."

He finally lifted his head and gave Davi his most genuine smile, then took a deep breath. The composition of the words still wasn't right in his head, but the moment was perfect and he couldn't *not* do this now.

"I want to be with you," he said.

"But you—"

"No. Not just sex. I want to be with you, only you. I want you to move in with me, and if something happens to the club, I want to take care of you. You're not going back to Portugal. I need—no, I want you to stay here. I want you to stay in my life."

"You are certain of this?"

"Absolutely positive. I've never been more sure about anything in my life." He swallowed, nervousness getting the best of him. "Say you'll stay. Please, say you'll be with me."

"I will." Davi's grin widened. "I will be with you."

"Does that officially make us a couple?" Lance said, laughing softly because his nerves *had* gotten the best of him.

"Sim, I think it does."

"Good."

Lance pulled Davi as close as he could get him without having his new boyfriend in his lap. Their fingers remained tightly twisted as Lance pressed their lips together. There was nothing heated or sexual in the kiss, and yet it was one of the most passionate kisses he'd ever had. It made his heart beat faster, then slower, made him want to yell from the rooftops about how he'd finally found Mr. Right. It made him feel like he was floating. It was the kind of kiss great romances were made of and it marked the beginning of something too beautiful for words, something Lance never expected to find.

32

MORE THAN a week had passed since Dorian had been released from jail, and things finally seemed to be returning to normal. At night, when they slept, Dorian curled around Jansen's body protectively like he used to, not waiting flat on his back for someone to attack him in the middle of the night. They talked more, laughed more, hung out more. They even talked about making a surprise stop at Sin & Seduction for the Thursday night show... which led to another subject Jansen had yet to broach with his husband.

Staring down at his dinner, Jansen absently pushed green beans around on his plate as he thought about how to tell Dorian he planned to dance in Jason's big closing show. Dorian vehemently opposed Jansen dancing at Sin. He'd said he hated the idea of all those people touching his man. Only one set of hands belonged on Jansen's business. While having Dorian so possessive of him and his "business" was flattering, at times, Jansen hated the jealousy.

"You're quiet," Dorian said before wiping the food away from his mouth with an overpriced table linen. He folded the cloth in his lap, then reached for his glass of wine. "Everything okay?"

"I have a lot on my mind," Jansen responded. He scooped the green bean he'd been playing with into his mouth, chewed, and swallowed.

"Like?" Dorian arched a brow.

"Sin & Seduction might be closing."

"What?"

Jansen nodded.

"When did this happen?"

"About a month ago, I guess." Shrugging, Jansen picked up his glass of wine and took a long sip. He didn't savor it like the enthusiasts did. It was nothing more than a means to wet his suddenly dry mouth. "Jason told me while you were still in jail."

"Jason," Dorian said flatly.

The conversation dragged to a stop. That wasn't the best way to approach this subject with Dorian. Even before the wedding, way back when Jansen and Dorian had first started dating, Dorian had decided he didn't care for Jason one bit, and apparently, he still hadn't changed his mind.

"Yes, Jason. He's trying to save the club."

"Well that's valiant of him."

"Valiant?" Jansen frowned. "Why valiant?"

Dorian laughed softly. "That club's a disaster. People know what goes on in there. Cops. Crooks. They all know. Why do ya think no one goes 'round that place anymore? Everyone's scared to death of gettin' busted."

"But it's always been like that...."

"Right, but the owners stopped payin' their 'dues.'" He air-quoted.

"Dues. Right. Well, none of the dancers want to see the club go." He paused, waiting for Dorian's rebuttal. When his husband didn't say anything, Jansen saw the quiet as a perfect opportunity to segue into the worst part of the plan to save the club. "He's putting on a show New Year's Eve. Bringing back all the old dancers."

Dorian laughed again. "Oh yeah?"

"Yeah." Dramatic pause. "I'm dancing."

And all the air was instantly sucked out of the room.

Dorian's jaw rippled, he clenched his teeth hard. His brown eyes darkened and his nostrils flared. Jansen could tell by the coloring of his knuckles that he was gripping the stem of the wineglass hard enough to break it. He didn't say a word, though. Just sat in his chair taking steady breaths and fuming from the ears.

"Say something," Jansen said. "I know you don't want me dancing there, but—"

"Then what's left to say?" Dorian let go of the glass, deposited the linen from his lap onto the table, and stood from his seat. "You're going to do the *one* thing I don't want you doing, and I'm not going to stop you because that'll make me an unloving asshole, right? Isn't that how it works?"

"No." Jansen rose to his feet. "I was hoping you would be supportive and come out to the show, maybe... I don't know. Dorian"—he took a step closer—"come watch me dance, and when it's done, I'll come up to the VIP booth and we can...."

Dorian exhaled and lowered his head. His jaw relaxed and he unclenched his fist. In a much softer voice, he said, "I love ya with everything I am, but I can't. I can't sit back and watch those people puttin' their hands on ya. I'll... I'll blow up, and I can't do that."

"Fine. Whatever." Jansen crossed his arms over his chest. "But I'm going to help my friend and you're not going to stop me."

"I didn't plan on it."

"Good."

Dorian didn't say a word.

Frustrated as hell, Jansen stormed by him and up the stairs to their master suite. He planned to just gather the shit he needed for tonight and hit the road before Dorian decided he wanted an argument, but when he swung back around with his trusted old duffel bag on his shoulder, Dorian was standing in the doorway looking like a little boy who'd lost his kitten. And dammit all to hell if that wasn't a heartbreaking sight.

"I'm still going," Jansen insisted, chin kicked up a little higher than normal, head cocked just enough to prove his resolve.

"I know ya are. Now, can ya drop the attitude for one second so I can talk to ya?"

"There's nothing to talk about."

"Isn't there?"

Jansen arched a brow, but didn't lose any of the "attitude" Dorian claimed he had. He stood stock-still, save for the slight tapping of his right foot against the floor. That was purely impatience and they both knew it. The tap, tap, tapping meant Dorian had better come with something damn good.

"So talk."

Dorian stepped inside the room and closed the door behind him. He sat down on the edge of the immaculately made king-sized bed they shared and patted the spot beside him. At first, Jansen refused to move, but then Dorian broke out his most heartfelt, pouty-eyed stare and put his big browns to work. Jansen couldn't resist when Dorian looked at him like that. He tried. Boy, did he try. He just couldn't help himself.

When he sat down next to Dorian, he kept his stare straight ahead, but from the corner of his eye, he saw the edge of Dorian's mouth lift in a pleased, sort of cocky, half-grin that he was apparently trying to restrain. Yes, he won. He broke Jansen's will. Big shocker, that one. Not.

"Like I said—"

"Talk. I know." Dorian reached down and wrapped his fingers around Jansen's hand and held on nice and tight, just in case Jansen got it into his head that he wanted to pull away. Dorian knew him so well. "What are the stipulations for saving the nightclub? Do you know?"

"I think he said he had to prove to the owners he could carry the club for an entire month."

"Okay. Makes sense, I guess." Dorian turned toward him. "I hate ya dancin' there. No surprise, right?" Jansen shrugged. "Well, we both love that place and I honestly don't wanna see it go. You don't wanna see it go. So how about I make a deal with ya?"

"I'm still dancing," Jansen insisted.

"I assumed."

"So what's the deal?"

"I'm gonna go with ya for the closin' show. I'm gonna be in the VIP booth, but I ain't watchin' ya dance. When you're done, we'll meet up there."

"What does that have to do with the club?"

"Nothin'… 'cept while you're dancin', I'll be negotiatin' with the owners to buy controllin' interest… for you… and your friend if ya want."

Jansen's eyes widened and his mouth gaped. "Are you serious?"

"Only if you're not gonna get mad," Dorian cautiously said.

"Why would I get mad?"

"I dunno."

The smile on Jansen's face grew so large the stretching of his mouth and the rise of his cheeks made his jaw hurt. He threw his arms around his husband's neck and planted one hell of a hard kiss on Dorian's lips. Jansen kissed him so deeply their mouths felt as though they could meld together.

Laughter erupted from the kiss. Dorian had the most beautiful grin on his ruggedly handsome face. He had the wonderfully lively sparkle in his eyes that Jansen had missed so much.

"I love you so much," Jansen whispered, lips touching lips.

"I love you too. Keep this thing about me buyin' stock in the club a secret. Even if the owners decide to let me do it, I don't want my name to sully what you guys are tryin' to do there. Understand what I'm sayin'?"

"I do. And I'll keep it a secret, but Dorian, you know how rumors spread there. It only takes one dancer finding out; then the whole freakin' world will know."

"So…." His brow creased hard. That look meant he was thinking of a way to do this without word getting out about his involvement. "If I'm a silent partner and you have control over the stock I buy, people will put two and two together. That won't work."

"What about Jason?"

"What about Jason?" Dorian countered, voice holding a bit of unnerving gravity.

"Put him in control of your share. He'll do the right thing. He loves that place. Always has. You just… you need to get over not liking him and trust me. Trust him."

Dorian didn't say anything, but he didn't have to. His silence meant he was actually thinking about it. Had he immediately launched into a roaring argument, then the suggestion would've been a no-go.

Nope, the silence was good.

33

The day before New Year's Eve

THE BED moved, but Lance didn't wake up. He was living in a dream right now—a Caribbean paradise, making love to a sexy Portuguese man under a palm tree with the ocean crashing against the seashore. Seagulls sang a song from a crystal-blue sky. Who would want to wake up from a dream like that?

Moments later he smelled freshly brewed coffee and the unmistakable scent of cooking bacon. He heard a voice singing from his kitchen and peeled open one eye. It was Davi singing, and Jesus Christ, that boy had an amazing voice. Whatever the song was, it was sung in Portuguese and Lance didn't understand the words, but it sounded a hell of a lot like a lullaby.

He sat up on the bed and wiped the sleep from his eyes, watching his lover move about the tiny kitchen with the kind of grace and form he'd only witnessed in Davi. And his sweet beauty was oblivious to his staring.

"What are you doing?" Lance asked from the edge of the bed.

"Is it not obvious?"

"Well, yeah." Lance rolled his eyes. "I meant… well, why are you up and cooking? Why aren't you still in bed?" *We were having sex on a beach for God's sake.* He stood and crossed the room and met Davi just as he rounded the edge of the island with a cup of black coffee. "I would've preferred you stay in bed with me a little longer," Lance said as the cup of joe was pushed into his hand.

"We cannot lie about in bed all day, Lance. There is much to do."

"Much to what?" Lance arched a brow.

"I have a plan." Davi grinned wide as he scooped a massive helping of eggs onto Lance's plate. "We're going to decorate the club. It needs to be regal. People should feel like royalty when they come see us dance. Sim?"

"Royalty?" Lance half laughed. "Do you realize what Sin & Seduction is? We're there to make them horny. The club is there to get them high. It's not about feeling important or regal, it's a place for them to do the shit they wouldn't do in their day-to-day lives."

"And that is the problem."

"Come again?"

"It's not a welcoming place." Davi added two pieces of toast and two slices of bacon to Lance's eggs, then slid the plate across the bar. He kept talking as he took to making one for himself. "People feel like criminals."

"Most of them are," Lance muttered around a forkful of eggs.

"See!" Davi wagged his pointer finger in Lance's direction. "That kind of thinking runs people away."

"Sweetie," Lance said as he laid his hand over Davi's. His lover raised those wonderfully innocent eyes of his. "Sin is an unsavory place filled with unsavory characters. It always has been, always will be. Our job is to entertain them. That's all."

"And that is the very reason the club is falling apart. Why can't we make them forget the bullshit for one night? Why can't we give them their dreams?"

Oh, but Lance had, hence the nice little nest egg he had tucked away.

"Trust me," Davi whispered. "On this, I know what I say."

"You know what you're talking about," Lance corrected with an amused grin.

"That's what I say."

They quietly finished their breakfast over talk of Davi's plans to decorate the bottom level of the club to have the same formal air as the VIP booths upstairs. The idea was to make everyone feel exactly like the rich people with overflowing pockets who wasted their money away on booze and cheap thrills. No one but Davi would've thought about something so simple. Every other dancer in the club seemed to be more out for themselves, and it'd been that way for as long as Lance could remember. At some point, it had truly stopped being about entertaining and welcoming everyone, and more about landing the richest possible man just so the dancers could have their own pockets lined.

Lance pressed his lips to Davi's cheek. "I think I love you," he said with a smile.

"I think I love you too."

Warmth spread through Lance's body. He couldn't remember the last time someone had said the big *L* word to him and actually meant it. Hell, he wasn't sure Davi meant it, but it felt good to hear.

"Join me in the shower?"

"But of course." Davi's grin widened.

The shower was quick but still sensual—little kisses stolen between massaging and bathing and shampooing. They took turns scrubbing each other's backs and washing each other's chests. Lance could admit the day had started off great, that having someone around when he woke up—someone to eat with and someone to shower with—made the world feel like a brighter, happier place. He could admit to liking his new status, and definitely admit to falling for Davi. And if today was any indication of how the rest of his life would end up being, he'd take it in a heartbeat.

They climbed out of the shower, dried off, and quickly tossed on some clothes suitable for work—something loose, but not hazardous and not favored, something already virtually ruined. They each wore a pair of nylon workout pants and a plain white T-shirt, sneakers, and a messy coiffure atop their heads.

Clean, dressed, and ready to go, they hauled down the stairs and around to the back door of the club. It was still early in the afternoon and the only car in the back lot belonged to the DJ. *Perfect*, Lance thought. Not only could they surprise their colleagues, but they'd have a little music to work to.

"I have an idea," Lance said, grabbing Davi's hand. With an enthusiasm he didn't have before, he dragged his lover back through the club to a far corner no one ever really went to unless they had something less than ethical on their minds. It was a storeroom, long forgotten by the likes of the dancers. The busboy would frequent that darkened hole to retrieve bottles of booze, but other than that, it was pretty much abandoned.

"What are we doing?" Davi asked.

"You'll see. Just trust me."

Lance reached inside the little room and blindly felt around on the wall until his hand brushed over the light switch. He flipped it on and the room came to life. The fluorescent lighting above flickered and choked for a moment before settling down enough to light up the closet. It was a huge room—shelves full of booze to the right, racks of old worn-out costumes to the left. But in the very back, beyond temptation and passing fads, was a small mountain of goodies ranging from Christmas lights to table linens, papier-mâché palm trees, and plastic coconuts to balloons and confetti.

Davi went inside first. His eyes lit up like the Fourth of July. "This is perfect," he gasped.

The pure joy on his face gave Lance a warm and fuzzy feeling. Who knew seeing someone else so happy could make him feel so good?

He stepped up behind Davi and wrapped his arms around his lover's waist, resting his chin on Davi's shoulder. "There's a ton of stuff in there, stuff we used to decorate with back when everyone had a sense of pride in the club, before we all got so wrapped up in our own shit. That was a pretty magical time for Sin."

"Then we'll make it look magical again," Davi said in a voice equally as soft and sincere.

Lance wholeheartedly believed in Davi. He seemed to be really tenacious when he wanted something, had a zeal about him when he believed in it. It was inspiring to witness, so inspiring Lance believed they might actually pull off something incredible.

He splayed one hand over the small of Davi's back and tugged him closer, and their mouths met in a kiss. And though all their kisses turned him on in some way, this one stoked the flame warming Lance's heart. It was a sincere kiss, a loving kiss, the kind of kiss that made relationships feel unbreakable.

"We should gather some of this stuff up," he said airily. "I would love to have it all done before Jason and the rest of the crew gets here."

"I think that idea is perfect," Davi murmured.

Reluctantly, Lance released his lover, and he watched as Davi made his way toward the pile of decorations tucked away in the corner and forgotten. Davi sorted through the piles. It seemed as though everything he picked up excited him, and that wondrous excitement was absolutely contagious. Now Lance couldn't wait to get the decorations out and put a little life back in the club.

34

THE THUMPING bass pouring out from somewhere in the bottom of the house roused Dorian from the half-empty bed he'd woken up in and drew him downstairs to the first floor of his sprawling mansion. He wasn't quite awake yet, probably could've used another hour or so of sleep, but the noise and lack of warmth beside him made getting any more shut-eye a pipe dream.

"Coffee, Meester Dorian?" Maria asked.

Dorian barely managed a nod as he scrubbed the sleep from one eye with the butt of his palm. Words were out of the question right now. Coherent thought was out of the question. Thankfully, Maria knew not to hold Dorian up, to give him the small necessities of his life and let him be on his way. He pressed on, padding across the living room, following the loud, thudding hum of club music.

A thin beam of bright white light slipped through the slightly open door to the weight room on the backside of the house. Normally, the blinds would've been closed to keep the hot sun from soaking up all the cool air. Dorian pressed his palm to the door's surface and gently eased it open so as not to startle the person he assumed was in there.

In front of a wall of mirrors, Jansen spun and shimmied and gyrated through his routine, moving in perfect rhythm with the music. He didn't miss a single beat, not that Dorian could tell, but what did he know about dance?

It wasn't about dance. It was about the sight of his love gliding across the floor and the utter enjoyment painted on Jansen's beautiful face. He hadn't seen an expression quite like that in a long time, and honestly, Dorian missed seeing that happiness. He missed watching Jansen enjoy the simple things in life—like twirling around in circles and moving his arms through the air like flowing ribbons, like becoming one with the music and living to entertain. Dorian knew it was his fault Jansen didn't have that anymore, not with Sin & Seduction, and not since those pretentious assholes at the New Orleans Dance Company didn't want to be associated with lowlifes and criminals. Their words. Not Dorian's.

For a brief moment, Dorian thought he could give it all back, that he could tell Jansen to return to the club if he wanted to, but Dorian also knew the first hand that touched Jansen's crotch would have five broken fingers. That was something he couldn't help right now.

The light from the wall of windows beside him made the sweat on Jansen's face and chest glisten. It cast shadows along his body. Toned muscles wound down his legs, rippled across his chest, and spilled down into his arms. They weren't bulging and ridiculous like a bodybuilder's, but perfect for Jansen's smaller frame.

Dorian leaned against the doorframe, arms crossed over his chest, watching the grace with which his husband moved. Jansen was still as beautiful as he'd been the first time Dorian had laid eyes on him. He had the most elegant form, as if he'd been sculpted by an artist's talented hands.

When Jansen twirled around on the ball of his foot and his gaze landed on Dorian, he stumbled forward, falling out of the rhythm he'd been so great at keeping up. A gasp slipped past his lips. Surprise painted his face. "How long have you been standing there?"

"Long enough to watch my baby do his thing." Dorian held out a hand. The edge of his lip kicked up in a half-grin. "I'd forgotten how good ya are at that."

A soft blush crept into Jansen's already rosy cheeks. It was the cutest damn thing Dorian had seen in a long time, cute like Jansen used to be when they'd first gotten married, back when things were close to being fairy-tale perfect. Oh, Dorian knew life with him hadn't been the greatest lately and he'd broken his promise to always make Jansen happy, but plans were presently in the works to change all of that.

"You always were a smooth talker, Mr. Grant," Jansen said as he pressed the length of his body to Dorian's.

"And you's always sexy as hell, Mr. Grant," Dorian said with a playful growl.

About the same time Dorian closed his mouth over Jansen's, the scent of freshly brewed coffee wafted up from behind them. The coffee he one-handedly dismissed. All it took was a flick of the wrist and Maria disappeared. But when he heard Angelo's booming voice calling his name, all bets were off. The kiss would have to wait.

"Gimme a minute," Dorian yelled back. He gave Jansen a weak sort of smile. "Baby, I got business to deal with. Ya mind practicin' a little longer? Then we can play."

"Sure."

Though he agreed, Jansen didn't look too happy about having to wait for Dorian's affection. To be honest, Dorian would've much rather stayed in that room watching his man move. But the business he had to tend to would hopefully keep the two of them together a hell of a lot longer.

Dorian gently closed the doors to the weight room, spun around, and found Angelo standing not five feet behind him. The mammoth gave him a start. "Personal space, man, for Christ's sake."

"You couldn't reach out and touch me."

"What the hell does that matter?"

"Personal space is your arm's length from your body."

Dorian glowered.

"Wha...? It's true."

"When ya sneak up behind me, and you're close enough for me to attack ya, you're in my personal space."

Dorian walked on by, waving two fingers in the air so Angelo would follow him. They stomped their way upstairs—the slapping of Dorian's bare feet contrasting Angelo's heavy leather boots. Upstairs, Dorian closed the office door behind them and they both took their normal seats.

"So...," Dorian led.

"So," Angelo drawled, clearly taking his time. Most likely because he knew Dorian wasn't going to be happy with anything he had to say. "I found out who was pulling Leo's strings."

"Okay...."

"The man's name was Norman Horton."

What the hell kind of name was that? Who the hell was Norman Horton? Dorian didn't even know a single person with that last name. Boy, if he wasn't confused before....

"Wait. Was? Did you say was?"

Angelo nodded slowly.

"What happened?"

"He's dead."

"No shit, Sherlock. The *was* is kinda indicative of the fact, don't ya think?"

Shrugging, Angelo relaxed on the couch, but not before eyeing the ashtray on the side of Dorian's desk. The half a joint he'd left there was gone. Dorian had pitched it in the trash right after Angelo had left last time. Since Dorian had been staying off the drugs, it was best for temptation's sake not to have the shit around.

"So.... Ya gonna tell me what the hell happened to him?"

"I'm getting there," Angelo said. "According to the coroner's report, he committed suicide. He was found after Leo Cabrezzi."

"What the—"

"I know, boss."

Dorian sat back in his chair and pressed his thumb and forefinger to his eye sockets. He rubbed small, tight circles, but the pressure didn't dull the budding throb inside his skull.

"Damn, Angelo," he whispered. "This wasn't what I was hopin' to hear."

"I know, Dorian. Trust me. I know."

"What's the big deal?" A voice asked from the door.

Angelo and Dorian whipped their heads around and they found Jansen standing in the opening. Apparently, neither of them had heard him open the door, and God only knew how long he'd been standing there listening. It wasn't like the off-limits subjects—like drugs, murder, and violence—had come up. They weren't plotting to kill someone. By the look on Jansen's face, though, he assumed they were.

"C'mere," Dorian said, wagging his fingers in the air.

Jansen stalked around to the back of the desk. There was a hint of hesitation in his step, as if he knew he wasn't going to like anything Dorian had to say and they would probably end up fighting but he would comply anyway. When he reached Dorian's side, Dorian took his hand.

"Leo Cabrezzi had been dead hours, maybe close to a day before Angelo went to his place. So—"

"So Angelo didn't kill him either," Jansen finished for him.

"I'm as innocent as a Boy Scout," Angelo chimed.

"Yeah, right," Dorian and Jansen said in perfect unison.

"The point is, when Angelo found Cabrezzi dead, he left and thought it'd be a good idea to keep that shit to himself."

Jansen frowned. "Why would *that* be a good idea?"

Rolling his eyes, Angelo threw his arms in the air. He popped up to his feet and very loudly argued, "The guy was fuckin' dead. That's what Dorian asked for. That's what Dorian got. I told him it'd been handled. Well, it had been. Besides, his head was somewhere else. He didn't need to know the details."

"Calm down, buddy." Dorian held up his free hand.

"There's a point to all of this, right?" Jansen asked.

"When we found out Leo was dead already, we thought we could find his killer and clear my name. I thought...."

Dorian stopped long enough to swallow and Angelo interjected.

"Leo's murderer killed himself."

"Wow." Jansen's eyes widened. "Sounds to me like he couldn't take the guilt of being a killer and offed himself. Right?" Dorian looked up at Angelo.

Angelo shrugged. Jansen continued, "Rebecca needs to know that. Couple this with the alibi from the hospital, I'll bet Dorian never serves another day in jail."

"Damn, I love the way ya think," Dorian said as he tugged Jansen down to his lap.

"I'm just gonna leave you two alone." On that note, Angelo hightailed it out of Dorian's office as if his ass had caught fire. While he didn't mind the fact his boss was into men and never made a big deal about it, Angelo was very hetero, and like most hetero men, the only same-sex couples he cared to watch making out were women.

From the corner of his eye, Dorian watched Angelo scurry. He kept his mouth locked over his husband's and wrapped one hand over the nape of Jansen's neck. When the door loudly slammed behind them, every bit of Dorian's attention turned back to his love.

"God, I want ya so fuckin' bad," he all but purred. He could feel Jansen grinning against his lips.

"You could have me right now...." Jansen reached back and casually rubbed the tip of his finger along an indentation in the wooden edge of Dorian's desk.

Dorian almost chuckled. He could feel his lips tugging at the edges. The night they'd made that mark had been hot as hell, though clumsy in its own right. A laptop and a desk lamp had gotten utterly destroyed, not to mention the mess that had been left for Maria. Damn, though, it'd been worth every second.

Jansen eased up from his lap and turned to move the laptop, bending at the waist just enough to push his ass out. He was so close to Dorian's face, close enough Dorian could smell the cocoa-butter lotion Jansen put on his skin twice a day, close enough he could smell the mix of sweat and cologne clinging to Jansen's clothes. What a turn-on.

Any restraint Dorian might've had was now gone. He reached up and hooked his fingers on the waist of Jansen's light workout pants and the briefs beneath, and he pulled down, exposing Jansen's ass, inch by immaculate inch. The sight was so awe-inspiring Dorian couldn't help dropping a kiss on Jansen's cheek.

"Such a tease," Jansen said from over his shoulder.

Dorian looked up to meet his husband's wicked stare. "Tease?"

"Just a kiss? One kiss on the ass? That's all I get?"

"Ya want more?"

"Like you have to ask."

It wasn't until the tip of Dorian's tongue met the valley of Jansen's ass cheeks that Dorian finally dropped his gaze. Their stares remained locked until the very last second, when physics and science and biology made looking at each other while licking Jansen's hole absolutely impossible. What Dorian wouldn't give to see the look on his lover's face as his tongue swept along Jansen's pucker.

The sound of Jansen's moaning played into Dorian's imagination. He could almost picture each little indentation and the whitening of skin as Jansen bit down hard on his bottom lip. He could picture the hooded eyes and the way Jansen gripped the desk.

God, that turned Dorian on.

With his thumbs, he spread Jansen's cheeks wider just so he could get a little deeper. He kissed and tickled and licked his way along that glorious path, up, up, up until his lips found the small of Jansen's back.

Dorian pushed up to his feet, reaching into a desk drawer to the right of Jansen's hip to grab the bottle of lube he kept there for emergencies such as this. With the other hand, he fumbled the button, then fumbled the zipper of his jeans until they fell open and slid down his legs. His hard-on burst free, ready for action.

Lube coating his palm, he gripped his shaft and started to pump. He slipped a single finger from his free hand into Jansen's hole. "That okay, baby? You good?" he rasped, voice hoarse with need.

"Yes. Yes. Oh, hell yes."

"God, I love you."

"I love you too...." Jansen's voice trailed into a high-pitched moan as Dorian slid the second finger in.

He planted kisses along Jansen's back, adding a sense of sweetness to the heated thrusting of his fingers. He scissored them open and closed, open and closed again. Each and every motion elicited a moan or a whimper or gasped breath. It was beautiful. Making love to Jansen was beautiful.

"I'm the luckiest man alive," Dorian whispered airily, more to himself than the man his fingers were making love to. And Dorian absolutely believed every single syllable of those five words.

With one hand at the base of his shaft, Dorian removed his fingers from Jansen's hole and stepped in to take aim. At just the right angle, he pressed the blunt head of his cock to the beautiful, readied rosette and he gently pushed while his lover took slow, even breaths. Dorian buried himself to the hilt, sac resting comfortably on the warmth of his lover's precious rounded ass, and nothing in the world could've made him happier.

35

"I LOVE you too," Rebecca said, voice dripping with exhaustion. She was supposed to meet her wife for dinner at their favorite restaurant and had to cancel thanks to a last-minute meeting with Dorian Grant's head goon. "Hey, sweetie, why don't you pick us up an order of the usual to-go? No reason we can't have dinner in bed." The request was warmly received. "I want to feed you with my bare hands and—"

A meaty fist banging on her office door cut her off before she got to sexual innuendos and methods of carnal gratification. She let out a sigh. "He's here. I'll be home as soon as I can. Keep the lo mein warm, please."

After hanging up the phone and pushing back her temper as much as she could, she called out to whoever was behind the door, "Come in."

One of the largest, most intimidating men Rebecca had ever met in her life stepped through her door. It didn't matter how many times she came face-to-sternum with Angelo, his size always made her knees knock a little, made her throat tighten. He was big enough and strong enough to end her fragile little life, and everyone who knew anything about the New Orleans crime scene knew he was Dorian's enforcer. It went without saying that a visit from Angelo would never end well. Thankfully for Rebecca, Dorian still needed her.

"Go ahead," she cautiously said, holding an arm out over her desk, fingers pointing at the empty chair across from it. "Sit down. I don't bite."

"Ah, c'mon, lawyer," Angelo teased. "Maybe I like it rough."

Rebecca rolled her eyes.

He did as she asked. The wooden chair groaned in protest. Angelo was too heavy and too wide, and she thought for sure the antique would fall apart at any second.

In the dim light of her office, his eyes looked much darker than usual, like a man who'd seen too much bad shit, a guy who didn't value human life, who'd kill a man just because he could, then possibly devour a cheeseburger after or maybe lie down for a good night's rest. He didn't have that thing most human beings had, the thing that knew right from wrong. He didn't have a conscience as far as she could tell.

"So, what was so urgent?" she asked.

Angelo didn't look too comfortable, as if he had some gross mound of confession to make, but instead of telling a priest, he intended to spill all his dirty deeds to her. She certainly hoped he wasn't that fucking stupid.

"I need to talk to you about Cabrezzi."

Apparently, he was that fucking stupid.

Rebecca held up both hands—a "whoa, boy, wait just a damn minute." "Angelo, I *really* wish you wouldn't say anything else about what happened to Cabrezzi."

Angelo frowned. "Why?"

"Seriously?"

"It ain't what ya think, I promise. I didn't off Cabrezzi, and neither did Dorian."

"It isn't?" Rebecca knew she sounded doubtful, but she couldn't help it. Dorian Grant didn't get along with a single person in the Cabrezzi clan. The fact wasn't a secret at all. He'd been in half-a-dozen fights with one or more of the Cabrezzi boys over the years. Logic leaned toward his wanting Cabrezzi dead. It just made sense.

"No. It ain't."

Angelo leaned forward and lifted the top of the candy jar at the edge of Rebecca's desk. She kept a bowl of what she liked to call stress relief. Usually M&M's, but sometimes she liked to switch it up. Sometimes, chocolate got passed over for something fruity like Skittles. Angelo dipped his fingers in the bowl and pulled back a handful. She used to love that candy.

She watched as he pitched colorful bits of chocolate in his mouth, waiting for him to say something enlightening and pertinent, something worth missing dinner with her wife for. Waiting. Waiting.

"Angelo?"

"Huh?"

"Please tell me you have something important to say."

"Oh, I do." He tossed the remaining candy in his mouth, then sat back in the chair. It groaned again. "Ya need to have the DA look into Norman Horton as a suspect."

"Norman Horton?" Rebecca frowned, reaching across her desk for paper and a pen to jot this down. She would forget otherwise. "Why is he significant?"

"I'm gonna tell ya everything I know, and you can use it however ya want, but it's all important."

"Okay…" she drawled, curious caution coloring her tone.

"I went lookin' for Cabrezzi's killer. See, Dorian told me to take care of that piece of shit when Jansen was still in the hospital. Back then, when Dorian said to take care of someone, that meant—"

"Stop. Stop right there." Rebecca closed her eyes tightly and shook her head. "I don't want to know this stuff, Angelo. I don't. So, just stop."

"This is important."

"Please don't tell me anything that might incriminate my client, okay?"

Angelo's face contorted, like half of it scrunched up and the other sort of deadpanned. He didn't understand, or at least, it didn't look like he understood. The notion irritated the piss out of Rebecca. She could've been home right now, having Chinese food finger fed to her by the most beautiful woman on the planet, but noooo, she had to be here with a Neanderthal.

"Cabrezzi was already dead by the time I got to him," Angelo said. "Norman Horton killed him."

"How do you know?"

"I can't tell ya that."

"Then I can't do anything with the information."

"You're gonna have to trust me."

Rebecca snorted. "Right."

"I'm serious."

"Me too."

Angelo let out a sharp sigh. His entire body slumped. "I got a guy. He's a nerdy type. He finds people who don't wanna be found. When I asked him to find Cabrezzi, he already had all his info, said some guy had just come lookin' for him. After some pretty—" Angelo's head waffled from side to side as if he was thinking of a neutral way to say what he needed to say. "—effective persuasion, he gave me Horton's name."

"Look, Angelo, I appreciate what you're trying to do, but this sounds very circumstantial to me. I don't see how it'll do any good."

"I'm tellin' you. He did it. The evidence is there. Ya just gotta dig for it."

"How are you so certain?"

"I just am, okay." Angelo stood from the chair. Thankfully, it didn't collapse. He didn't say another word about anything he'd told Rebecca, and he sort of left her with a bit of WTF. He stopped, reached for the door, and said, "By the way, Norman Horton is dead. The coroner can fill you in on what happened."

Make that a lot of WTF.

Exhaling, Rebecca sat back in her chair. She pressed her thumb and forefinger to her eye sockets and gave them a thorough rubbing. It didn't help, though. The monumental headache brewing in the front of her brain didn't let up. She knew she needed to call Wheeler and let him know what Angelo had told her, but she also knew having that info would make her sound shady, if not utterly crazy.

Before picking up the phone, she mentally arranged all the information Angelo had dumped on her, compiled and processed, and put everything into legal jargon. Maybe she could spin this in such a way Wheeler wouldn't ask a million questions. Maybe she could actually get her client off for good. She finally picked up the phone and pressed the speed dial for the DA's office. This time of night, the best she could hope for was an answering service, but something was much, much better than nothing at all.

36

New Year's Eve

HANDS SHAKING, palms sweating, Jason paced the backstage area of the club, checking the clock every few seconds. The dancers should've started arriving already, but not a damn one of them was there. Where the hell were they? They all knew tonight was the big night. Do or die. Raise the money or fail so big the club had no choice but to shut its doors forever.

"Dammit," he said on a sharply exhaled breath. His nerves had been getting the best of him for over an hour, and the more time wound down, the more his stomach knotted. His hope was slipping away with every single brutal tick of the minute hand.

The door at the end of the hall squeaked open and Jason's head whipped back. He watched closely, waiting to see who would be the first to finally emerge from the darkness. Waiting. Waiting. It seemed like an eternity before a shadow appeared in the light cast over the concrete floor.

It was Jansen, and Jason couldn't have been happier to see anyone in his life.

He held out both arms. A smile stretched his lips as he charged forward and closed the distance between them. He pulled Jansen into a tight hug and clapped his hand against his best friend's back.

"You okay?" Jansen asked.

"No." Jason half laughed as he pulled away from the hug. "I feel like I'm gonna fuckin' hurl."

"Don't do that. You have a show to put on."

"Yeah." Jason sighed and scrubbed his hand over his face.

The door opened again, and this time voices and laughing came with it. The footfalls were plenty. From the darkness emerged four more men, two dancers from Jason's heyday and two of the new ones. Hope was slowly coming back. Now he only waited for Lance and Davi and a few others, but at least he had enough to make a show if no one else bothered to come in.

Music from the club trickled in through the stage curtains and cinder-block walls. It was something slow, something sweet—a song no one would've ever danced to. Jason frowned. A sense of dread pushed up through his wavering hope. If the DJ was having a "breakup" night like he often had, the music would blow, but even worse, if it wasn't the normal DJ he wouldn't know which dancers performed to what songs.

"What the hell else can go wrong?" he groaned, throwing his hands up in the air.

Every set of eyes in the place watched him as he stormed toward the front stage. He didn't know what he expected to find, but it damn sure wasn't what he saw.

Every single table in the place was covered with a white cloth and lit with a tiny candle inside a frosted globe. Shimmering black-and-silver confetti littered the dance floor.

Lance had his head on some guy's shoulder, arms around his waist. His eyes were closed. They slowly swayed with the music. He'd never seen Lance look so content, and almost felt bad about snooping until he saw who the guy in his arms was.

"Davi?" he gasped.

They both raised their heads, turning their wide eyes toward Jason.

"What are you...." Jason frowned, forefinger waffling between a frozen Davi and Lance. He tilted his head. "Are you...?"

Smiling wide, Lance took a step forward. It was a genuine smile, something Jason hadn't seen from Lance in a long time. Sure, the guy grinned and laughed at stupid jokes, cut up with the other dancers, and put on a happy face for the world, but beyond the façade, Jason knew for a fact Lance wasn't happy. It looked as though Davi changed that for him.

"We're together," Lance said, and he shot a glance over his shoulder, back at Davi, who appeared to be completely at peace. "I think I...."

"Love him?"

"Yeah." Lance grinned harder. "Yeah, I think I do."

Jason immediately closed the distance between them and he threw his arms around Lance's shoulders, absolutely relieved Lance had found someone who did it for him. "I'm happy for you," he said into the crook of Lance's neck, and it was true. One hundred percent.

When Jason had hooked up with Brad, it'd left Lance the odd man out—with feelings and desires and a whole lot of things Jason couldn't do for him. He'd stayed pretty scarce for a while after that. In fact, for a few weeks, he didn't even bother coming in to work. Jason had worried, but what could he do?

Now, Lance was happy again.

Good.

He let his friend go and stepped back so Lance could find his lover's side again. Truth be told, Lance and Davi looked good together. They fit. Somehow, they made sense.

"What do you think of the decorations?" Davi asked, breaking the silence.

Jason took another quick look around. He'd glossed over the "decorations" the first time in the surprise of seeing Lance and Davi together. They'd hung long, sparkling curtains in the doorways, tied back with black ropes. The flickering candles reflected in the disco ball above and tossed a soft golden glow onto the glimmering confetti below. The place looked clean and neat and regal.

He reached out and pulled Lance into a hug first, splaying his hand over his friend's shoulder to bring him in tight. He kissed Lance on the cheek. "Thank you," he said softly.

"I didn't do it alone," Lance replied.

"I know." Jason released him from the hug and stepped over to give the same to Davi. It was awkward for them both. While Jason had spoken to the kid many, many times, he'd never actually touched him, not even so much as a quick clap of hands, and now he had Davi in his arms. "Thank you too," he said before quickly letting him go. The hug didn't linger at all like it had with Lance, but in Lance's case, there were a hell of a lot more emotions in the background of that manly, friendly, half-hug.

With a relieved sigh, Jason straightened and dropped his arms to his side. The other dancers began piling out of the back room. They lined up along the side of the stage, Jansen leading the line with a smile. It was good to see old friends coming out to show their support, to help Jason pull the club up out of the muck and save a place they all loved so much.

"So." Jason clapped his hands together. "Let's get started."

37

"DORIAN GRANT," Hank said, offering his plump, shriveled white hand for a shake. His huge gold rings clanked together when Dorian gave it a squeeze. Sad thing was, Dorian knew he'd look just like Hank in the next twenty years if he didn't take better care of himself. "To what do I owe this honor?" Hank sat down behind his desk, arm extended, offering Dorian a seat at the desk right across from him.

"I'm here to make a business proposition."

Dorian tugged his slacks up as he sat down in the seat. He crossed his legs, ankle-to-knee, and leaned on one elbow against the armrest. That was his no-bullshit pose. Most people didn't argue and didn't question when Dorian threw that one on them. It had been a while since he'd used it, so he wasn't sure he had the clout to pull it off anymore.

"A proposition, huh?"

"Yep. I'm gonna be frank with ya. Ya been on everyone's radar for a while, man. I don't know why ya stopped payin' the cops, but that's why they're screwin' with ya business."

"And what do you propose to do?" Hank asked.

"I wanna buy ya out, let ya walk away from the club free and clear."

Eyeing Dorian hard, Hank pressed his forearms against the desk and leaned his rotund body on its surface. The wood creaked and whined under his weight. The dim light hanging overhead caught all of Hank's wrinkles just right. He looked a hell of a lot older than Dorian had remembered him.

"Why would I want to sell my place to you?" he finally asked.

Well, wasn't that just fucking laughable?

"You're serious?" Dorian asked.

Hank nodded.

Dorian shook his head. "Ya been lookin' for a buyer for more than eight months. Ya had no intention of lettin' Jason keep this place open. Didn't matter if he pulled off everything ya asked for. The doors're closin' tomorrow morning. Tell me they ain't."

If a man could've turned white as a ghost, Hank would've been the one. All the color fled from his face. His expression deadpanned as if Dorian wasn't supposed to know about that plan. Maybe he wasn't. Didn't change the fact he knew every single little detail about what would go down tomorrow morning. Angelo had eyes and ears in all the right places. While Dorian had been taking a backseat to the business and keeping his nose as clean as possible for Jansen's sake, Angelo had been doing the dirty work and Angelo knew things.

"I didn't wanna sell the club. I *don't* wanna sell the club," Hank finally admitted.

He sat back in his chair. The little bit of strength he exuded deflated with the breath he exhaled. The look on his sullen old face made Dorian believe Hank was telling him the absolute truth.

"So," Dorian drawled, waiting for the punch line. "Why ya lookin' for buyers, then?"

"It's Smitty. He wants out and he don't give a damn how he gets out. Problem is, I ain't got the money to buy his share. I'm barely stayin' afloat as it is."

"Then, why ya tryin' to hang on to this place?"

Hank shrugged. "I've spent my entire life here. This club used to be a warehouse my pops owned. Wanna know what he did here?" Dorian arched his brow. "Seafood and fish packing. Boats brought loads down the Mississippi. Pops had contracts with a few of them. He'd pack and ship their product and split the earnings with the captains—minus overhead, of course."

"Of course."

"This is all I got left of my old man, Dorian. I can't let it go. That's why I wanted to give Jason a chance. Smitty, he...."

"Don't worry about Smitty."

"Dorian...."

The dismal tone in Hank's voice wasn't lost on Dorian. He'd known Hank in a roundabout sort of way for a long time, long enough to know what was going through the old man's head. Normally, Hank would've been right. Normally, "Don't worry about someone" meant the crocs down in the swamp would feast well. Not in this case. Not since Dorian had promised Jansen no more violence.

"Hank, I'm simply gonna make an offer Smitty won't wanna refuse."

"How can you be so sure?"

"He wants out, and I got money. I got enough dough to give him a very, very comfortable retirement."

"Why are you doin' this for me?"

"I'm not doin' it for *you*. Jason's gonna be your new partner. I'm just his backer. Understand?"

Hank nodded.

"Once Jason has made back my investment, I won't be involved in the place anymore. The thing is, Hank, ya gotta keep my name outta all this. Nobody can know I'm involved."

"Should I ask?"

"Nah, it's not important."

"Okay."

"So," Dorian said as he stood from his chair. Hank rose with him—a great show of respect. "Where can I find Smitty? I want his name on a dotted line before the night's out."

"Home maybe? I'm not sure. There's a strip joint in Gretna. He likes to hang out there. The Black Cat Club? I think. He has a thing for ethnic women."

"Yeah, I know the club. Gimme his home address. We'll check there first."

Hank scribbled on a bright blue sticky note. His writing looked like an incomprehensible mess of swirls and lines, chicken scratch not much different from Dorian's. When Hank finally handed the note over and Dorian started to inspect it, he couldn't make out the first word or number.

"What the…?" Dorian frowned, wadded the paper, and pitched it into the wastebasket next to Hank's desk. "Why don't ya just text it to me?"

"Right," the old man said with a chuckle. Dorian turned on his heel and started out the door when Hank's gravelly voice stopped him. "Thanks, Dorian. I mean that."

"Ya can thank me when I get the other half of ya club."

"Well, even if you don't, thanks for tryin'."

"Oh, I'm gonna do more than try, so don't ya worry 'bout a thing."

38

FROM BACKSTAGE, Jansen peeked through the curtains, watching as the club started filling up. People were slowly trickling in, consuming empty spaces from the front of the stage to the back of the bar. So many faces. Much like the first time he'd ever graced that stage so many years ago.

A soft breath on his cheek and a pair of strong arms wrapping around him stole his attention away. "Almost feels like old times, huh?" Jason whispered.

Jansen didn't move a muscle. He looked down and found Jason's hands straightening the bow tie around Jansen's neck. The costume he'd picked turned him into an absolute nerd, complete with fake glasses. It was the thing now. People went crazy over hot men in glasses, for the geeks with their bow ties and their high-water slacks.

"You were so afraid that first night you danced up there. I fed you Ecstasy, swatted your ass, and sent you on your way."

"Yes, but not before adjusting my business."

Jason retracted his arms and put a few comfortable inches of space between them.

With a frown, Jansen looked over his shoulder, and the expression on his friend's face wasn't exactly sorrowful nor was it sardonic, but a confusing mix of the two. It felt as though Jason really missed the past, but loved the present too, like maybe part of him would've changed things if he could've. Jansen turned around to fully face him.

"I can't read you anymore," he said.

"What do you mean?"

"Well, you start reminiscing about the past and the expression on your face makes me believe you wish it wasn't the past."

Licking his bottom lip, Jason averted his stare, dropping his gaze somewhere distant. Jansen followed but only found the dirty, blackened edge of the white back curtain.

"I don't know," Jason finally said with a sigh. He hugged himself, brushing one hand up and down his forearm. "I do miss the past, but not like you think. I miss our friendship. I miss dancing and watching you dance. But I'm worried about the future too. You know? I see people trickling in and from here, it looks like we're doing great, but this is my last chance. Jansen, if I don't make it tonight, I let all the people who work here down."

"Don't think like that." Jansen wrapped his hand over his best friend's chin and lifted until their stares met again. "It'll work out. I promise."

"How can you be so certain?"

"Because Dorian has a plan."

"Dorian?"

"Yeah. Dorian. Is that a problem?"

Jason pinched his lips shut and shook his head. "Nah. Not a problem at all if he can save our jobs."

"Good to know."

Jansen eased by Jason and headed over to the mirror for one last check. He had about fifteen minutes until he had to waltz his ass out onto that stage and dance the best solo performance of his life. The idea was to keep all those faces in the crowd coming back so Jason could make Dorian's money back. The idea was to bring life back to the club and turn it into what it was two or three years ago when it'd been nearly impossible to squeeze through the crowd on the lower floor.

"You're going to do great," Jason said. "You were always one of the best dancers I knew."

"I'm probably the only one with any formal training," Jansen joked. He shot Jason a sideways grin.

"You're definitely more confident than you were back then."

"I've been doing a lot more professional dancing since then. That group Dorian got me involved in was good for me."

"That's good."

"Yeah," Jansen mumbled, running his hands down his abs as he stared into the mirror. They were slick with the oil each dancer usually coated their skin with. It was all for effect and nothing more. The oil made their sweat bead and made the light glisten on their flesh, giving off something as attractive as pheromones, thus making the people in the crowd go wild. They would thrust their dollar bills into the air with eagerness, begging for a chance to stuff the paper down some lucky dancer's Speedo.

This wasn't about the money for Jansen. Unlike before, being on that stage had nothing to do with money. It had to do with something so much bigger and more important than his wallet. How he'd matured in those years.

Thank you, Dorian Grant.

Dorian. God, how Jansen wished his husband were backstage with him right now, giving him a kiss for good luck, telling Jansen how proud he was. But Dorian hadn't been seen all night—which could mean something good or something bad, depending on which one of Dorian's issues were being dealt with at the moment.

"You ready?" Jason asked.

Jansen pulled the white button-down over his chest, buttoned it up until the bow tie stuck out from behind it. The idea was when he ripped the shirt open, the bow tie would still be where it belonged. That was kind of hard to do when worn the right way. He tucked his shirt in his tear-away slacks and said, "As ready as I'll ever be."

He jogged up to the edge of the curtain and listened as the music changed from the subtle house-mix crap the club kept at a low enough volume people could still talk over. The music got louder and more intense when the shows started.

The bass dropped with a thunderous boom and kicked Jansen's heart rate into high gear. He wasn't sure if the rapid thump, thump, thumping in his chest was from the music or his nervous pulse. He didn't have the benefit of drugs to keep him calm this time around.

"Takin' it back to old school tonight," the DJ announced. "You knew him way back when and loved him then. Help me welcome to the stage…." Insert dramatic pause while the patrons clamored to know whose ass would be put on display tonight. "Sah-weeeeeet Heeeeeat!"

With that, Jansen ripped open the part in the curtains and sauntered onto the stage. He stopped right in the middle, hooded his eyes with a flattened hand, and looked the crowd over. With his free hand, he waved his fingers in the air, rousing them all to yell louder. They did. He grinned, reached down, and tore open the white button-down shirt covering his slick chest.

He stalked straight up to the pole, grabbed it with both hands, and thrust his crotch out while throwing his head back. He rolled his hips, up and down, fucking that pole with purpose. Cheers roared up from the crowd. Thankfully, the stage lights were so bright he couldn't tell how many people were actually out there. Had he known, he might've lost all his conviction.

Somewhere between the pole and the end of the stage, and in time with the way the music crescendoed, he ripped the slacks away from his legs. The fabric burned his skin, but he didn't let it stop him. He twirled and turned and gyrated his way to the edge of the stage, planted both feet, and when the bass hit again, Jansen dropped to his knees.

Jesus, that hurt a hell of a lot more than it used to.

Another reminder he was getting too old to be playing around in strip clubs and his lewd dances were best left to the softness of a bed, in the privacy of a bedroom.

He thrust his groin toward all those waving hands, pumping against the air as they filled his Speedo. Their fingers reached for parts untouched by anyone other than Dorian in years. He could feel them stealing not-so-subtle gropes. It knotted Jansen's stomach. While he'd been so mad at Dorian for not wanting him to dance on that particular stage, now he understood. Now he wanted off it.

39

THE RED pitchforks over the front door of Sin & Seduction glowed with intensity against the black backdrop of night sky. Lance loved the sight of it, but even more, he loved seeing the line of people waiting to get inside stretching down the sidewalk, all the way down to the edge of the building. He couldn't remember the last time he'd seen the line so long, but it still wasn't what it had been in the club's heyday, and honestly, Lance doubted it would be enough to save the place he loved.

For the first time in God only knew how long, Lance caved to his need for a smoke. It was nerves, purely nerves, but lucky enough for him, one guy standing in line had been sucking down cancer sticks one right after another. Lucky for Lance, the guy was willing to share to get in the club quicker. Lance pulled him out of line and took him right up to the bouncer. "This guy's a friend of mine. Let him in."

The doorman nodded his massive, neckless head.

Everyone privy to what had just happened booed.

Lance shrugged it off and happily smoked his way to the side of the building.

The rusty door creaked open at the exact same time he pitched the butt of his cigarette toward the chain-link fence. He looked up in time to catch Davi walking through. Lance wasn't sure if his lover had caught him smoking or not, but he really hoped not.

"What's up?" Lance asked.

Davi closed the space between them, reaching for Lance's hand. He leaned in to steal a kiss and Lance immediately pinched his lips together. As if Davi wouldn't smell the smoke clinging to his skin and clothes. That had been part of the reason Lance had given up the habit in the first place. It was filthy.

"I didn't see you backstage." Davi frowned. "You've been smoking."

"Yeah." Lance turned his head and not so subtly sniffed his shirt. Sure enough, he smelled like an ashtray. "Come upstairs with me so I can freshen up. You got time?"

"Sim, four dancers are before me. I have time."

"Good."

Holding Davi's hand, Lance led him around the back of the building and up the rusted fire escape, then down the hall and to the last apartment on the left.

Inside, a few lights had been left on, as well as the stereo. It played acoustic music at such a soft volume the pounding and thumping from the club below nearly drowned out the sound. Lance stripped off his shirt, but kept it balled in his hand.

"I'll be right back," he said as he headed over to bathroom.

If Davi acknowledged him, he didn't hear it.

Lance stood in front of the mirror, staring at his harsh reflection. While he wasn't an old guy by any stretch, the crow's-feet at the corners of his eyes and the dimpling at the edges of his lips told him with stark realism that the time for being flighty and childish had passed. He'd admitted to being in love with Davi already, but somehow that just didn't feel as final as making a commitment to him. Marriage was out of the question right now, but there were so many other ways Lance could commit. And if things didn't go well with the club, he needed Davi to know just how committed he truly was.

He turned on the water, cupped his hands under the flow, then splashed some on his face. It woke him up, but didn't do a damn thing for his nerves. Nope, those guys were bent on letting him know he was on the verge of losing his damn mind.

"You can do this," he told his reflection.

He spritzed on some cologne, then tousled his hair. Happy with his appearance, he returned to the main room, but instead of joining Davi at the island, he went straight to an armoire on the far wall. The window beside it overlooked the street below, and from up there, it looked as though the line had actually dwindled. Not a good thing. And all that did was reaffirm the fact that Lance needed to make sure Davi had no reason to leave.

In the corner of the drawer, under a pile of T-shirts, awaited a single key for a very special situation. It was a key Jason had once had, one Lance swore he would absolutely never give to another soul. But he also never thought another soul would be special enough to have his heart.

He locked his hand around the key after settling a fresh T-shirt in place; then he spun around and returned to the island where Davi so patiently waited for him. Lance stepped up close, hips between Davi's knees.

Davi took a long, hard whiff along Lance's neck, pulled back, and grinned wide. "Much better."

Without saying a word, Lance lowered his head and pressed his lips to Davi's. The kiss was short and sweet, but as meaningful as any other kiss he'd ever given Davi. Maybe even more so, considering what he was about to do. Right as their lips parted, Lance said, "I love you."

"I love you too."

"Davi, I want you to live with me."

"What?" Davi straightened. His expression contorted in disbelief.

"Live with me. You don't have to pay any rent or anything else really. Maybe just pitch in on the groceries from time to time. I want you here with me."

The longer Davi remained silent, the more worried Lance became. Maybe he'd moved too fast. Maybe this was too much. But he couldn't help it. Lance had always been the kind who acted upon things without really thinking, well... until he met Davi. Then he started doing a whole lot of thinking and no acting upon. So this had to be right, then. Right?

"Davi...."

"Are you sure this is what you want?"

"I couldn't be more certain."

"Why? Are you afraid, Lance? Do you think I'm going to leave?"

"Yes," Lance said without thinking. Davi lowered his head, averting his eyes as if the truth genuinely hurt his feelings. Lance hated the thought. He hated the idea that his blundered words and good intentions had caused even an ounce of pain in the man he loved. "But," he continued, "I want you here. I want to wake up beside you every morning. I want to sleep with you every night. I want to laugh over omelets and cry together while watching sad movies. I want to adopt a pet and have a life with someone I love, Davi. You're that person. I love you. Please... please, move in with me."

Davi laid his hand over Lance's curled fist, prompting Lance to release the key he'd been holding on to. The worn bronze color was a sight to behold in Davi's palm. It was a very real, very tangible show of love and trust, and a sight Lance planned to remember when they slipped into old age together.

"I'll live with you," Davi finally said. "But if the club closes...." He swallowed hard, then licked his bottom lip. "If I can't find another job—"

"Then you'll let me take care of you and we'll figure it out, because that's what people who love each other do."

Davi nodded.

Lance wrapped both arms around Davi's body and pulled him into the tightest hug. He pressed his lips to Davi's forehead, letting them linger simply because he couldn't remember the last time something felt so incredible, so right and perfect, and he wanted to relish it before returning to the reality happening below them.

40

HUFFING AND puffing, Jason galloped off the stage as the song he'd coordinated his routine around faded out to its end. He could feel his heart rapidly thudding and the ache in his lower back was already creeping in, meaning the early-morning hours after the club shut down and people went home would be spent either lying on a heating pad or facedown on the bed while Brad massaged out the pain. The latter was preferable.

Applause erupted, a lower, much thinner applause than what he'd gotten as he left the stage. He looked up to find all his dancers and the ones who'd left the club a long time ago standing in a tight line. They all smiled and cheered, and he gave them an exaggerated, low, sweeping bow. With a hard wince, he righted himself again as the small crowd started to disperse, but one remained exactly where he'd been standing the whole time.

Jansen had a proud smile on his face. He held both hands clapped together at his sternum. "You were incredible," he said. "Now I remember what I loved about watching you dance. You're so graceful and artistic, even when you're getting half-naked." He laughed.

A lighthearted laugh from Jason followed. He stepped farther into the room, and into the arms Jansen now held open. They were in a sweaty, mostly naked hug. The heat off their bodies melted together. Jansen's groin pressed to Jason's, crushing a wad of singles into his crotch.

As uncomfortable as the bills were scratching against Jason's skin, he wasn't ready to let Jansen go. It was silly really. He'd made up his mind that no matter what, he would never look at Jansen as more than a friend, that Brad was his be-all and end-all, that he would never love another man like he loved his soon-to-be husband. But as he stood there holding his best friend in his arms, Jason knew beyond a shadow of a doubt, Jansen was someone he would never be completely over. Jansen still held a little piece of his heart, and frankly, Jason didn't want that piece back. He didn't need it.

"You okay?" Jansen asked.

Jason nodded against his shoulder.

"Promise?"

"Yeah, I just...."

As soon as Jason raised his head, he saw Brad standing where the hallway opened to the backstage dressing area, holding a bouquet of perfect red roses in his arms. He had a surprised, yet extremely hurt look on his face. It was heartbreak. No doubt about it. What Brad caught Jason doing there—as innocent as it might've been—broke his heart.

"I gotta go," Jason said as he released his best friend.

He hurried past Jansen, rushing without running to Brad.

As quick as his feet carried him, though, it felt as if he were moving in slow motion, or running through a tunnel and the light at the end was getting farther rather than closer. He had a whole lot of apologies on the tip of his tongue and couldn't get to Brad fast enough to say them.

Brad set the roses on the edge of the vanity closest to him, then tucked his hands in his pockets and turned on his heel to leave. He had his back to Jason. Now, Jason felt the pain of being hurt firsthand.

"Wait," he said. "Don't walk away."

Brad stopped where he stood, but didn't turn around. "Tell me how I'm supposed to feel about that," he said, "because I'm not sure I know."

"Brad...."

One breath, then another, Brad didn't say a word and he didn't move a muscle. Jason thought for sure finding him and Jansen in a hug would be the final straw for Brad, and their relationship would very much come to a crashing halt. On the other hand, the hug had been purely innocent and they'd been friends forever. It was perfectly acceptable to hug his friend. Wasn't it?

Brad finally turned around. "Had I caught Melody like that when we were still together, I... I don't know. I don't think I would've thought anything of it, but you...."

"Me?" Jason arched a brow. A hint of anger pushed up inside him. "What about me, Bradley? What makes me different?"

Brad didn't answer him.

"Is it because I used to be a stripper? Because I work in a nightclub? Because I'm not a saint and don't go to church like Melody?"

"Jason...."

"No. Don't 'Jason' me. What the fuck makes me different from her?"

"Because she's never been in love with someone else," Brad growled back.

And that was exactly what it boiled down to. Nothing more. Nothing less. A simple matter of telling the truth coming back to bite Jason in the ass.

"Can we go in my office and talk, please?"

Without waiting for an answer, Jason unlocked his office and turned on the light. It flickered and clicked, until finally the bulbs warmed up and the fluorescents settled down. He stood in the doorway, waiting until Brad took a seat. Jason moved to lean against the desk in front of him.

"Yeah, I loved Jansen at one point. I was honest with you about that. But I also told you those feelings were in the past. What more do you need from me?"

"I don't need to find you both half-naked, hugging each other like—" Brad shook his head, voice lowering significantly. "Like you still love each other."

Jason knelt down in front of his fiancé and he looked Brad straight in the eyes. "Look, part of me will always love Jansen. We were so close for so long. We have this incredible history together, difficult history. When we had no one else, we had each other, and nothing will ever change that. I'm sure you understand."

Brad gave a barely noticeable nod.

"That doesn't belittle my feelings for you. We were half-naked because I had just come offstage."

"I know. I watched you perform."

Jason half smiled. There was more than a hint of surprise there. "Really? You did? What did you think?"

"I think… it was incredible. I haven't seen that kind of passion in you in a long time. You really like dancing, don't you?"

"Yeah, I do. I always wanted to be a professional, but…."

"You're still young."

Jason snorted as he rose to his feet. He sat down on the edge of the desk, legs dangling off the side. "I'll give you that. I am still young, but I promise, after tonight, I won't be able to move for a few days."

"Maybe once we get married I can get you on my insurance. Then we can get your back looked at."

"You still wanna marry me?"

"Of course I do." Brad reached for his hand. "I'm sorry I jumped to conclusions about Jansen. I'm normally not jealous like this. I just…." He took a deep breath. "You're such an amazing person I often wonder why you're with me. I mean, people pretty much called me a piece of shit for what I did to Melody, and I half believed them."

"People suck."

"Maybe." Brad laughed. "That's not the point."

"That's exactly the point, Bradley." Jason tightened his grip on Brad's fingers. "Not one of those assholes lived your life. They didn't know what you were going through. They didn't know how scared you were of the truth and of hurting Melody. It took a lot of strength to finally come out. And look, Melody respects you for it. She's happy and you're happy. You *are* happy, right?"

"Couldn't be happier."

"Good."

"Wait. That's a lie."

Jason frowned.

Brad stood from his seat and he wrapped both arms around Jason's shoulders, bringing them together until their mouths met. Brad spread his lips and Jason followed; then he tasted Brad's tongue on his. Jason closed his eyes, giving in to the feel of his fiancé conquering his mouth in the sweetest possible way. He slid his hands down the small of Brad's back.

When the kiss broke, Brad said an airy, "I'll be happier when I finally call you my husband."

41

"WALK," DORIAN commanded, nudging Smitty in through the back door of Sin & Seduction. Angelo followed behind them, playing lookout like he always did, even if that was a bit of overkill in a situation like this. Dorian hadn't been able to convince him war tactics weren't needed here.

Dorian had had about all he could stand of Smitty already, and the sooner all the legal shit was handled, the better. Another second of listening to that old man complain and Dorian would've considered doing Smitty a favor and putting him out of his misery.

They slipped by the few dancers hanging out close to the steps leading up to the main offices. Dorian stole a quick peek and didn't see Jansen in the crowd. Good thing. Jansen was the kind of guy who would've had his feelings hurt if knew Dorian had come to the club but chose not to stay for the dance, even if Dorian had told him he wouldn't. Right now, Dorian had other things to worry about. He couldn't deal with hurt feelings on top of business dealings.

At the top of the steps, Smitty breathed harder, like he'd just run a freakin' marathon or something. "Ya need to quit smokin', old man," Dorian said. Not only did Smitty have a smoker's wheeze, but the yellowing of an otherwise white moustache meant he'd had the habit for a long damn time.

"I already gave up the booze," Smitty rasped. "I ain't givin' up my cigars."

"It's your life."

"That's right. It is."

"Don't get smart."

Dorian reached out and pounded the edge of his fist on the office door. It immediately opened as if they'd all been sitting on the edge of their seats, waiting for Dorian to come back.

"Glad to see you made it back in one piece," Rebecca said. She moved out of the doorway, making room for Dorian and the much wider Smitty, and the much, much wider Angelo to squeeze into the cramped office.

"Thanks for comin' out so late," Dorian leaned in and murmured to her. "I'll pay ya double for this."

"Dorian, we're friends."

"I know, but I ain't takin' advantage of that."

Smitty immediately flopped back in his seat, like that'd been the only thing he'd been looking forward to since they'd arrived at the club. His chest rose and fell, rose and fell. Each breath louder than the one before it. He was probably clinging to life by a thread. No wonder he wanted out of the business.

"Smitty here decided that sellin' the club is in his best interest," Dorian said, clamping one hand over Smitty's shoulder. "Didn't ya?"

"Do I have a choice?"

"Mr. Smith, you always have a choice," Rebecca said. She eyed Dorian hard. "You're not entering into this contract under duress, are you?"

"Nah," Smitty said. "I don't want this place no more."

"I'm buyin' it at fair market value," Dorian said. "I ain't strong armin' him."

"Then, I suppose we should sign contracts," Rebecca said.

Dorian took a look around the room. Angelo stood behind Smitty, keeping his eyes locked on the old man like he was bent on not missing a single wheezy breath Smitty took. Rebecca stood beside the kid—the scrawny, nervous attorney who represented the business and was overseeing the dissolution of the partnership. Then there was Hank, sitting on his side of the desk, glowing like someone had given him a second chance at life. Sure, this had first been about saving something Dorian's husband loved, but it was Hank's sad story that really tugged at his heartstrings. This might very well be his first good deed in a while.

"Angelo," Dorian said, "go get Jason. He's gonna be Hank's new partner. He needs to be the one who signs this shit."

"Right, boss." Angelo left the room, taking a hell of a lot of heat with him. His absence made the air in there a bit easier to breathe.

"I'm gonna find Jansen."

Rebecca gave him a nod; then Dorian left the room too.

Instead of heading back the way he'd come in, he took a left outside the office, in the direction of the VIP balcony. It was pretty nice the way the club was laid out. It wasn't a full two stories, but more like sixteen-foot high ceilings with a ledge running along the walls, leading to offices. Back in the days of it being a factory, the ledge and the balcony had been metal mesh hanging high enough for management to look over the workers. Now it allowed the bosses to check out the party below.

As soon as Dorian rounded the corner, he saw Jansen leaning against the railing with his hands locked together. His stare was focused on the show below. Dorian recognized the kid on the stage. Golden Boy, they'd called him—one of the men Dorian had once had a fling with back when he was fighting not to fall head over heels for the man he'd ended up marrying.

He sidled in behind Jansen and wrapped both arms around his husband's waist as he pressed his lips to Jansen's nape. He could taste the sweat on Jansen's skin. "Enjoyin' the show?"

"I am. You?"

"I'd rather be enjoyin' you, baby."

Jansen purred.

He turned around and Dorian pressed more firmly against his body. With the thin robe and the thin Speedos, Dorian felt the soft bulge of his husband's flaccid cock. Oh, but if Dorian had his way, it wouldn't stay soft long.

"Easy boy," Jansen teased. "I have another routine to perform."

"Later, yeah?"

"Abso-freakin'-lutely." Jansen reached up to run his hand down the line of buttons along the front of Dorian's dress shirt. He came damn close to brushing that hand over Dorian's crotch, but stopped short. "Did you see me dance?"

Lie.

Truth.

Lie.

Truth.

"I, um." Dorian stiffened. He shifted from one foot to the other. "No, I missed it."

Jansen immediately deflated.

"But," Dorian continued, "I told you I wouldn't, remember? Besides, I had a damn good reason."

"Okay...."

"Smitty is upstairs with Hank signing over his partnership in the club to Jason. So, regardless of the numbers tonight, the club's not closin' down. Jason now owns the controllin' half of Sin & Seduction. Any decisions made about the business will ultimately be his."

Silence. Jansen didn't immediately say anything. He opened his mouth, closed it, and smiled wide. He got that silly grin he often wore when something made him just the right mix of surprised and happy. This shouldn't have been a surprise, though. He'd told Jansen about this plan a while ago. Maybe Jansen just didn't have enough faith in him.

"What?" Dorian asked. His voice trailed off into a breath as a grin much matching Jansen's tugged at the corners of his lips.

"I can't believe you did it. You *actually* did it."

"You didn't think I would?"

"I didn't say that." Jansen pushed his hands around Dorian's waist and dipped them into his back pockets. "I'm surprised and excited, and I love you so much."

"I love you too."

There was still something going on Dorian couldn't quite put his finger on. While Jansen was doing the touchy-feely thing and making smiles, he wasn't saying something he obviously had on his mind. Dorian knew this by the way Jansen wouldn't quite look him in the eyes.

"Baby, what's wrong?" Dorian asked.

Exhaling, Jansen leaned back against the railing, but he kept his hands on Dorian. He looked over his shoulder, back down on the stage, but he didn't immediately look back. It felt like Jansen actually missed being on that stage, dancing and having all those men adore him and want him. Did Dorian not give him all of that already?

"You were right," Jansen finally said.

Dorian was just about to launch into a whole bunch of apologies and promises, and anything that would make Jansen happy, but those three words sent his brain into a tailspin.

"Wait. What? What exactly was I right about?"

"Having all those hands on me. I didn't like it. It felt wrong. When I was on that stage, I kept thinking about how I only wanted you touching me."

"Baby...." He embraced his husband fully without saying a word. Admittedly, that news relieved him more than he'd ever really acknowledge. "I hate you had to experience something painful to get what I was sayin', but I'm glad ya get it now. I was bein' a jealous ass when I said I didn't want nobody touchin' ya, but I'm glad ya feel the same way now."

"I know, Dorian. I just want you to know that you don't have to worry about me dancing in a club like this anymore. I don't want it. I only want you touching me."

"Then that's what you'll have, Jansen Grant. That's what you'll always have."

42

THE NIGHT wound down with a whole lot of exhaustion on every side of the room. The club had emptied out about an hour ago, leaving a bunch of trash to be picked up, tables out of place and pushed together. The DJ had gone home, but music still played at a low volume. A stack of pizzas had been set on the edge of the stage, bought by "The club's secret admirer," and signed, "To the gorgeous dancers, with love." Dorian had set three six-packs of the good stuff out beside the food and told the bartender to put it on his tab.

Admittedly, Jason would've never expected the night to turn out like this. He never expected to see Dorian Grant hanging out with the little people, buying them beers and having a good time. He never expected to see Brad and Jansen having what looked to be a really great conversation. But the icing on the cake was seeing Lance holding someone so lovingly and truly being happy for the first time since Jason had met him. It was beautiful. Utterly beautiful. So even if all the effort to draw in some old clientele ended up being futile, at least they'd all made some pretty great memories.

"All right, kiddos," Hank called from the balcony. "Rebeccer and I just finished tallyin' tonight's numbers."

Every single body in the room stilled. Every head turned up toward the voice in the sky. No one breathed. No one spoke. No one even batted a lash. Everything froze—time, air, Earth. Everything stopped except for the music.

"I just want to say," Hank began again, "that y'all really came out and showed me how much this place means to ya. I'm honored to call every one of ya my friend."

He paused again. If Jason didn't know better, he'd think Hank was having a hard time delivering his little speech. The balcony was too high up to actually see whether Hank's eyes had begun to redden like Jason suspected they had. He couldn't tell from down there if Hank's voice held any tremble. Historically, Hank wasn't an emotional man, but things changed. People changed.

"So you gonna tell us how we did?" one of the dancers called back.

Jason couldn't be sure from where he was sitting which one had asked the question, and by the time he looked up, they were all laughing and smiling.

"Accordin' to Miss Rebeccer here, the numbers tonight were…"

Hank glanced back to the woman behind him. They whispered something to each other. Chatter rose from the dancers below.

"Tease," someone yelled.

More laughter followed.

Jason could barely breathe now. He nervously wrung his hands, wondering if he'd pulled off the numbers—even if it didn't matter anymore—or if the night had been a total flop as he'd expected it to be. A hand brushed up and down the small of his back and nearly made Jason climb out of his skin. He looked over his shoulder and found his fiancé settled in place behind him.

"You guys almost tripled the numbers tonight," Hank finally said.

Every single soul in the place cheered and yelled and hoorahed. There weren't many people left there, but enough noise filled the room to make it sound like they were in the Superdome in the middle of a Saints game. At least, that's how it felt to Jason. He had yet to process how well they'd actually done. He had yet to let go of the breath he'd been holding.

"Did you hear that?" Brad asked. "You did it, baby. You did it!"

"No, we all did it."

"And you thought you didn't have what it takes to run this place."

"I know, and like always, you were right."

The slow, wicked grin Brad often boasted when he was feeling especially frisky spread across his face. "Tell me I'm right again." He began to slowly back away, keeping his playful stare on Jason. He held up both hands, wagging his fingers in a come-and-get-it sort of motion.

Oh, Jason had every intention of coming and getting it.

Jason charged forward, and Brad took off in a run toward the VIP section. Great thing about being an owner, he could play wherever and whenever he wanted to, and he had Brad there to play along with him.

"HEY, DORIAN."

Dorian raised his head, swung it back, and locked his eyes on Rebecca. She was making her way across the room, sauntering with the kind of grace and poise he'd come to respect and expect from her.

"You have a minute to talk?" she asked.

He took a quick glance around. Neither Jansen nor Angelo was anywhere to be seen. Who knew where Jason and Brad had run off to: probably the VIP booths upstairs. Everyone hid up there. Even the other dancers had vanished. He was alone now, sitting at a bar he'd just paid for, sipping on the only glass of Scotch he'd had in months. But he wasn't drinking to get wasted. He was drinking to celebrate. Hopefully, Rebecca had more good news to add.

"Yeah, sure. What's up?"

She sat down beside him, reached for the bottle and one of the turned-down glasses beside it. She poured a two-finger, slammed it back, then poured another.

"Angelo came and talked to me," she said.

"Judgin' by the way you're drinkin', it wasn't a good visit."

"I didn't say that."

"No, you didn't have to." Dorian polished off the rest of his drink and topped up his glass. This time, he went a little heavier, thinking he actually needed to get toasted now. "So, what's up?"

"I called the DA. I asked him to pull the evidence from the Cabrezzi crime scene. I don't know what good it's going to do. I don't know if they still have the evidence from the Horton suicide."

"I understand."

"Do you?"

"Yeah." Dorian turned on the stool to face her, and he leaned in close. "I'll bet it says on the report what caliber pistol was used in Horton's suicide, and I'm willin' to bet everything I have to my name that it's the same caliber, even the same manufacturer."

Rebecca held up both hands. "I believe you, Dorian. I really do. I'm simply telling you that this may not play out the way you hope. There's still a distinct possibility of you going back to trial."

"Just promise me one thing, Rebecca."

"Dorian, don't ask me to make promises."

"I'm innocent. I don't wanna go to jail, especially not for something I didn't do."

"I know, and I promise to do my best to make sure that doesn't happen."

LANCE WATCHED Davi peel away his T-shirt, slowly exposing his incredible body. He watched as Davi reached for a warm, wet towel and the soap to wash the oil away. It seemed like such a waste.

"Don't," Lance called from the edge of the room. The sound of his voice made Davi jump. "Leave it. We'll go upstairs."

"Mmm… Do you have something planned for me, *cônjuge*?"

Lance licked his lips, eyes fluttering as Davi's native language sibilated in the sexiest possible way. The word rolled off his tongue, sending ripples of heat and excitement through Lance's body. For all he knew, Davi could've been calling him an asshole, but boy, did he sound sexy as hell doing it.

"You're going to tell me what that means, right?" Lance asked, tugging Davi toward him.

Davi only laughed.

"That's not a good sign."

"It means partner, like a spouse."

"Is that how you see me? As your partner."

"Sim, I thought it was better than *namorado*."

"And what is that."

"Boyfriend." Davi nipped at Lance's bottom lip. "Lover."

God, that gentle teasing and toying at Lance's mouth sent waves of heat and contradicting coolness rippling all through his body. He dipped a hand deep into the back of Davi's loose pants, down deep until the tip of his forefinger found the valley of Davi's wonderfully round ass. He kept going, reaching for Davi's pucker. Davi pushed his body against Lance's. They *had* to get out of there soon, real damn soon.

"Hey, Lance."

The voice cut off the sounds of their moans and purrs soft laughter. Lance jerked his head back and found Jason standing there looking fish-faced. "I, uh... I'm sorry. I, uh...."

"It's okay," Lance said, retracting his hand from Davi's firm, warm ass. "We were just—" Davi snickered. Heat rushed Lance's face. Nothing like getting caught by the boss to turn two grown-ass men into silly schoolboys. "Um, never mind. What's up?"

Jason dragged his hand back and forth across the nape of his neck as he stepped farther into the overhead light. His coppery hair was dark at the roots, sweat clinging to his scalp and beading on his brow. The club was still pretty hot, even a little over an hour after the bodies cleared out. Though most of the sweat probably came from that last badass routine they'd all danced together.

"Since we pulled off the show tonight," Jason said, "I wanted to make sure you still wanted to be a stage manager."

Stage manager. The position would bring in enough money to make ends meet. Barely. The upside was not having to sell his body to men who weren't Davi. Jason had promised he could still dance, which meant he'd have the tips every night. Davi would have his tips. They could make it. They could do this.

"Yeah, I'll be the stage manager," Lance said. He shot a grin over to Davi. "This'll be good for us." He kissed Davi's sweaty temple. "It'll be great for us."

"Awesome." Jason nodded. "Very awesome. I guess I'll see you Thursday."

"Sure thing, boss."

43

Three weeks later

SPREAD OUT on the couch, Jansen rested his head on Dorian's thigh as he absently stared at the movie playing on the big screen. Dorian ran his fingers over and over through Jansen's hair. It nearly put him to sleep ten minutes into the movie. He put up a good fight, though, even with his eyelids growing heavier and heavier. His mouth stretched into a yawn. His lids fluttered again. He was right on the edge of dozing when Rebecca's voice startled him. He jerked straight up, wide-awake in a triple venti sort of way.

"Dorian, I've got news," she said.

Not great news. Not good news. Just news.

Dorian stiffened, sitting straight up on the couch.

Jansen scrubbed his face, trying to get rid of the sleep so he could focus on his husband's future. If he tried to listen to anything right now, he'd only hear a bunch of *blah, blah, blah.*

"So spill," Dorian said.

He started in with the rapid tapping of his foot. Dorian did that when he got nervous. Shook the whole damn couch sometimes. If he'd had shoes on, a rhythm would actually accompany the bouncing. And Jansen wanted to reach over and grip his knee so badly, make it stop before the shaking drove Jansen insane. Before Jansen's nerves got the better of him, though, Dorian popped up to his feet and started to pace.

"Wheeler had his clerk go back and look at the evidence from the Cabrezzi crime scene and the Horton suicide. He met with the investigator and, Dorian—" He jerked his head up, stopped right where he stood and waited for her to keep talking. She smiled and said, "The bullets in both bodies came from the same gun. They'd ruled Horton a suicide because of the GSR on his hand."

"GSR?" Jansen frowned

"Gunshot residue," Dorian and Rebecca said in unison.

"Oh," Jansen said. "So what exactly are you telling us?"

"I'm telling you Wheeler is willing to accept that Norton killed Cabrezzi. All the evidence adds up. I guess the cops didn't put it together because there was no reason to connect the two. Norman Horton wasn't a criminal that anyone could tell. He didn't hang out in Cabrezzi's circle. He was a respectable member of the community, a husband and father. Hell, he even went to church every Sunday."

"Sounds like a good front to me," Dorian said. "If I was a bad guy who didn't want to get caught...."

Jansen narrowed his stare. He didn't want to even fathom the inner workings of the criminal mind, and he certainly didn't want to hear his husband talking about it. "Anyway," he said, turning the floor back over to Rebecca Chambers.

"Wheeler still wants to know where I got the information."

"What did ya tell him?" Dorian asked.

"Well, I said a little bird told me, but he wasn't buying it." She laughed. "So I told him I hired a private investigator. I said his buddies at NOPD weren't known for being the best at solving homicides."

"Thank God for that," Dorian muttered.

"So, he's free and clear? No more cops barging in? No more jails and judges? No more trial?"

"Not for this crime. If other ghosts from Dorian's past creep up, then we'll have to deal with them, but for the Cabrezzi crime, Dorian's name is clear."

"You're beautiful, Rebecca," Dorian said, opening his arms wide. She stepped in to hug him, and he planted a chaste kiss on her cheek. "Stay and celebrate with us. I'll have Maria cook up an amazin' meal. We'll uncork a bottle of the good stuff."

"I can't, Dorian. I would love to, but I have a wife at home who hasn't seen much of me in the last month and a half."

"Tell her," he whispered, "that I appreciate her sacrifice. That's sincere."

"I will, Dorian. Thanks."

"No, thank you."

When he let go of her and she left, Dorian stood in the center of the room sort of staring into space with an even mix of shock and relief. No one would've known he'd doubted justice. He'd had all this confidence. He was innocent and fate would work out in his favor. Innocent people didn't go to prison, not for good. But boy, when Rebecca told him he was off the hook, he gave away the extent of his worry. He'd been terrified.

"Come here," he said, holding out his hand, fingers slightly curled. He licked his bottom lip as if he were readying his mouth for the kiss of a lifetime.

Jansen didn't hesitate. In fact, he ran to Dorian, ran to his husband and collided with his body. A lesser man would've toppled over on impact. Not his Dorian. That man stood firm and solid and unmoving, and he caught Jansen against his chest and wrapped him up in the tightest hug. Jansen finally let out a sigh of relief.

"Let's move away," Dorian said in a soft voice. "We could move to Mexico or the Caribbean somewhere. Let's go someplace where they won't bother us anymore."

"What about your businesses?"

"I'll sell 'em."

"What about Maria and her husband?"

"They can go with us. I'll need 'em at our new place."

"What about Angelo?"

"Jansen." Dorian raised his head. A frown wrinkled his brow. "Don't ya wanna leave this place with me? Find paradise somewhere else?"

"I...." He'd never really thought about leaving New Orleans. This was home. This was where his family and friends were, where his life was. Oh, but wasn't Dorian his life now? Wasn't Dorian his family? "I...."

"We don't have to. I just thought—"

"No, I think I'm okay with leaving. Honestly, anywhere you are is where I want to be."

"That sounds amazin'. How about we start with goin' to the bedroom?"

Jansen could've sworn he'd seen a glint of sinfulness in his husband's big brown eyes, the wickedness he'd fallen in love with years ago. It was the same raw heat reminiscent of the old Dorian Grant, the mysterious bad boy Jansen both feared and lusted over.

"Mmm... going to the bedroom sounds like a fab idea."

Without another second of hesitation, Jansen took off, bare feet slapping against the cool floor. Another set of feet pitter-pattered close behind him, chasing him up the stairs and onto the carpeted hallway. The sound died then, and he wasn't sure how close Dorian was now, making the chase twice as intense and twice as exciting as it had been before. Jansen knew as soon as he turned around, he would be face-to-face with his lover. He knew it and he turned around anyway, and Dorian caught him in a tight hold. Jansen squealed like a twelve-year-old girl watching a horror movie. His pulse rushed and his breath hitched. It was all one great big turn-on, and he couldn't wait to get Dorian in the bed.

The greatest thing about all of this was finally having the man he'd fallen in love with. Well, the man minus the violence, anyway. Dorian had become fun again. He smiled again. He was playful again. All those things Jansen had missed. For a brief moment, he hadn't been sure he would get any of them back, but as he stood there being stripped of his clothing, he knew he did have Dorian back, and this time, he doubted he'd ever lose him.

EPILOGUE

Six months later

"CÃO, C'MERE, boy," Lance called, patting his free hand on his upper thigh. In the other, he held a leash and bags just in case the puppy needed a potty break on the way to the Riverwalk.

The eager beagle mix came running full speed ahead, ears flapping, tail wagging like crazy. He practically jumped right into Lance's arms. They'd had him for about three months, had adopted him from a rescue group and made him part of the family. He was malnourished and half-alive when the group had found him, and was just now reaching his proper weight. Now he was the cutest, happiest little pup to ever live, and the first thing Davi and Lance had gotten together. They'd lovingly named him the Portuguese word for dog, appropriately pronounced "cow," considering the beagle had all the right colors.

"He loves you," Davi said with a laugh.

As soon as the beagle heard his other daddy's voice, his excitement became tangible. He bounced and hopped, running in circles.

"Looks like he loves us both."

Lance raised his head and he got a good look at his partner for the first time since Davi had disappeared to go take a shower. He wore a thin, off-white pullover shirt with a loose neck that showed off his very defined collarbones. Those deep ridges begged to be kissed. The shirt hugged his slim waist and met at a pair of relaxed-fit dress slacks. A pair of leather loafers finished the look. And while their outfits might've matched almost perfectly, Lance doubted he looked as handsome and debonair as Davi did.

But the thing that really, really turned Lance on was the fact Davi had left his hair down. He'd left it just long enough to kiss the edge of his jawline, and a few thick black locks always fell forward when Davi tucked his hair behind his ears. Oh, and the smell. How could Lance forget the smell? His cologne was spicy and musky and delicious, a scent he'd only smelled on Davi, and Lance thought it had more to do with Davi's fiery DNA than it did some cologne any old Joe could run into a store and buy.

"You okay?" Davi asked.

"I'm better than okay."

"Better than okay?" Davi quirked a brow.

"Yeah. I'm… the best I've ever been."

The puppy yelped and whimpered, running figure eights around their legs. Lost in Davi's stare, though, Lance paid the pup little attention. The sound wasn't much more than background noise. Lance just needed a minute to take stock of how far he'd come and what he had, how after he finally gave in to his heart, he was the happiest he'd ever been in his life.

He had a wonderful man who loved him. They had a real home on the edge of the French Quarter, not some dingy studio above a nightclub. Lance managed the dancers on the weekend, but during the day, he managed one of Dorian Grant's check-advance places and made great money doing it. The money was so good he could help put Davi through school. Now that Davi had his green card, the sky was the limit for anything he wanted to do.

Life couldn't be better.

"Are you ready?" Davi asked.

"Yeah. I'll take care of Cão. You grab the gift."

With the square box in hand, Davi joined Lance and they headed out to the compact SUV Lance had never bothered driving before he'd moved away from his converted warehouse apartment.

No sooner had Lance gotten the hatch open than Cão was diving into the back. The puppy got all trip-over-his-own-four-legs excited when it was time to go somewhere with the guys. It didn't matter if they were taking a quick trip down to the Quarter or to the park in their neighborhood. Cão was always excited to go. Lance laughed and shook his head as he closed the door. Cão popped his head up and ran his wet nose along the back glass.

"C'mon, Cão. I just cleaned that window," Lance whined. He heard Davi cackling behind him. Lance swung around and narrowed his eyes. "And what's so funny, mister?"

"You. O Cão will not listen. He is a puppy and he needs to be taught the right things to do. He needs to be trained."

"I'm aware. And he will be when one of us gets the time to take him."

Davi leaned in and stole a kiss before making his way to the front passenger's seat.

Lance savored the taste of his sweet lips for a moment—cherry Chap Stick and mint mouthwash. The mixed flavors didn't sound so great, but something about the way Davi applied them to Lance's lips made the flavor taste better than homemade apple pie from Brad and Jason's place.

"YOU LOOK as handsome as you did on our wedding day, Bradley Britt," Melody said as she straightened his tie. She checked his boutonniere and his vest, checked his cufflinks and his belt.

"Everything okay?" he asked. His voice held a bit of a nervous quiver and rightfully so. He'd been married one other time in his life, and that hadn't worked out so well.

He'd once sworn that if things didn't work out with Melody, there was absolutely no way in hell he would go through the whole wedding crap again. For Jason, though, he was more than willing—eager even—to make an exception. Unlike the first time he'd gotten married, this felt right. It felt like a perfect chapter to add to their fairy-tale romance.

"Wow, whatever you were thinking about," Melody said, "keep thinking about it."

Brad let out a light laugh. One corner of his mouth kicked up into a crooked grin. A flutter of heat hit his cheeks. "Why?" he asked cautiously. "What did I do?"

"You finally stopped shaking and that happy gleam came back to your eyes."

His smile widened and he pulled his ex-wife into a tight hug. Bradley couldn't do much more than cling to her at the moment. He was so incredibly thankful for her taking the news of his sexuality the way she did. Everything could've gone so badly. She could've kept him from seeing his daughter, and she didn't. For that, he would always be thankful.

"I still love you," he whispered. "You're my very best friend, Melody."

"I know, Bradley." She lifted her head. "We're better this way. We're happier."

"We are."

She pushed up on her tiptoes and placed a chaste kiss on his warm cheek. Her hand splayed over his pec. She used him to help keep her balanced, and he truly didn't mind.

"Come on, handsome. We have a wedding to go to," she said with a wink.

"WHY ARE you still here?" Hank asked, wobbling his way back behind his desk.

The sound of his gravelly voice made Jason raise his head. Between his thumb and forefinger, he held the white calla lily boutonniere by its stem. He'd spent the last God only knew how long staring at that flower while trying to stave off the intense cold feet he started rocking when he climbed out of bed that morning.

"I'm just"—Jason shrugged—"thinking, I guess."

"'Bout what?"

"I'm getting married today, Hank. I'm about to vow to spend the rest of my life with someone, to love them no matter what. In sickness and health and all that shit. I don't… I just don't know if I'm ready."

"Then why did you say yes?"

Jason shrugged.

"Here's the deal, kid." The wooden chair Hank plopped his rotund ass in creaked under the weight of his body. "In about thirty minutes, you're going to have about twenty of your closest friends waiting at the Riverwalk, expecting to hear you say I do. So, I suggest you decide what you want to do and soon. But, Jason…."

"Yeah?"

"Make sure you know for sure it's what you want, because you can't just leave a man at the altar and expect him to stay with you."

Shit.

"Well, I… I don't want to lose him."

"Then I suggest you work it out, kid."

Right. Work it out.

Jason stood from his desk and gave Hank a two-fingered wave from the brow to let him know he was heading out. Of course, he'd see Hank again in a few minutes. Well, Hank was supposed to be at the wedding, that didn't necessarily mean Jason would see him. Jason might not have the presence of mind to notice anyone when it came time to take his spot in front of the officiant.

Outside, the sun held high overhead. In all honesty, they couldn't have asked for a more beautiful day. It wasn't muggy outside. It wasn't so hot the pavement fumed. A perfect summer day had found the Big Easy. Those were few and far between in the deep, deep South. That was a sign, right? A sign that this marriage was meant to be and everything would be okay, that his cold feet could go ahead and start warming up now. *Any minute now. Just warm right up.*

IN THE back of the sedan, Dorian held Jansen's hand tight, so tightly Jansen could barely feel his fingertips anymore. He wiggled his digits, but Dorian didn't take the hint. Jansen cleared his throat. Still nothing. Dorian was lost to scenery passing by outside the window.

"Dorian!"

Dorian's head jerked up. He looked right at Jansen, or maybe right through him. He blinked a few times as if he were trying to focus but couldn't quite make it happen.

"What is your deal?" Jansen asked.

"Sorry. My mind is… It's not all here."

"So where is it?"

A hard sigh pushed through Dorian's parted lips. Apparently, he'd been holding his breath for a while, because as soon as it escaped his body, his shoulders rounded and his chest deflated. He did *not* resemble the powerful, confident man Jansen had fallen in love with.

"Dorian?" Jansen said his name again, softer, more cautiously this time.

"I'm thinkin' 'bout leavin'. I'm gonna miss this place. Everything I've ever known and love is here. I'm sellin' the house I grew up in."

The house had already been on the market for close to five months and Dorian had talked every single interested buyer out of the place or wouldn't budge on the price. He didn't want to let go of it. Jansen knew he was holding on. He was just waiting for Dorian to admit he didn't truly want to leave New Orleans forever. In all honesty, neither did Jansen. He'd agreed to go because Dorian had needed him to. Long trips and journeys to faraway places were fine, but New Orleans was home.

"Dorian, you don't have to. You could keep it, and we could come home every once in a while."

"I suppose we could." Dorian turned in the seat and took both of Jansen's hands into his. For a few long, silent minutes, he simply looked Jansen in the eyes. "Would you be willin' to do that? Come home I mean?"

"Of course."

A relieved smile tugged at the edge of Dorian's lips. "I still wanna get rid of all the businesses. I have enough money stashed back that I can cover us for another lifetime. The house is paid for. The cars are paid for. I have investments that bring in more money every week than some people make in a month. It's sickenin' the amount of money I have… *we* have. We could make this work without me havin' to deal with a buncha bullshit. We could still afford to travel and everything. We ain't getting' no younger, baby."

Jansen snorted out a little laugh. But it was true. They weren't getting any younger. Jansen felt the years in his achy muscles every time he came offstage. And the moves he did with the production company weren't anything like the moves he used to pull at Sin & Seduction. This was like geriatric dancing.

"You can still be a businessman and not be a criminal," Jansen countered. Dorian gave him a let's-not-go-there look. Fine, Jansen knew when not to argue. Two businesses had been handed over to Angelo already. There were four more left, not including the loan Dorian had given to Jason for the nightclub. Jansen was getting exactly what he'd always wanted, so he would take it in whatever packaging it came in. "So sell the rest of the businesses, Dorian. Just… do me a favor."

"Yeah?"

"Can you give Lance first option on the place he's running?"

"Sure. Hell, he can have it. I really got nothin' invested in it. We'll clear up the debts and I'll sign it over to him. He'll make a killin' there. Broke people will spend a fortune for a loan." Dorian gave Jansen's hand another squeeze.

Jansen arched his brow. Apparently, there was more coming.

"I want to adopt a kid too."

"A what?"

"A kid."

"Right. Why?"

"I dunno." Dorian shrugged. "I always wanted to be a dad. Wanted to be a better old man than mine was."

"A kid, huh?

"Yeah." Dorian nodded. "A kid."

Jansen thought about it for a long moment. Brad and Jason seemed to be happy with their kid, and Hope was a sweetheart. She always wanted her Uncle Jansen when he came to visit. Come to think about it, all kids seemed to like him. Maybe he could do this whole being-a-daddy thing. "Okay." He nodded. "Okay, yeah. Let's get ourselves a kid, Dor."

"GOD, WHERE is he?" Lance muttered. He'd been pacing the cobblestones for what felt like forever. Davi silently watched every step he took. As Jason's best man, if the groom didn't show up, Lance would have to deliver the news to the other groom—the unsuspecting, newly heartbroken one. No one in their right mind would want that job.

He raked his wrist over his brow, and only then realized how badly he'd been sweating. It wasn't even hot outside. Where the hell was the sweat coming from?

"You should calm down," Davi said, locking both hands on Lance's shoulders.

"I'm trying. I swear, I am, but I don't want to be the one to tell Brad that Jason bailed on him. I... I... I can't do it. I can't. It'll devastate him."

"Jason will be here."

"How can you be so certain?"

"They're meant to be together. They love each other. Can't you see that and feel it when you're around them?"

Lance shrugged. He'd never really given it much thought. They seemed like any other couple he'd ever encountered. Happy or not, he wouldn't have been privy to it. But he sorta, kinda had his own relationship to put all his energy into.

"I love you," Lance said before lowering his head to steal a quick kiss from Davi's plump lips. Their mouths lingered. Their eyes closed. Lance suddenly forgot all about the missing groom and the presumably doomed wedding still waiting to commence.

The puppy bouncing around at their feet barked for attention. Davi pulled away from the kiss first, and Lance reluctantly peeled back both lids. The light was too bright for a moment, and it haloed Davi in a sort of whimsical glow. Made him look like an angel.

"Am I too late for the party?" It was Jason's voice saying those very teasing words.

It took more than a second for things to click and Lance's brain to get with the program. "Jesus. Yes. Where the hell have you been? I've been a nervous wreck." He playfully socked Jason's shoulder. Of course, Jason only laughed.

"I'm... I needed a moment." Jason inhaled deeply. "I'm good now."

"Good, because I sure as hell didn't want to be the one to tell Brad you were ditching him at the altar."

"No need. Let's do this."

BRAD STOOD at the head of the aisle with the officiant, and his daughter stayed close to his side, hugging his leg as though she never wanted to let go. When he'd been asked a few months ago whom he wanted to stand by his side, she was the only person he'd even considered. Besides Jason, she was his entire world.

And she looked so precious in her little white dress and the pink and white ribbons twisting and flowing with her almost platinum-colored curls. She held a small basket of silk petals in her tiny fist. She was supposed to toss them out as she walked up the aisle with her daddy, but she hadn't wanted to let the pink petals go. Even now, every time the wind blew one of them out of the basket, she chased it down until she had it in her chubby little grip again.

THE FINAL SEDUCTION | 201

"Hope, be still, honey," Brad whispered. He could hear a few light laughs coming from the small crowd behind him. The officiant gave the little girl an endearing smile, and when he did, Hope hid behind her father's leg.

He looked back over his shoulder one more time, and he still didn't see Jason. Lance and Davi and their cute little beagle were heading up the cobblestones toward the river's edge, but they didn't have Jason in tow.

Brad's heart instantly sank.

He turned back to the officiant so the intimate group of friends behind him wouldn't see his panic. His throat knotted and he would've sworn every inch of his body trembled. He couldn't believe Jason would do this to him, couldn't believe the man he loved with everything in him would abandon him at the altar like this.

Brad lowered his head and swallowed back the tears he felt building. But as he raised his sights back toward the bright sky, he saw a faint smile on the officiant's face. Brad frowned. Then he followed the man's gaze, over his shoulder and beyond the small crowd, and there he was. Jason stood there looking more handsome than Brad had ever seen him. The sun cast copper highlights that shimmered throughout his hair. But his smile... wow, his smile was magical and contagious, and so wide it pushed dimples into his cheeks. That smile filled his eyes with the kind of joy he filled Brad's heart with every single day.

Jason took Brad's side and immediately he laced their fingers together. Everyone behind them settled down, leaving nothing but the sound of the Mississippi River churning in front of them and the sounds of New Orleans life behind them.

"Jason and Brad," the officiant said, "we are gathered here today to bear witness and share in the love you have for each other."

A CHILL rippled down Lance's arm. He tightened his hand around Davi's, looked over, and immediately pictured himself doing the exact same thing Jason was right now, what Dorian and Jansen had done years ago. All his friends looked so happy to step out of single life and into wedded bliss. It looked so easy to do, so natural, and the sort of big step that really showed one's love for another.

He leaned over and whispered, "Can you see yourself doing this one day?"

Davi's head jerked in his direction. His big brown eyes were wider than Lance had ever seen them. He opened his mouth and immediately closed it. Then he tilted his head and said, "Can you see *yourself* doing this one day?"

Lance thought about it. He pictured himself in the suburbs with a white picket fence and Cão all grown up. Maybe they'd have another puppy to chase him around, and there would be a bigger SUV in the driveway. Maybe Lance wouldn't be at the club anymore. Maybe they would try to have a kid somehow. He wasn't sure what the future held, but none of this freaked him out. Not in the least.

A year ago, Lance would've run the hell away from a commitment of any kind, but Davi was special. Davi was worth holding on to. "Yeah, I can," he finally said with a nod.

"It is my honor," the officiant said, "to introduce Jason and Bradley Britt."

Brad and Jason pressed their lips together. From where Lance stood, it looked as though their mouths had melded together. He couldn't be happier. There weren't two people in the world who deserved this more than Jason and Brad. And every single friend, their tight-knit little family, roared with joy.

It all started with a dream that made her heart wrench and a set of mesmerizing eyes that begged to be seen, and ALLISON CASSATTA the writer was born. A techie by trade, the daydreamer in her wanted to sail away from the mundane, while the hopeless romantic in her searched for the perfect love story. Many poems and short stories were written before her first attempt at a novel, and once that piece of her soul spilled onto paper, there was no stopping it.

She has an eye for the visually stunning and a mind that screams to bring that beauty to life. She gives her readers something they can feel in the depth of their hearts, creates worlds they can touch, and characters who become your best friend or worst enemy.

Born and raised in Memphis, Tennessee, big-city life was a rat race that kept her busy in her career. It took moving with her new husband to a sleepy Mississippi town to make her realize that dreams can come true, and did they ever. She found herself a published author. She found her perfect romance.

Visit Allison at
http://www.allisoncassatta.com, http://www.facebook.com/pages/Author-Allison-Cassatta/158938557051, and
http://www.goodreads.com/author/show/4417507.Allison_Cassatta.

Also from ALLISON CASSATTA

ALLISON CASSATTA

LIES & Seduction

http://www.dreamspinnerpress.com

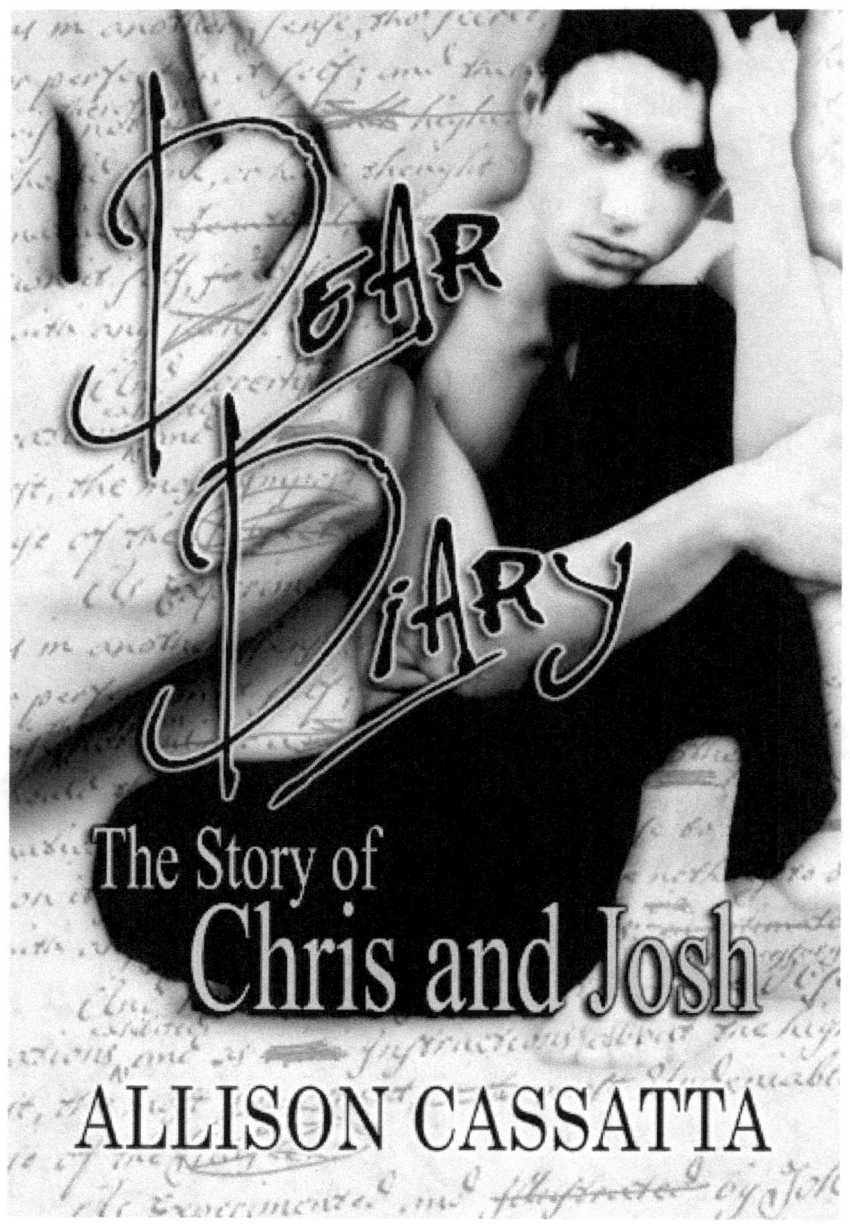

Dear Diary

The Story of Chris and Josh

ALLISON CASSATTA

http://www.dreamspinnerpress.com

The Dear Diary Series from ALLISON CASSATTA

http://www.dreamspinnerpress.com

The Dear Diary Series from ALLISON CASSATTA

Another Chris & Josh Story

Dear Diary

RELATIONSHIPS

101

ALLISON CASSATTA

http://www.dreamspinnerpress.com

Also from ALLISON CASSATTA

http://www.dreamspinnerpress.com

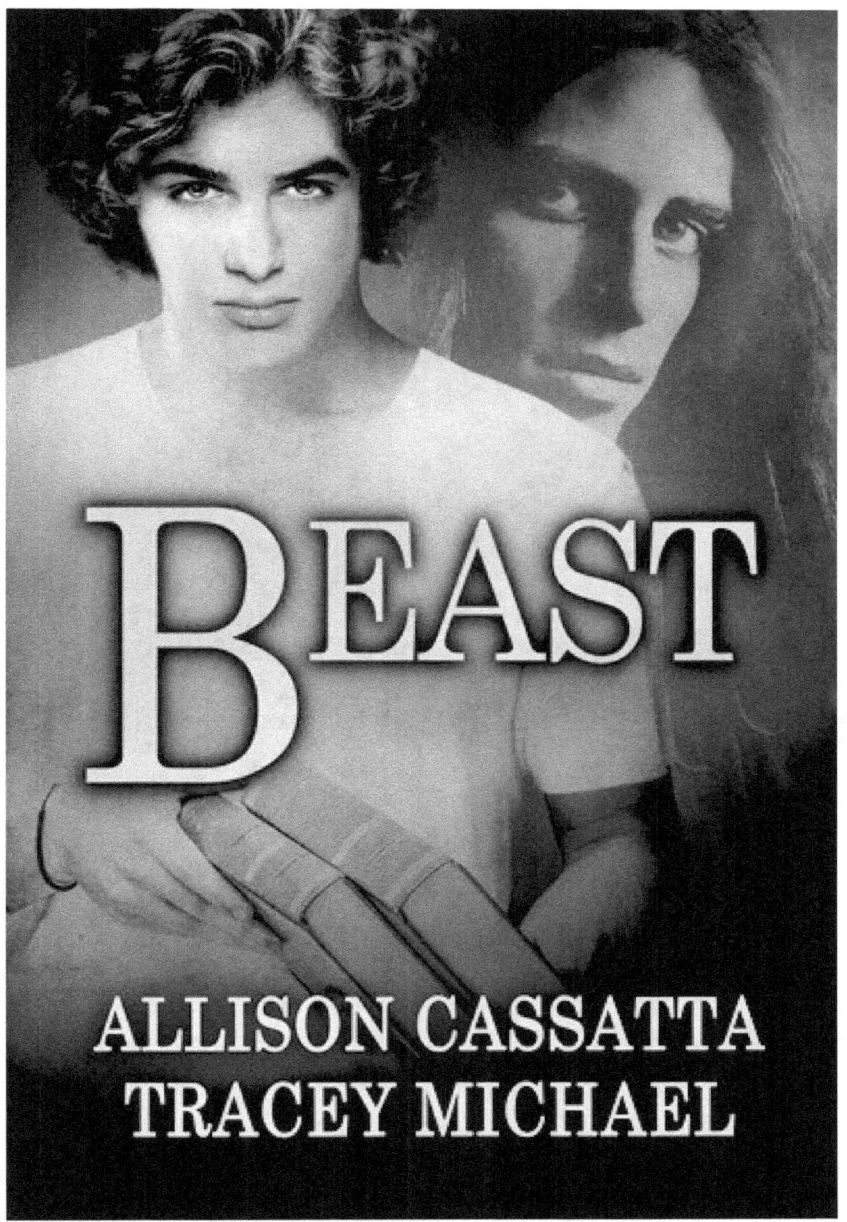

Also from DREAMSPINNER PRESS

After the End

ALEX KIDWELL

http://www.dreamspinnerpress.com

Also from DREAMSPINNER PRESS

http://www.dreamspinnerpress.com

Also from DREAMSPINNER PRESS

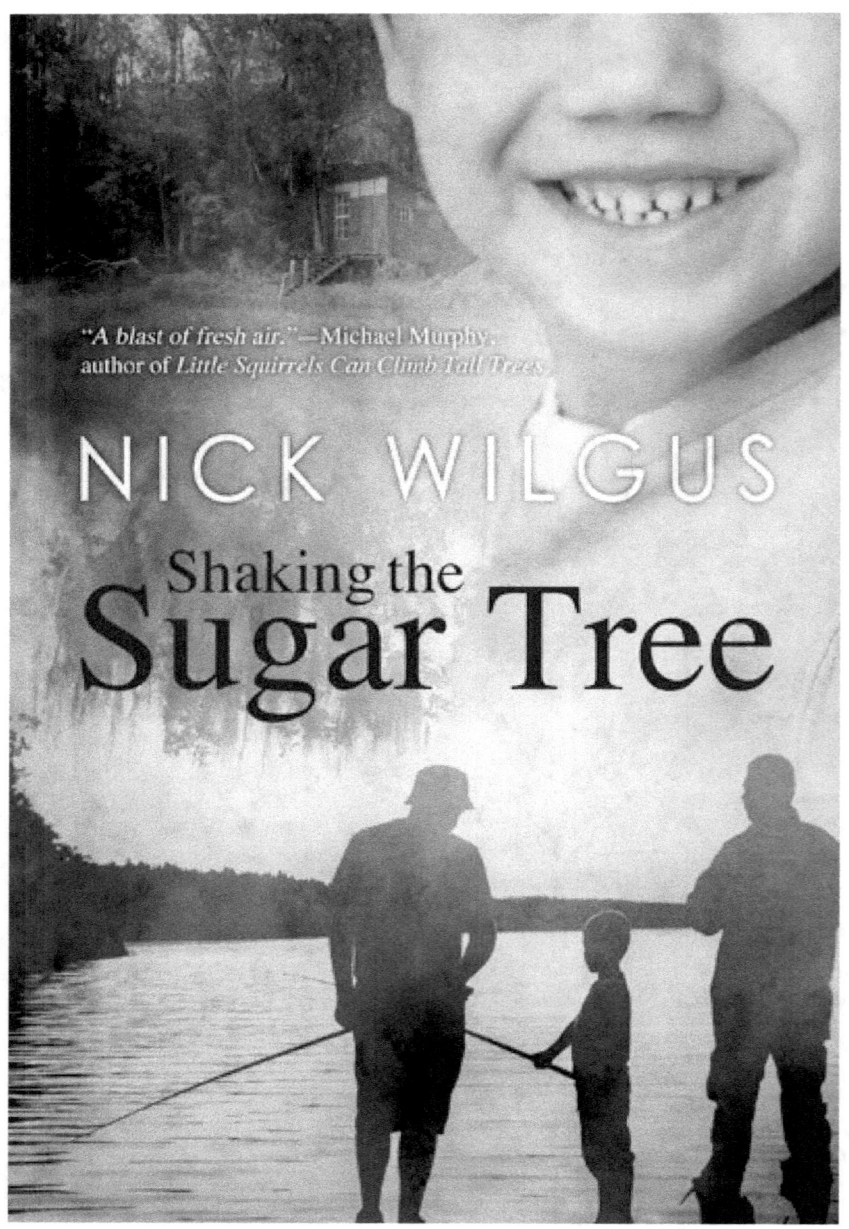

"A blast of fresh air." —Michael Murphy, author of *Little Squirrels Can Climb Tall Trees*

NICK WILGUS

Shaking the
Sugar Tree

http://www.dreamspinnerpress.com

Improves with Age

Lavinia Lewis

Also from DREAMSPINNER PRESS

http://www.dreamspinnerpress.com

Also from DREAMSPINNER PRESS

http://www.dreamspinnerpress.com

www.ingramcontent.com/pod-product-compliance
Lightning Source LLC
Chambersburg PA
CBHW071328250626
47159CB00004B/1512